SCREAM QUEENS OF THE DEAD SEA

SCREAM QUEENS
OF THE DEAD SEA

GILAD ELBOM

THUNDER'S MOUTH PRESS
NEW YORK

SCREAM QUEENS OF THE DEAD SEA

Published by
Thunder's Mouth Press
An Imprint of Avalon Publishing Group Inc.
245 West 17th Street, 11th Floor
New York, NY 10011

AVALON
publishing group incorporated

Library of Congress Cataloging-in-Publication Data is available

ISBN: 1-56858-322-2

9 8 7 6 5 4 3 2 1

Book design by Abacus Print & Sign Solutions
Printed in the United States of America
Distributed by Publishers Group West

CHAPTER 1

I don't know why I'm writing this book in a foreign language when I have at my disposal such a beautiful mother tongue. It's not a perfect tongue, I know. It's been dead for the past two thousand years, and it goes from right to left, and we constantly have to come up with new words for simple things like oranges and submachine guns and encryption software. But it's the language of the Bible, the dialect of the Divine, the words in which the world was created. So why am I writing in English when I have this native language good enough for God?

My mother says that I'm being ungrateful. She says that I have a responsibility, a commitment to our history. I also have a degree in comparative literature and linguistics, but she says that it means nothing. I don't know. I'm actually proud of my degree. So proud that I decided to leave it untouched. Never traveled, never tried to speak any of the languages I'd studied at the Hebrew University. Instead, I got a job as an assistant nurse at a mental hospital. I'm not a registered nurse, of course, but basically I do a nurse's job.

I have to go to work. It's a bad day to go out, but I have to be at the hospital at three. It's always bad when it's quiet. You know they must be planning something big. And when you finally hear the blasts and sirens, you feel redeemed. It happened elsewhere. You'd hear about it on the radio: the blood, the severed limbs, the names. But if the daily disaster is over, and your name is not on the radio, it's safe to go out again. Safe to go to work.

My mother thinks it's a dead-end job. She says that I'm neglecting my intellectual ability. She says that I should start thinking about my future instead of wasting my life playing Florence Nightingale. And it's not just my mother who says that. The patients also think that I should stay at home.

Two-fifteen. It's raining. I'll give it another ten minutes. If I don't hear anything, I'll take my chances and drive to the hospital.

When the space shuttle didn't make it back to earth, everybody felt redeemed. We hadn't had anything for days. It was scary. What are they waiting for? They must be planning something really big. And then it happened. Columbia exploded. Everybody sighed in relief. It was safe to go out again.

I put side A of *Symphonies of Sickness* on the old turntable and start getting dressed, but halfway through the first song, stage-diving into an imaginary audience in my underwear and Iron Maiden T-shirt, there's a knock on the door. I put on my work clothes: my old jeans, the ones I don't care if the patients puke on, and the nice sweater that Carmel got me for my birthday, just to show them that even though I might get dirty, I still dress like a normal human being.

"Mezuzah inspection." A stocky man in a long black coat, rain-soaked beard dripping on my doormat. "Can I come in?"

"I'm on my way out."

"It'll only take a minute."

"I don't think there's anything wrong with my mezuzahs."

"I'm sure they're all kosher, but you never know. The ink wears out, letters get erased. The tip of the smallest letter starts fading, and the whole thing is an abomination. Your house is not protected."

"I'll take the risk."

"Especially in times like these. *Write them upon the posts of thy house, and on thy gates.* And it's free. You can give me a small donation, if you wish, but it's all for heaven's sake."

"Maybe some other time."

"Might be too late."

The phone rings.

"I have to go."

"I'll come again next week, in case you change your mind. In the meantime, be very, very careful."

I close the door and pick up the phone. It's Carmel.

"I knew it."

"Knew what?"

"The space shuttle. Finally, after four thousand years of humility and humiliation, after four hundred years of enslavement in Egypt, after forty years of wandering in the desert, we've been given the chance to create our very own Icarus: the first Israeli in space, the pioneer Hebrew astronaut. So why send a scientist or an astrophysicist when we can send a soldier? And not just a soldier. A pilot. A colonel in the Israeli Air Force."

"Carmel, I have to go to work."

"Wait. According to his illustrious military record, celebrated in every corporate Judeo-Christian newspaper in the world, the brave starblazer bombed Iraq in 1981, then bombed Lebanon in 1982. Unfortunately, they don't tell you how many refugee camps he bombed. For some reason, probably because of self-hating defeatist propaganda, dropping bombs on houses owned by relatives of potential terrorists is considered now a shameful crime rather than an act of pure self-defense. Or maybe it's just that such acts—or operations, to use a more professional term—have been reduced to a daily routine that diminishes their uplifting effect on the national morale. Dead Arabs don't make us happy anymore. We need to put a Jew on Mars to elevate our spirits in such hard times."

"Stop it, Carmel. Please."

"Why?"

"People wouldn't like it."

"They could always skip it."

I hear a siren. Did I hear an explosion? I'm not sure. Just one siren, somewhere in the distance. Must be a routine call. When something big happens, the sirens don't travel alone.

"Did you hear anything?"

"No."

"I have to go. Patients are waiting."

"Go. I'll call you later."

For some reason, maybe because systematic vilification of those who try to help them is one of the symptoms of their illness, all my patients seem to hate me. They say I'm the worst nurse they've ever had. But Dr. Himmelblau tells me that the best thing to do when dealing with the mentally ill is to keep a distance. Which, considering the fact that our ward is so small, is not such an easy thing to do. In fact, it's so small, in terms of both space and population, that they don't even call it a ward. They call it a unit. The rehabilitation unit. Which, of course, is just a nice euphemism for *Home for the Incurably Insane*. I know I don't have a lot of experience when it comes to treating mental patients, but as far as I can see, none of the inmates in our unit has the slightest chance of ever getting reincorporated into society. As far as I can see, they're just a bunch of hopeless ghosts who require minimal daily maintenance.

Which is probably why they say that I'm cruel. But Dr. Himmelblau, who's even crueler than I am, tells me to treat them as professionally as I can.

I put my shoes on. But before I go on, I think I should mention that Dr. Himmelblau is a woman. I don't know if it's a relevant piece of information at this point, but I just thought I should make it clear that she's not a male doctor. Because whenever I mention her name, people tend to automatically assume it's a man. I guess it has to do with the difference between Hebrew and English. In Hebrew you could never get confused, because the verb conjugates according to the gender of the noun. But in English I could write an entire novel about Dr. Himmelblau, and unless I use the pronoun, you wouldn't know if she was male or female.

Anyway, Dr. Himmelblau is a woman. And I actually appreciate her advice when she tells me not to befriend the patients. I even practice it outside the hospital, in my private life, on real people. People I really need to keep a distance from. Like Carmel, for example.

Carmel and I are now trying to be just friends. But it doesn't always work. Last night, twenty minutes into the sold-out premiere of the much-anticipated rock-opera production of *Tamburlaine*, we sneak out of the auditorium at the Jerusalem Interdisciplinary Theater, climb up to the empty, under-construction balcony, and engage in various inappro-priate activities to the sounds of a pseudo-psychedelic mish-mash of wailing guitars and off-beat drums. It was quick and sloppy, and I almost ruined Carmel's new denim jacket, but she insisted that in spite of our mutual decision to stay away from one another, we had a moral obligation to take revenge on the JIT for trying to make us sit through such an insulting, not to mention overpriced, fiasco.

But enough about Carmel. Time to go. I bring the needle up, turn off the computer, and lock the door. The hospital is thirty minutes away. At the first light, a mustached man in a green old Ford Escort, which we sometimes call Brenda, rolls down his window, motioning for me to do the same.

"You selling?"

"No."

"How much?"

"Not selling."

"I'll give you twenty."

The light turns green. I roll up the window and drive on. He couldn't see the scratch, otherwise he wouldn't have offered me twenty thousand. Or maybe he just didn't care about the scratch. I bet he would give anything for a white Subaru Justy. It's small, it's inconspicuous, it's innocent-looking. Would be perfect for stuffing full of explosives.

I have no idea how it got scratched. I woke up one morn-ing, about three months ago, and there it was: an ugly scratch across the driver's door, so deep it actually made a hole through the metal. And so fresh: it hadn't been there the night before, and now it was there, palpable and irre-versible. It was two or three days after Carmel and I had had a huge fight—I can't even remember what about—and the scratch looked so decisive and violent that I was sure she'd done it during the night. I never asked her about it, though.

But enough about Carmel. I should just mention that she's married. But I'll tell you all about it later. I'm approaching the hospital now, and there's something strange on the road. The hospital is strategically situated outside the city, on top of a high hill, surrounded by dark forests and empty roads. It's very quiet up here during the day, but dozens of jackals howl very loud and very close every night, which always scares the patients further out of their minds. Sometimes you can see the jackals crossing the road, but not today. Today there's something strange on the road. Looks like a military roadblock from afar, but when I get closer, it's actually a car accident: a blue Peugeot crushed against the mountainside, upside down, two people lying in the middle of the road, three police cars, two ambulances, flashing lights. Stupid Peugeot. Lost control taking one of those sharp uphill curves. Happens all the time.

I slow down. A policeman in a yellow rubber coat waves for me to keep driving. I look at the bodies on the road. Motionless. Are they dead? One of them is a woman, young, her pants pulled down, blood on her legs. The other one I can't see very well, but it doesn't look too good either. The face is covered with a blanket. I feel better now. Sometimes it's reassuring to know that people still die here just because they get into a car accident. At first I thought the Arabs had hit again. But that wouldn't make much sense. Why would you want to kill two people and a bunch of jackals on an empty road when you can stuff a Justy full of explosives and drive it into a shopping mall downtown?

It's good to know that people still get killed because of things completely unrelated to the war. People murder other people just for money, roofs collapse on guests in wedding halls, people burn to death when houses catch fire. Like in any other normal country.

Three o'clock. I drive into the hospital, park my car in the small parking lot, enter the unit, swipe my card, and walk into the nurse's station, where I listen to a three-minute update from nurse Odelia about the patients and what they did today and how they behaved. Odelia has been working here for fifteen years. She's slow and quiet and impatient and always talking about her kids and how she has to pick them up from school and feed them. The day has been uneventful, and Odelia takes her purse out of the medicine cabinet, where she hides it every morning, and leaves. I sit down at the Formica desk and start reading the newspaper. First I read an article about Eden, the band we're sending to the Eurovision song contest this year, then a story about the heavy winter gear the army makes the soldiers carry in case it snows in the West Bank.

Time to go check on the patients, but just as I step outside the nurse's station, the phone rings. It has two different rings: one for calls from inside the hospital (two short rings, sort of an iambic buzz) and another for calls from outside the hospital (one long ring, somber and ceremonial). This one's from outside. I step back into the station.

"When you think about it, the whole thing had nothing to do with the astronaut himself. More important than the man in space was his hand baggage: a drawing by a fourteen-year-old Jewish boy who perished at Auschwitz."

"Carmel, I'm trying to work here."

"Seriously, how can we travel light when we were chosen to bear the eternal burden of bringing light to the nations? If you ask me, the death of the drawing and its carrier was not a tragicomic twist of fate but a carefully planned, well-executed climax."

"I'm not asking you."

"Still, it's very clear that the purpose of this triumphant debut Jewish space voyage was not to land safely in Florida but to explode over Palestine, Texas, in an orgasmic display of emotional pornography: burnt body parts and Holocaust memorabilia raining from the heavens on peaceful redneck communities, washing both America and Israel in a glorious torrent of human debris and national mourning."

It's four o'clock, which means that all the patients congregate in the game room, which we sometimes call the TV room, to watch the daily soap opera. Commenting emphatically on the joys and sorrows of lives other than their own, their perpetual listlessness is ephemerally replaced by a pale gleam of fascination and excitement. After all, Ridge is about to be thrown in jail for a crime he didn't commit.

"Call me back in an hour, Carmel."

I walk out of the nurse's station and sit next to Amos Ashkenazi.

"You think he's guilty?" asks Amos Ashkenazi.

"I don't know."

"You don't think he did it," insists Amos Ashkenazi, "do you?"

"I told you: I don't know."

And I don't really care. As far as I'm concerned, guilty or not, Ridge can rot in prison for the rest of his life. However, when Sheila says to Taylor, "It's the waiting around and the not knowing that's killing me," I do feel obliged to torture poor Amos Ashkenazi with a detailed disquisition on the syntactic structure and semantic function of the cleft sentence.

"Take for example a sentence like *John ate the apple*."

"Who's John?"

"It doesn't matter. It's just an example."

"Maybe it wasn't John who ate the apple," says Amos Ashkenazi. "Maybe it was Thorne."

"Okay. Let's take a sentence like *Thorne ate the apple.*"

"Was he supposed to eat the apple?"

"Let's say he wasn't. And now someone wants to know if *you* ate the apple."

"Me?"

"Yes, you."

"I didn't do anything."

"I know. But let's just say that someone wants to know if you ate the apple."

"Who wants to know?"

"That's not the point. Let's just assume that we have apples, but they're not supposed to be eaten before dinner, okay?"

"We never have apples for dinner."

"It's a hypothetical situation."

"Okay."

"And even though the apples were not supposed to be eaten, John ate one."

"Thorne."

"Thorne. Thorne ate an apple. And when Dr. Himmelblau finds out about it, she storms into the unit, furious, and she wants to know if *you* ate the apple. Now what cleft sentence would you use to tell her you didn't eat the apple?"

"What would she do to me if I ate one?"

"She'll increase your medication."

"Could you tell her that I didn't eat the apple?"

"I didn't see who ate the apple."

"Then why are you picking on me?"

"I'm not. To use a cleft sentence, it's Dr. Himmelblau who's picking on you. And she won't stop until you come up with the right cleft sentence that says that Thorne ate the apple, not you."

"Could you give me an example of a cleft sentence?"

"I just did."

"I didn't get it."

"Then you'll just have to take more drugs."

I don't know why I like to pick on Amos Ashkenazi. I guess I shouldn't. I guess I'm supposed to be professional. But on the other hand, I don't want to treat the patients with fake compassion just because they're ill.

Amos Ashkenazi always wears faded purple T-shirts. He must have dozens of them, because every day you see him wearing a different shade of faded purple. He has bad teeth, oily hair, yellow fingertips, and a surprisingly big vocabulary. He says I'm *nefarious*.

Too close to Amos Ashkenazi, on the saliva-stained couch, sits Immanuel Sebastian. Immanuel Sebastian is one of the two murderers we have. The daily episode of their soap opera concludes, and a documentary on the crusades commences. Immanuel Sebastian says he was once a crusader himself.

"You actually went on a crusade?"

"Sure."

"And what exactly did you do?"

"Fought the Saracens."

"Did God tell you to do that?"

"I don't believe in God."

"You don't?"

"I don't believe in anything." Immanuel Sebastian shakes his head.

"Not even in God?"

"I have nothing against God. I just don't believe he exists."

"Why not?"

"I told you: I don't believe in anything."

"How come?"

"FDD," he whispers.

"What?"

"I have FDD," says Immanuel Sebastian, raising his eyebrows, half-closing his eyes. "Faith Deficit Disorder."

"Which means?"

"Which means that I'm incapable of faith. My belief mechanism is impaired. I can't believe."

"Can't believe in what?"

"In anything."

"You must believe in *something*."

"I wish I could," he sighs, "but I just can't help it. I believe in nothing."

"Nothing at all?"

"Nothing at all."

The phone rings again. I get up from the couch and walk into the nurse's station.

"Forget the stupid space shuttle," Carmel whispers. "We had fun last night, didn't we?"

"Oh, yes. I love Marlowe."

"We should do it again some time."

"Good idea. I think they're working on a stand-up comedy version of *The Jew of Malta*."

Carmel sighs. Is she getting tired of me? Or is it just my annoying witticisms that she's getting tired of? I don't know. Maybe I should stick to my original plan and not see her anymore. Put an end to this adulterous extravaganza. She, of course, says that there's nothing wrong with what we're doing, especially considering the fact that soon she won't be married anymore. Her husband has cancer. I know it sounds corny, as if I'm using my omnipotent position as the author of this book to give this poor guy cancer. But it's true.

Believe me. He does have cancer. Which means, at least the way Carmel puts it, that I'm having an affair not with an unfaithful wife but with a future widow.

"I know you're dying to do it to me again tonight."

"I am?"

"Are you kidding? I can hear you drooling."

"Which reminds me: I have to get back to work."

Immanuel Sebastian drools. Side effects. I hang up and walk back to the couch, where he's still sitting, watching the crusaders, rocking his knees up and down, awaiting my return. I like Immanuel Sebastian. I'd like to believe that I'm making him human by ignoring the fact that he's a convicted murderer and treating him nice. Just like I make Amos Ashkenazi more human by treating him bad, ignoring the fact that he's just an innocent patient.

"FDD, huh?"

"That's right," nods Immanuel Sebastian.

"Never heard of it."

"It's new. People have been suffering from it for ages, of course, but it wasn't officially diagnosed and classified by modern psychiatry until only a few years ago."

"Is it a mental illness?"

"No," says Immanuel Sebastian, "it's a personality disorder."

"What's the difference?"

"You don't know?"

"You've been here for ten years. I've only been here for a year."

"Okay," says Immanuel Sebastian, "let me put it this way. An illness is something you're inflicted with. If you have schizophrenia, for example, then you have schizophrenia. It's not your fault. It's like cancer: there's nothing you can do about it. You're sick."

"I see," I nod, my eyes wandering about the unit, catching a glimpse of Amos Ashkenazi chewing invisible food in silent concentration.

"Are you with me?" asks Immanuel Sebastian.

"Absolutely."

"Okay. A disorder, on the other hand, is something you're expected to have control over."

"Control?"

"Yes."

"Over what?"

"The symptoms."

"What *are* the symptoms?"

"Strange behavior," says Immanuel Sebastian.

"Is that the only symptom?"

"That's the only symptom."

It's five o'clock now, two hours into my shift, and everything—the greasy fingerprints on the TV screen, the sticky floor and tables, the cracked tiles in the kitchen, the almost invisible spiderweb above the medicine cabinet, the yellowing mortar dripping from the ceiling in the dining hall, the crooked little felt menorahs that they made in Occupational Therapy, still hanging from the curtain rods even though it's almost two months after Hanukkah—everything looks so stupid. Why am I sitting on this filthy couch, getting a lecture from the criminally insane while watching other crazy people half-watching another attempt to recover the Holy Land from the Muslims? Maybe they're right, all those nagging inmates and concerned family members. Maybe I shouldn't be here. I should go to Cardiff, work toward an advanced degree in Celtic languages. I should stop seeing Carmel, start looking for a new girlfriend. I'll find myself a nice Welsh redhead called Branwen or Goleuddydd, with beautiful slate-gray eyes and an interesting accent. She'll be soft-spoken and pale, tender and loving. And single.

"That's the only symptom," says Immanuel Sebastian.

"Of what?" I focus my eyes on a glistening drop of spit gliding down his chin. "Illness or disorder?"

"Both. In both cases—mental illness and personality disorder—the patient behaves in a way which society sees as strange or deviant. In both cases you operate outside the norm."

"So what's the difference?"

"The difference is that if you're mentally ill, no one can blame you for your behavior."

"And if you have a personality disorder?"

"Then you're held responsible for any strange behavior you choose to demonstrate. You're considered master of your symptom."

I like the way Immanuel Sebastian says "master of your symptom." He has a special way of pronouncing these words, in a deep, doom-like voice that makes it sound ancient and prophetic, almost evil. Reminds me of those old, ultra-heavy Black Sabbath tunes. I still listen to them almost every day. Which is another reason why my mother thinks I'm going nowhere. Heavy metal is not something an intelligent person should be interested in. She takes great pride in the fact that her own hobbies, the hobbies of the educated, are much more challenging: nineteenth-century Russian novels, classical music, dialysis. Heavy metal, she says, is making me dumb. She would be happy, of course, if I decided to go abroad to continue my education. Because the hospital, she believes, is also making me dumb. Not to mention the fact that it's dangerous. And it serves no purpose. So just quit your job—a year in a mental institution is more than enough—and apply to graduate school. Doesn't matter where, doesn't matter in what field—as long as you get your doctorate. But please hurry. I'd really appreciate it if you became a university professor while I'm still alive.

Carmel, on the other hand, doesn't believe in long-term goals. Recklessness excites her. If it's logical or reasonable or purposeful, she won't do it. Life is all about wasting, she says. Wasting and spending. Wasting money, spending time, squandering your energies, using up your resources. Just like children do. Always fritter, never save. This is the meaning of life, this is the essence of youth. Only the sick and the old are concerned with conserving energy.

But enough about Carmel. Supper will be served in about an hour, and the patients are already getting restless.

"Master!" shouts Hadassah Benedict. "I'm dead!"

"Stop shouting!" I shout back. "Can't you see I'm in the middle of a conversation here? And I'm not your master. I'm your nurse."

"Nurse? Aren't nurses supposed to be—you know— women?"

"I'm a male nurse."

"And they say *I'm* insane."

As a matter of fact, I can see why Hadassah Benedict would think that nurses must always be female. In Hebrew, just like in, say, German, we have no special word for *nurse*. A nurse is simply a *sister*. Same word. And a male nurse, of course, would be a *brother*. But not in English. An English nurse, as opposed to a Hebrew one, can be either male or female. Which is probably why Abe Goldmil often calls me a *Krankenschwester* behind my back, thinking that I can't hear him from the nurse's station, or that even if I could, I probably wouldn't know what it meant. But I haven't mentioned

Abe Goldmil yet, so you'll just have to be patient. In the meantime, let me take care of Hadassah Benedict.

I page Dr. Himmelblau, who comes down to the unit, gives Hadassah Benedict an extra dose of Halidol, and orders her to go to sleep.

"You're a monster," they say to me.

"If you could only practice some authority," Dr. Himmelblau maintains, "they would never allow themselves to talk to you like that."

Easy for her to say. She's the one in control of their treatment, not me.

"So what about treatment?" I turn back to Immanuel Sebastian.

"Same treatment," says Immanuel Sebastian. "The only difference is that if you're mentally ill, they *force* you to receive treatment."

"And if you have a personality disorder?"

"Then they expect you to *seek* treatment."

"What kind of treatment?"

"Therapy, I guess. And they probably have some drugs that can help."

"So there may be something you could actually do about your FDD."

"I guess."

"So why don't you see a psychiatrist?"

"I don't believe in psychiatrists."

"What *do* you believe in?"

"I told you. Nothing."

"There must be *something* you believe in."

"Like what?"

"I don't know. Nature. Elvis. Oral sex. *Something.*"

"I used to believe I was the Messiah."

"When was that?"

"Many years ago."

"And now?"

"Now I'm sure of it."

"What makes you so sure you're the Messiah?"

"God told me."

"I thought you didn't believe in God."

"I don't. But he insisted I was the Chosen One, and I just didn't want to argue."

"Why not?"

"Would *you* feel comfortable arguing with God?"

"But you don't *believe* in God."

"Still, I wouldn't want to make him angry."

"You're beginning to make *me* angry."

"Are you God?"

"Of course not."

"Then I don't mind making you angry."

I've changed my mind. I don't like Immanuel Sebastian.

It's suppertime, which means they all drop whatever they're doing and rush to the small dining hall. The food arrives from the main kitchen in big gray containers, and all I have to do is supervise the way they take it out of the containers, ladle it onto the blue plastic plates, lay it on the table, and eat. Today we have overcooked pasta, canned tuna, cottage cheese, hard-boiled eggs, and watered-down semolina porridge. They usually eat in an orderly fashion, but I still have to be around, just in case.

So here I am, standing in the dining room, watching them consume enormous amounts of hospital cuisine in determined silence, making sure they don't cut themselves with their knives or start a fight or swallow their tongues. When it's all over, and the daily designated patients-on-duty begin washing the dishes, I step back into the TV room, where

Amos Ashkenazi, Immanuel Sebastian, and Abe Goldmil are watching a movie. The crusaders are gone now, and Michael Caine is on, playing the bad guy. A burglar, I think. Or maybe a professional safecracker. Anyway, he's old and depressed, out of luck and out of work, but he keeps conjuring up all kinds of interesting plans for a quick profit,˙all the while displaying that dark, sarcastic humor so typical of old, depressed, out-of-luck, out-of-work British crooks.

Supper made me miss the beginning, but as far as I understand, Jack Nicholson is the one who finally hires Michael Caine's services. But I'm not quite sure what exactly it is that they're trying to do. Their basic plan, it seems, consists of breaking into some rich man's yacht, melting the safe open, and stealing an exceptionally big diamond.

All this could have been very simple, of course, if it wasn't for an exceptionally bitchy, constantly nagging, overtanned, overbleached, middle-aged woman—I think she's Jack Nicholson's wife—who had once been good-looking, it seems, but whose faded beauty has made her bitter and cranky and suspicious and vindictive. And there's also a hot-blooded boy of about eighteen, rowdy and muscular—I think he's Jack Nicholson's son—or stepson—whose role in the film mainly involves breaking the law and walking around with no shirt on.

And finally, there's an ultra-sexy, cute-but-dangerous teenage girl of about sixteen, with dark, inviting eyes, smooth, bronzed skin, and a perfect body packed into what looks like a nurse's uniform, although I'm not quite sure she's a real nurse. She looks more like a babysitter or a private tutor. Maybe a nanny. Or maybe a nurse after all. Anyway, if she *is* a nurse, she's definitely a female nurse. And even though she's hired by Jack Nicholson's wife to perform a certain job around the house, it somehow comes as no surprise when all she really does is parade up and down the set in a very tight blouse and a very short skirt, inadvertently driving her employer into being a bitter, cranky, suspicious, vindictive old bitch, while shamelessly seducing both father and son—or stepson.

It's still raining. I get up and stand by the window, looking for my Justy in the parking lot. But it's as dark as Egypt, as we say in Hebrew, and all I can see is the reflection of the TV screen. I walk back to my plastic chair. Amos Ashkenazi is dozing off on the couch, his head dropping intermittently on Immanuel Sebastian's shoulder. I bring my right knee to my chin and tie my shoelaces. They're wet at the ends. Abe Goldmil coughs. He pulls his brown notebook out of his coat pocket and hands it over to me. Out of the kitchen comes Uriah Einhorn, wearing dirty glasses and a green baseball cap that says *South Dakota*. Desta Ezra, today's patient-on-duty, is sweeping the floor in silence.

Everybody's here right now—which offers me a good chance to introduce them all, say a few words about each of them—but I promised to tell you about Abe Goldmil first, so just be patient: by the end of chapter 3 you will have met them all. The only one I don't really know much about is our new arrival, Ibrahim Ibrahim.

Abe Goldmil, on the other hand, is one of those patients you know too much about, probably because he always wants to show you something. Usually it's his poems, stupid little doggerels he writes in his little brown notebook. Actually, he's not such a bad poet, but for some reason, probably because he's mentally ill, he insists on wasting his talent composing hyperbolic love limericks to Julie Strain, a Hollywood B-movie actress, nude model, and porn star he happens to be infatuated with. I open his wrinkled notebook. He stares at me as I'm reading, eagerly awaiting my approval:

My yearning letters, characters of lust,
To show my hidden flame in verse are fain,
But it's my pining, lovelorn heart that must
Transcribe the brimming, overwhelming pain;
Constrain my weeping fingers not to wipe
Warm words that drip to paper from my vein,
Encrypt the secret passion into type:
Red ink which will perhaps unread remain.
Yet even if my pet deciphers not
My fervent hieroglyphs, they still are meant
To woo her endlessly. For every dot
Of crimson is an ardent ornament,
Each scribbled symbol is a ruby swain:
Strange jewels to adorn my Julie Strain.

This time he's sure she'll respond.

The yacht explodes.

"If *he* doesn't respond," Immanuel Sebastian sneers at him, "what makes you think *she* will?"

"He's watching a movie," says Abe Goldmil.

It's fun watching a movie without really being committed to it. Jack Nicholson and Michael Caine all of a sudden become enemies, but me, I just go on minding my own business. Let them kill each other. See if I care. I just check on them every few minutes, make sure they're still out there. And if they're not—because at one point Michael Caine does end up as a dead body floating in his own swimming pool—that's their own problem. I never promised I'd watch this movie from beginning to end. I never said I'd get excited or emotional in any way. Or even interested.

Carmel often says that I'm not really interested in her. Walking around naked in my apartment, she would put me to these little passion-tests, especially when I was busy doing something else. I'm sitting in the kitchen, doing my home-work, translating something from Latin or Arabic, sur-rounded by a battery of dictionaries, immersed in a particu-larly difficult paragraph, when all of a sudden she would appear, stark naked, examining my reaction. And I would always get confused. She had been fully dressed a minute ago, like a normal human being, sitting on the couch in the other room, reading a book—so what does she want from me now? And she has a funny way of administering these tests. She would get up from the couch without saying a word, go to the bedroom or the bathroom or who knows where, remove her clothes, and march back to the living room. She'd sit down and continue to read, naked, then get up and walk to the kitchen, open the refrigerator, get a peach or an avocado, a knife and a plate, get back to her book, eat the peach or the avocado, go to the kitchen again, wash the knife and plate, still naked, go back to the living room, read some more. And you know how hard it is to put the text aside when you just discovered that a syntactic irregularity you've mistaken all along for an accusative is—it's so clear now!—just a simple nominative.

She never says anything, just sits there with her book and her nakedness, waiting for me to respond. "In a minute," I'd say to her, "I'm on the verge of a breakthrough here." And then, when my homework was almost done, I'd wait for her to come to the kitchen again, where I'd kneel down on the floor and lick her for a long time, then get up and grab her arms and tighten my grip on her biceps and kiss her hard on the mouth, giving her a taste of herself, then make her turn around and bend over, her hands on the kitchen counter, and grab her by the back of her neck and push her head into the sink and stick it to her from behind, pumping her a little harder than necessary, then yank myself out of her, spewing on her ass and the small of her back, forcing her to go take a shower while I sat down and finished translating my paragraph.

Carmel claims that I sometimes have sex with her as if she's not there at all. She says that in order for me to learn to acknowledge her presence when we're doing it, we need to have a joint fantasy that will increase our awareness of each other.

But I'll tell you about this fantasy some other time. The movie's over now, and I already miss the little sexy girl. I kept hoping that somehow the action in the movie would revolve around her. And that she would take her clothes off. If she must be a minor character, at least let her be a *naked* minor character. And I can't help thinking that it would have been awfully nice, for example, if someone did something sexually violent to her. Not that I'm into nudity or violence, but if someone in the movie has to die naked and of unnatural causes, I'd rather it be someone other than Michael Caine. And I guess I'm asking for too much here, but it could also be nice if *she* did something sexually violent to others, preferably to the smug young boy and his irritating mother—or stepmother.

But then again, I wasn't really watching. So maybe something did happen. Maybe she did get naked. Maybe I just missed it. Or maybe she did hold a loaded gun to that strapping young lad's pretty head. Maybe she did order him to undress, did handcuff him to the pipes under the kitchen sink, did insert various objects—I'm thinking of the gun, but not necessarily—to different cavities in his body. I'm thinking, of course, about his mouth and nostrils—but not necessarily. Maybe it all happened while I was busy serving supper and reading poetry.

They say I'm inattentive, but Dr. Himmelblau says that I really have to learn to ignore them, even if they're making me angry.

"Do you enjoy making people angry?"

"I can't help it," says Immanuel Sebastian.

"Maybe someone can help *you*."

"I don't need help."

"Why not?"

"Because I'm not a criminal. My behavior is unusual, not illegal."

"It may not be illegal, but it's socially disturbing."

"Does that make me crazy?"

"Absolutely. If you operate outside the social norm, your social behavior is abnormal."

"Yes, but that's not a crime. I operate outside the norm, not outside the law."

"You never broke the law?"

"No."

"Never?"

"I wouldn't say *never*."

"So you did break the law."

"I guess I did."

"What did you do?"

"I killed someone. But I had a good reason."

"Who did you kill?"

"Who? I thought you were a writer."

"Whom did you kill?"

I knew I was making a mistake, but Immanuel Sebastian is an idiot; I didn't expect him to appreciate good English.

"My lawyer."

"And what was the good reason?"

"I don't believe in lawyers."

"So why didn't you just fire him?"

"I fired *at* him," smiles Immanuel Sebastian.
I told you. An idiot.
"Why did you do that?"
"Because he lied to me."
"What did he say?"
"Don't kill me. There's a law against murder."
"Isn't there?"
"There is, but it's flexible."
"The law?"
"Yes. It changes."
"How does it change?"
"According to the circumstances."
"What circumstances?"
"Historical, social, political, geographical."
"For example?"
"For example," Immanuel Sebastian takes a deep breath, "there were times—and there are still places—where it's against the law for a man to have sex with another man."

They say I'm sadistic. They say that I enjoy playing the prosecutor of the insane. They say that I maliciously interrogate them just to see if I can make them confess. But Dr. Himmelblau says that I ought to keep doing my job regardless of any protest on the part of the patients, because one of the most important objectives of the rehabilitation process in the unit is to teach them how to engage in everyday conversations.

"Have you ever had sex with a man?"
"No," says Immanuel Sebastian.
"Never?"
"I wouldn't say *never.*"
"Well?"
"Well, I did pick up girls who later turned out to be—you know—boys."

"And what did you do when you found out?"

"Nothing."

"Why?"

"Because our relationship had already reached a stage where it didn't matter."

"What do you mean?"

"It was too late."

"Too late for what?"

"I was already in love with her."

"But it wasn't *her* anymore. It was *him*."

"So?"

"So you *did* have sex with a man."

"Yes, but I didn't *know* it was a man."

"And once you did, you didn't care."

"Right, because there's always something: you meet a nice girl, you spend some time with her, you sleep with her, and then, all of a sudden, she confesses to being a vegetarian, or a communist, or a Jew, or a man. But you don't care. Because, like I said, you're already in love with her."

"But doesn't it bother you that she's not a woman?"

"Listen," says Immanuel Sebastian. "She's nice, she's smart, she's good-looking. So she's got male genitalia. Nobody's perfect."

Nine o'clock now. One hour to go. I get up from the couch and step into the nurse's station, where I sit for about twenty minutes and write the report. When I'm done, I step back into the game room, but everybody's gone, probably in bed already, except for Amos Ashkenazi, who still sits in front of the TV, watching an old Roger Corman film. I sit down next to him. Vincent Price lives with his young daughter in what looks like a medieval mansion. He wakes up in the middle of the night to go out to confront an evil magician who has challenged him to a duel. Seeing him getting ready to go, his concerned daughter asks him if he's going to fight that wicked sorcerer. "Yes, dear," says Vincent Price, "it is to his castle that I must go."

I say nothing.

And in any case, if Dr. Himmelblau asks, we'll tell her that it was Ibrahim Ibrahim who ate the apple.

But enough about Ibrahim Ibrahim. My shift is over now, and just before I leave, Carmel calls. She's in her own hospital. Her husband's hospital.

"They put him in intensive care again. I have to spend the night here."

"I'm going home."

"Don't go to bed yet. If he doesn't make it through the night, I'll stop by on my way home."

CHAPTER 2

My shift starts in twenty minutes, so I leave side B of *Symphonies of Sickness* playing on the faithful Luxman—I like the idea of the assiduous, gyratory motion of the thick metal plate lingering in my apartment after I'm gone (the needle will come up automatically)—and I get in my scratched Justy and drive to the hospital. I'm running late, so I'm driving a little faster than usual, but after five minutes I get stuck behind a big yellow tractor, probably on its way to the nearby kibbutz, which forces me to drive painfully slow now. At first I'm angry and impatient, and I curse the powers responsible for putting this rusty monster on this road at this critical moment, and I try to pass it, and I honk my horn once or twice, but the road is too narrow, so I finally make peace with the fact that my speed is reduced to almost a walking pace and decide to devote the rest of this drive to inspecting all those scenery-related details that I usually can't pay attention to when I'm driving at normal speed.

It's a typical winter day, bleak and turbid. The bare mountains into which the road is hewn are the color of the sky. The pines that stretch along the hilltops are a murky shade of green. Animals are crossing the road here and there: the jackals and gazelles of the northern Judean Mountains, some big snakes, and occasionally a fox or a porcupine. They usually come out of their hiding places on a cold day like today. And I can also see a big brown bird of prey hovering above the road like it owns it, probably a falcon.

Sometimes I expect to find escaped lunatics crossing the road, but I don't think our lunatics ever attempt to escape. Most of them are petrified by the thought of having to cope on their own outside the hospital. And those who do wish to escape don't escape to the woods. They normally escape to the city, to beg for cigarettes downtown before they take the bus back to the hospital.

I'm looking for leftovers from yesterday's accident, some telltale signs on the road—broken glass, tire marks, blood on the shoulder—but everything has been cleaned up by the police and washed by the rain.

We're getting close to the kibbutz now. They have a little petting zoo here called Imprinted Creatures. I went there once, when I was working for *The Capital*, one of two local weekly magazines that we have here in Jerusalem. In addition to writing about heavy metal, I was also the editor of the Minor Attractions page, and when they opened Imprinted Creatures a few years ago, I went to the kibbutz to see if it was worth a piece. I thought it was interesting. Imprinted animals, which meant that you could pet them all, even the little foxes and fawns. The only animal you couldn't really touch was Judith, an old female baboon, a former employee at the Weizmann Institute of Science. Her job at the WIS was to sit in front of a computer and click a button in response to visual stimuli on the screen. The scientists had trained her to hit the button every time a pair of letters belonging to a fixed set appeared, and to not hit the button when a pair of letters belonging to a different set came on. All the letters were English consonants. The letters that required her response were such that if you put a vowel between them, they would make a real word: CR, DG, PT, and so on. The nonresponse letters were consonants that did not make any sense if you stuck a vowel in between them: XD, MQ, ZH, and so on.

When Judith retired, they relocated her to Imprinted Creatures, where she spends her days in her little cage, playing with children through the bars. The whole place looks like a secular, low-budget, run-down version of the official Jerusalem Biblical Zoo, where they have every animal mentioned in the Bible. The Biblical Zoo is big and nice and generously state-funded, but since the Old Testament doesn't say anything about computer-literate monkeys, Judith had to go to the kibbutz. They put a double-monitored computer in her cage, and the kid sitting opposite her, outside the cage, would have to do exactly what she'd been taught to do: click the button if a vowel would make the letters into a word, not click it if it wouldn't. The winner was whoever clicked first. Judith was always faster.

"I want you to go to the kibbutz," I said to one of my reporters. "Play with Judith. I need four hundred words."

When he came back with his four hundred words, I told him I had the perfect headline for his piece: MAN PLAYS COMPUTER GAME AGAINST MONKEY—AND LOSES.

"No, please," he said. "Don't use it."

"Why not?"

"It's insulting."

"It's a fact."

"I know, but I'm begging you, please. My mother will be reading it—what would she think?"

"Who cares?"

"Please. I don't want her to open the newspaper on Friday and find out that a monkey knows English better than her son."

We're past the kibbutz now, getting close to the hospital. You can't really see it from the road. It's nestled among the trees like a secret military base, hidden from curious eyes as if it were an important place. You have to get off the main road and take an even narrower side road, almost unfit for vehicles. It winds up and around an exceptionally high hill, until you find yourself in front of an anachronistic, manually operated gate, a lobotomized watchman, and a small, crooked, blue-and-white, four-line sign that says:

State of Israel
Ministery of Health
TRANQIL HAVEN
Mental Health Center

The *Ministery* I can understand. If you're a minister, you're in charge of a ministery. Makes sense. And I can also understand the *Tranqil*. If Q is always followed by U, the U becomes redundant. Arabic, for example, like Hebrew, is a language that distinguishes between male adjectives and female adjectives. Female adjectives are usually formed by attaching a suffix to the male adjective. But the Arabic word for *pregnant*, for example, doesn't have that suffix. If you don't have to distinguish it from a male adjective, why add the female suffix? Technically—or morphologically—it's a male adjective. But the fact that we know that the word *pregnant* applies only to women is enough to make it—semantically—

31

female. So if you don't have to distinguish between a Q that is followed by a U and a Q that is *not* followed by a U—simply because there is no Q that is not followed by a U—then what do you need the U for? Plus, Hebrew speakers are very uncomfortable with diphthongs, which makes *Tranqil* even more logical. But what I don't understand is the *Haven*. It makes perfect sense: the mental institution is traditionally referred to as a sanctuary, a shelter, an asylum. But considering the erratic grammar of the Israeli Ministry of Health, maybe what they really meant was *Heaven*.

My father used to say: Never trust a government that can't spell its own official signs.

But I'll tell you all about my father later, because I'm already late for my shift. I enter the hospital, waving a small thank-you to the guard as he opens the gate for me, but his face, as always, remains expressionless. I park in front of the unit and walk into the nurse's station, where Odelia is sitting with her purse in her lap and a reproachful look in her eyes. She doesn't say anything, just looks at her watch, sighs, and gives me a speed-of-light summary of her shift before she storms out of the unit, home, to her hungry dependents:

Immanuel Sebastian: ate, took his medicines, watched TV, quiet.

Abe Goldmil: ate, took his medicines, wrote in the kitchen, quiet.

Uriah Einhorn: ate, took his medicines, sleeps most of the time.

Amos Ashkenazi: ate, took his medicines, mumbles to himself, quiet.

Hadassah Benedict: ate, took her medicines, says she's dead, quiet.

Desta Ezra: quiet.

Ibrahim Ibrahim: ate, took his medicines, hardly comes out of his room, quiet.

I sit down and reach for the newspaper, but before I get a chance to glance at it, the phone rings. One long ring. Must be Carmel.

Is her husband dead?

Carmel got married when she was nineteen in order to avoid the otherwise compulsory military service. She had originally intended to divorce her disposable spouse once he would have fulfilled his function as an army waiver, but when it was time for them to officially split up—when she was twenty-one, he twenty-seven—he was diagnosed with brain cancer, and Carmel decided to postpone the divorce. That was three years ago. Her friends and family—especially *his* family—admire her endlessly for taking care of him the way she does, so angelically and altruistically. But Carmel says that the real reason she stays with him is because a young widow is universally acknowledged as significantly more attractive than a young divorcée. And besides, why bother with all the paperwork when you can let nature take its terminal course?

"Sorry I couldn't make it last night. He's still alive."

"Maybe next time."

"But I really wanted to see you. Fresh out of work, with all those schizophrenia germs still on your body."

"They're still on my body."

"Good. Then I'll come over tonight, with all the cancer germs still all over *my* body."

"What makes you think it turns me on?"

"You're attracted to sickness. You're aroused by disease."

"I am?"

"Of course you are. That's why you work at a hospital."

"It's a job."

"You're not doing it for the money."

"What am I doing it for?"

"You're doing it because being close to illness excites you on the most basic carnal level. Being surrounded by patients helps you get in touch with the most primary needs and urges of your body."

"But they're *mental* patients."

"Even better. Fucking with someone's brain is always sexier than just fucking."

"Are you trying to say that I use the company of sick people in order to satisfy a personal desire?"

"That's exactly what you do. You exploit innocent, helpless victims for your own gratification. You're a pornographer."

"I have to get back to work."

"So we'll do it tonight?"

"Do what?"

"Play nurse and gravely ill patient."

"I'll call you when I get home."

"Don't take a shower."

"I won't."

I step into the TV room. They're all watching their soap opera. I go back into the nurse's station and look at the newspaper. First I read a report on the activities of the Jerusalem Front for Bicycle Lanes, then a special epistle from the Minister of Tourism to Israelis traveling abroad:

> *It would make me very happy, in light of the terrible tourism crisis from which we are suffering these days, if you chose to vacation this year in the Negev, at the Sea of Galilee, in Jerusalem, or at the Red Sea. We have been blessed with a beautiful country and world-famous hospitality, so why do we insist on embarking on*

long journeys to foreign lands? Why do we roam the planet so restlessly, aimlessly exploring other countries, seeking peace of mind in outlandish places? Perhaps we have developed this national tendency to be drifters when the Children of Israel wandered for generations in the desert on their way to the Promised Land. Perhaps we became such hopeless nomads due to the prolonged vagrancy forced upon us during two thousand years of exile. Perhaps it is merely the wish to take a break from military duties in the army and on reserve and relieve security-related stress.

In Israel, everybody has to go to the army. And if, for some reason, you don't, they say you're wasting yourself. A person who can't be conscripted—someone with a serious physical disability, for example—is considered a waste of a soldier. I got out of the army about a year ago, after four years of active duty and four years on reserve. You're usually on reserve until you're fifty-five years old, but I managed to get out. I think I deserve to waste myself a little.

My mother, of course, abhors wasting. I once dropped an ice cube on the kitchen floor. When I picked it up and threw it in the sink, she yelled at me: "Don't waste the ice!"

"Mom, it's just an ice cube."

"It's a good ice cube. If you dropped it—just wash it and put it in your glass."

"It's frozen water, Mom."

"It's food. You don't waste food."

It's funny that my nephrectomized mother, criticizing my decision to work as an assistant nurse, reprimands me for wasting myself while she's the one who's wasting away. And my father, who had a mitral valve replacement last year, is not the epitome of health either. But I'll tell you all about it later, because right now I have to make sure that everything's okay in the unit before I actually begin my shift.

Amos Ashkenazi is sitting on a plastic chair in front of the TV, watching a movie, wiping his nose on the sleeve of his purple T-shirt. Uriah Einhorn is on the couch, green baseball cap turned backwards, glasses exceptionally dirty. Immanuel Sebastian and Ibrahim Ibrahim are playing Monopoly on the carpet. The air is dense and stale, smells like a nauseating mixture of dust, sweat, and cigarettes. I open the windows, even though I know they'll try to close them in a minute or two. They're always cold, even in the summer. Even when it's a hundred degrees outside, they still walk around in coats and sweaters. Except for Amos Ashkenazi, who always wears a purple T-shirt.

"Don't open the windows," says Hadassah Benedict. "Please, I'm cold."

"Put another sweater on."

They say I'm abusive, but I don't care. Dr. Himmelblau says that I have to learn to ignore them.

The phone rings again. What does she want now?

"Make no mistake. The mission has not failed. On the contrary. It succeeded in delivering a strong and clear message to all those who doubted our right or ability to rule the cosmos: now that we've conquered all the land we could get our hands on, it's time to move on to outer space."

"Carmel."

"Now that we've turned Jewish suffering into a successful marketing strategy, it's time to take it to other planets."

"Carmel, please."

"And while you've been wasting your time replanting uprooted olive trees or standing in line for a special travel permit to see your doctor in the next village, we've managed to manufacture a man who can see the world from God's point of view."

"I'm not listening."

"And not just a man. A Jew. A real Jew, the kind that asks for kosher food on the space shuttle. By the way, are there stewardesses on American spacecrafts, strutting down the aisles in miniskirts, distributing little plastic trays to the astronauts?"

"He's dead, Carmel. Give the poor man a break."

"The kind of Jew that tries to keep the Sabbath even though he's secular. And by the way, do you think you could really light the Sabbath candles or keep the prayer shawl on your shoulders in zero gravity?"

"Carmel, you're making zero sense."

"The kind of Jew that understands that when the Bible promised us the Land of Milk and Honey, it actually meant the Milky Way."

"I told you, Carmel. This is not what people want to hear."

"Edit it out."

"Why don't you just talk about something else?"

"Like what?"

"Anything. Where are you?"

"At home."

"And what are you doing?"

"Looking at the book you got me."

"Which one?"

"*More Housewives at Play.*"

"There you go. Now why don't you describe one of the pictures for me."

"I thought you didn't want me to take your mind off work."

"I don't, but I'd rather be distracted by *Housewives at Play* than by paranoid political propaganda."

"*More Housewives at Play.*"

"I'm sorry. *More Housewives at Play*. Go ahead."

"Okay. I'm looking at a picture of a young girl penetrated from behind by a woman wearing an artificial penis. The penetrating woman is in her late twenties, maybe early thirties. She has blonde hair, perfectly combed, big smile, perfect teeth. She's a happy housewife, which means that she probably eats meat every day and goes to the gym every morning, to keep her body full yet trim, her breasts round yet firm. The penetrated girl looks fifteen, very pretty, long hair, cute face. She's on the floor, on her hands and knees, wearing white knee socks, her panties rolled down, her shirt pulled up, small nose, puffy lips, pain wrinkles on her forehead, tears coming out of the corners of her eyes. You can't really see, but it looks like she's being penetrated anally. She has small, pointy breasts, one of which the penetrating woman is squeezing with a perfectly manicured hand. In the background stands another woman, tall, athletic, naked, older than the penetrated girl, younger than the penetrating woman, wearing the same kind of leather-strapped rubber penis, her hands on her hips, observing the scene, approvingly, waiting for her turn."

"You see? That's much better. A little offensive, sure, but not nearly as bad as the space shuttle drivel."

"Whatever. It's your book."

"Could you call me later? I think they're fighting out there."

I hang up and step out of the nurse's station. Immanuel Sebastian and Abe Goldmil are punching each other.

"What the hell is going on here?"

"He started it," says Immanuel Sebastian.

"Me?" says Abe Goldmil. "You hit me first."

"Yes, but who finished the toilet paper?"

"I didn't finish it. I used it."

"To wipe your ass or write your poems?"

"I have needs, both bodily and intellectual. I have a right to use the toilet paper in the unit."

"All of it?"

"I go through a lot of drafts."

"Stop fighting," I cut them off. "Abe Goldmil, go get a new pack of toilet paper from General Supply."

"Me? I can't go."

"Why not?"

"What if they get me?"

"Who?"

"The terrorists."

"Don't be ridiculous. There are no terrorists in the hospital."

"I'm staying in the unit."

"It's not like I'm asking you to risk your life or anything. It's two buildings away. It'll take you a minute to walk over there and a minute to come back. Nothing is going to happen to you, I promise."

"It's raining."

"Immanuel Sebastian, you go."

"They don't give supplies to patients."

"Tell them I sent you."

"They won't believe me."

"So what are you going to do? Not go to the bathroom?"

They both shrug their shoulders.

"How do you expect to make it in the real world with this kind of attitude?"

They shrug again.

"Forget it. I'll go get it myself."

I put my coat on and step out into the rain. I'm not supposed to leave the unit unattended, but the chances that someone dies or that they smash the TV within the next two minutes are pretty slim. I walk over to the General Supply Room. Adiva, the woman who runs it, is sitting behind a big wooden desk, counting thumbtacks.

"I need some toilet paper for rehab."

"Tell the nurse to send someone from personnel."

I show her my hospital employee card.

"Oh. Sorry. You new here?"

"It's been almost a year."

"So you're new here."

"I guess."

She gives me a pack of toilet paper, for which I have to sign in duplicate. I walk back to the unit, distribute the pack in the restrooms, and sit on the dirty couch with the newspaper in my lap, pretending that I'm watching TV and reading at the same time, but actually making sure that nobody touches the windows. A black-and-white movie is on. Four struggling comic-book artists are making their first steps in the business. Two guys from New Jersey, who do a dumb comic-book but are unhappy with their commercial success because they feel they can produce better, more meaningful books. A cute blonde, with whom one of the guys is in love, but it turns out she's a lesbian. And an African-American guy from New York, who preaches militantly against whites and whiteness in front of ecstatic audiences of black kids, but off-stage, in real life, he's timid and effeminate and openly gay, and his best friends are the two white guys from New Jersey.

After delivering another aggressive, anti-Caucasian sermon at a comics convention in New York, he's strolling down the aisles of a downtown record store with one of his white friends, when a little black kid comes up to him, asking for his autograph. He turns to his young fan and, signing one of his comic books, points at his white colleague and issues a paternal warning in a deep voice: "See that man right here? He the devil."

"He hates him," says Amos Ashkenazi.

"No, he's his friend. He just pretends as if he hates him."

"Why?"

"Because his friend is white. And he's black."

"He's black?"

"It's not that hard to see."

"I'm not sure," mumbles Amos Ashkenazi.

"How can you not be sure? You don't even have to look at him. Just listen to the way he talks."

"What did he say?"

"Take for example a sentence like *He the devil.*"

"Who's the devil?"

"Nobody. It's just an example. *He the devil.* That's typical black English. White English doesn't have that kind of sentence."

"Is that why the movie is in black-and-white?"

"No. Listen to me. In standard English, like in most Western languages, you can't just put two nouns next to each other."

"Why not?"

"Because then you wouldn't have a complete sentence. You need a verb. He *is* the devil."

"And the black man has no verb in that sentence."

"Exactly."

"Because in comics you can do whatever you want. You can break the rules."

"No, it has nothing to do with comics."

"So what's the movie about?"

"The movie is about comics, but the point is that the black guy speaks a different language."

"Is it dubbed?"

"No, of course it's not dubbed. They all speak English. But the black man's English is different from the white man's English."

"Of course. It's full of mistakes."

"No, it's not. It's just a different language. In black English it is perfectly correct to say a sentence like *He the devil.* In black English, like in many other languages, nominal clauses are very common, and they form grammatically complete sentences."

"Such as?"

"Such as what?"

"You said other languages."

"Oh. Most of the Semitic languages, like Hebrew or Arabic, and even some Indo-European languages, like Welsh."

"Do black people speak Welsh?"

"No. But in black English, just like in Welsh, you can have a sentence without a copular verb—and it wouldn't be a mistake."

"Why not?"

"Because that's how the language works."

"I think I got it."

"Good. So now you see why black people can say a sentence like *He the devil?*"

"Yes. It's because they have thick lips, right?"

Sometimes it's hard to tell whether Amos Ashkenazi is genuinely stupid or just enjoys playing the numskull. It's also hard to tell if he knows that he wears only purple.

And speaking of cleft sentences, I should tell Amos Ashkenazi about the pseudo-cleft: *What Ibrahim Ibrahim needs now is an apple.*

But I'll tell you all about Ibrahim Ibrahim in a little while, because Hadassah Benedict is starting to act a little weird again.

42

"I'm dead," she says, scratching her nose.

"How do you know you're dead?"

"I smell of death."

"Take a shower."

"It won't help. I'm rotting from the inside."

"So what do you want me to do?"

"Nothing. I'm going to kill myself."

"I thought you were already dead."

"But I'm still moving."

"I don't get it. If you're dead, how come you're moving?"

"I don't get it either," she says. "Dead people should not move."

"That's true."

"Which means that I have no choice but to kill myself."

"Sounds like a good idea," I say, and I page Dr. Himmelblau, who comes down to the unit, gives Hadassah Benedict an extra dose of Clozapine, and tells her to watch TV.

They say I'm inhumane, but Dr. Himmelblau tells me to ward them off as soon as they start getting on my nerves. They also say I'm ugly, but Dr. Himmelblau tells me to keep in mind that they all tend to use a projection mechanism.

Dr. Himmelblau goes back to her office upstairs. Hadassah Benedict comes back to the game room.

"The doctor told me to watch TV. What's the movie about?"

"Ask Amos Ashkenazi."

For some reason, they all seem to think that talking to another patient would be stooping too low. Unless, of course, they're having a fight, in which case they have no problem communicating with each other. So when I tell them to talk to each other, it actually serves a therapeutic purpose. It's rehab. If you can't talk to your fellow inmates, how can you expect to be able to function in society? And

GILAD ELBOM

besides, I don't want to be disturbed. If it's not an emergency, don't bother me. Just leave me alone.

"What's the movie about?" asks Hadassah Benedict.

"I'm not sure," says Amos Ashkenazi.

She sits down, but next to the set, not in front of it, watching Amos Ashkenazi as he watches the movie.

"Would you like to read another one?" Abe Goldmil comes up to me, handing me his brown notebook:

If God dictated that she be a star,
Then her celestial body's every curve
I, heathen, vow to worship from afar,
Her every golden rule pledge to observe;
Just as a great, green, grateful tree would serve
The light that gives it life, the long, warm hand
Which plucks its frozen flowers' each numb nerve
And lifts it up, and makes it understand
That every leaf it boasts is like a band
Of saintly seraphs singing songs of praise,
Of pliant players strumming string and strand,
Who their melodious echo wish to raise
Like sacrifice to glorious rays that reign
In heaven and on earth spread their sweet Strain.

The blonde lesbian is showing her tongue to her male suitor.

"He's watching a movie," says Hadassah Benedict.

"He's reading the newspaper," says Amos Ashkenazi.

Abe Goldmil takes his notebook back and sits down next to Uriah Einhorn, who pushes his dirty glasses up the bridge of his nose with his index finger and starts telling his life story again. It's a stupid story, and I wish I could spare you the details, but Uriah Einhorn insists on telling it at least once a week, and considering the fact that there's nothing better to do here right now, you might as well join us and listen to it. Just keep in mind that Uriah Einhorn is not the most stable person in the world, so today's version might be either excruciatingly boring or incredibly fascinating, depending on his current mental state.

* * *

I used to be the best sleeper in town. I used to wake up every morning at seven-thirty, take a shower, put on my suit and tie—I had nice clothes back then—and go to work. I used to work at the best sleep clinic in Tel Aviv. I'd arrive there every morning at nine o'clock, take my clothes off, put on my pajamas, and go to bed. I was one of twenty professional sleepers working at the clinic, supervised by the best psychiatrists, neurologists, psychologists, and lab technicians. Every morning they'd attach electrodes and gauges to our bodies, and we'd plunge into the deepest, most blissful slumber. Conducting advanced research on the cognitive process of dreaming, the scientists would watch us sleep, map our eye movements, monitor our brain waves, scan our central nervous systems—and at five o'clock they'd wake us up.

I'd put my clothes on and drive home, tired and hungry after another hard, long day. My wife would make me dinner, and I'd sit and eat it at the kitchen table, then rest a little in front of the TV, exhausted. She'd suggest that the two of us go out for a while—movie, coffee, a walk in the park—but I'd usually say no. Not tonight. Had a tough day at work. I'm beat. And I have to make an early start tomorrow.

* * *

Dr. Himmelblau, who doesn't want me to use psychiatric lingo when I write the report, has a variety of nonmedical, semiprofessional terms for a patient like Uriah Einhorn. *Par-*

rot is one of them, because the patient repeats the same thing over and over again. *Glue* is another one, because the patient attaches himself to you like a leech, refusing to let go. *Tick* is yet another useful, self-explanatory term. In other words, a *nudnik*.

* * *

One morning I arrive at the clinic and find the whole place in turmoil. Rumor has it that some unexpected cuts in personnel are about to be made, and everybody's in a panic. My sense of alarm grows into massive hysteria when I find out that the basic criterion for the evaluation of the employees is the quality of their dreams. I come back home in a state of anxiety and tell my wife that I'm about to lose my job. My dreams are dull. I know I'm going to get fired.

My wife tries to cheer me up. "You always underestimate yourself," she says. "I'm sure you have very interesting dreams."

But I know that my dreams are no good. They're all superficial, trite, insignificant, predictable: I'm going back to school, but I can't find my classroom, and I'm wandering up and down the halls, lost, scared, mortified. Or I'm walking down the street, and I keep finding crisp hundred dollar bills on the sidewalk, and I pick them up and put them in my pockets, but when I get home, they're all gone. My pockets are empty. Can you get more boring than that?

* * *

"It's boring," says Amos Ashkenazi.

"What is?" I ask him.

"The movie."

"Boring? Look at the way these two girls kiss."

46

"That's disgusting," he says, getting up from his plastic chair, walking away. Hadassah Benedict hurries up and takes his seat. He stops and gives her a furious look, not sure whether to deliberately ask for his seat back and resume watching the movie, or stick to his original plan and go look for something better to do.

"You tricked me," he says to Hadassah Benedict, his voice shaking. "You'll regret it."

"Spoiled child," spits Hadassah Benedict. "What makes you think the whole unit belongs to you?"

"Could you two keep it down?" says Uriah Einhorn, fixing his green baseball cap on his forehead. "I'm trying to tell a story here."

* * *

So my wife has an idea. "If your dreams are not interesting enough," she says, "then you'll just have to *make* them interesting. We'll go out to a bar tonight, have a few drinks, meet some people, and I'm sure that tomorrow, at work, you'll dream much better dreams."

But I know it won't work. I know that if I went out at night, I'd go to work tired the next morning, perform my job inadequately, and damage the quality of my sleep.

* * *

"I'm going to sleep," says Hadassah Benedict.

"I thought Dr. Himmelblau told you to watch TV."

"It's boring."

"What is?"

"The movie."

As soon as she gets up and goes to her room, Amos Ashkenazi makes a glorious return and proudly recaptures his seat. He smiles at me, victoriously, but when he sees that I don't smile back, his face becomes blank again.

Desta Ezra comes out of her room. She looks sweaty. She sits on the floor next to Immanuel Sebastian and Ibrahim Ibrahim, trying to join—or at least watch—their game of Monopoly.

"Go away, Seed of Satan," Immanuel Sebastian growls at her. "What did you come here for? To mongrelize our race?"

"Immanuel Sebastian," I warn him.

"What?"

"Stop it."

"She can't hear me."

"Says who?"

"Look at her: deaf, dumb, and black."

Desta Ezra doesn't speak. She came from Ethiopia a few years ago, when the Israeli government paid the Ethiopian government to get all the Ethiopian Jews out of Ethiopia. They'd been living there for more than two thousand years, a community of black Jews who consider themselves true descendants of the lost tribes of Israel, strictly observing all the Jewish laws and holidays. One day the Israeli Air Force came, landing in the middle of the desert with great secrecy and jumbo jets, and ordered all the Ethiopian Jews to quickly pack their most valuable possessions into small bags, gather outside their villages, and prepare to be airlifted to their new homeland.

Once they arrived in Israel, the Ministry of Interior Affairs demanded that they convert to Judaism, because who knew if African Jews were really Jews. The Ministry of Health flushed all the blood they had donated for victims of Arab terror down the toilet, because who knew what strange African diseases these pseudo-Jews might have been carrying. The army drafted them without any questions.

Dr. Himmelblau says that according to Desta Ezra's family, she'd been a perfectly normal girl before they left Ethiopia. She was sixteen when the airplanes came, happy and excited to go. But as soon as she landed in Israel, she fell silent and never spoke again. Her family thought it would pass—just a temporary muteness due to immigration shock—but when two years went by and Desta Ezra still didn't speak, they had her committed.

I like Desta Ezra. She's shy and slow, always moving about the unit with cat-like suspicion. And when you give her food, even if it's just breakfast or supper, she always seems very grateful.

But the rest of the patients don't seem to be very fond of her. I once caught Hadassah Benedict making Desta Ezra clean her room for her. And when they think I don't see or can't hear, they tease and taunt her:

Black as coal
You have no soul
Serves you right
You Yemenite

* * *

So my wife has another idea. "If they're looking for some good, interesting dreams," she says, "then you'll just give them exactly what they want. You'll go out and buy the most recent books on the theory of dreams, read them carefully, and dream precisely what they expect you to dream. You're going to show them all what a structured, meaningful dream looks like."

At first I didn't like the idea. Sounded too much like cheating. But then I realized that I had no choice. Not if I wanted to keep my job.

* * *

"You can't build a house if you don't own all the streets in the city," says Immanuel Sebastian.

"What about a hotel?" asks Ibrahim Ibrahim.

"Let alone a hotel."

* * *

So I start looking for professional literature on dreams. I go to the public library, I photocopy dozens of academic papers from psychological journals, I stay up late, reading, analyzing, memorizing. And gradually, at the clinic, though not effortlessly, I start having better dreams: I'm climbing up a grassy hill, I'm falling down into a wishing well, I'm on a train that goes through a dark tunnel—

But it's not good enough. A few weeks go by, and I'm summoned to the boss's office to be informed of my dismissal.

* * *

In any case, the globetrotting People of Israel are going abroad in hoards. So have a nice trip, lovely experiences, and a good vacation—and come back to our stormy little country relaxed and revitalized, ready and eager to participate in the ongoing struggle against our enemies. But here is where I get to the point of this letter. There are too many reports of Israelis abroad acting rudely and violently, defaming Israel, adding fuel to the unjustified fire of hatred and hostility toward our peaceful country. We have enough troubles defending our political and military stand, explaining our position to an unfriendly world. It is hard for us to explain ourselves to the Gentiles not only because they have interests in favor of our enemies, but also because we have always been bad at explaining. So why give our enemies more reasons to hate us? Why should we have to relieve stress by sabotaging hotels and restaurants all over the world? Why should we have to steal towels, faucets, ashtrays, and doorknobs? Why should we have to be rude to waitresses and chambermaids, urinate and vomit out of windows, or yell and spit in the streets?

* * *

"We feel that your dreams lack integrity, character, and depth," the clinic director says to me. "They offer no emotional output."

What a mean, wrinkled old man! He had the most hideous hairless head and the biggest, thickest pair of glasses I've ever seen. I hated him! But I didn't say anything. I just left the clinic for the last time, slowly headed home, and went to bed.

The next morning I felt better. I got up and went to the nearest employment agency. When the interviewer, a young girl about half my age, asked me what I could do, I simply said: "Sleep." She blurted out a rude laugh, but I insisted: "I have years of experience. I sleep in a dedicated, responsible, professional way. And I also have references." She gave me a nasty look and asked me to leave.

So I go home. I go over the want ads in the paper. I find nothing. I go to bed. My wife calls. Wakes me up.

"How did it go at the agency?"

"Not too good."

"Don't be too upset, honey. You'll find something. Now how about lunch? Feel like going out?"

"I'm sleeping."

"For free? Sucker!"

I know she was just teasing, but I wasn't in the mood for jokes. I hung up on her, extremely offended. But after thinking about it for a while, I said to myself: She's right. If this is what I do for a living, then I shouldn't be doing it for free. I must find a job.

Determined never to sleep again without proper pay, I decide to leave my wife and embark on a cross-country journey in search of a job. I wander from one remote sleep clinic to another, I visit obscure research institutes in numerous small towns, I check out dozens of hospitals in godforsaken places, I go through an endless series of job interviews, always presenting myself as a loyal, reliable, efficient worker.

But I keep getting rejected. There's this place, for example, where they tell me that the line of work I have chosen for myself is a very demanding one, and that I look worn out. They tell me that I look a little nervous, a little irritable. They say that they doubt I could sleep at all in this jumpy state of mind. "Maybe you ought to take a vacation," they suggest. "Have you ever considered a change of profession? And besides, to be honest with you, we've heard that your dreams are pretty lame."

But I just wear my usual mask of restraint and self-control, thank the interviewers, leave their offices in a graceful, dignified manner, and get back on the road. Overcome by fatigue, I doze off on the train, on the bus, on my motel bed, over my table at the local diner. And it's then that I start having these mad, fragmented dreams: I come home and beat my wife to death for making fun of me over the phone. I slit my boss's throat and run his bald, decapitated head through the paper shredder at the clinic. I handcuff, whip, and brutally rape the girl at the employment agency.

And then, scared, screaming, all sweaty, I'd wake up. For I had sworn never to sleep for free again.

* * *

One last interruption. I don't know if this thing with the three asterisks is working. The whole point was to give you a story within a story, like they often do in literature, but since the patients can't sit still for more than five seconds, I constantly have to cut it off, overusing these poor asterisks to the point where they're more confusing than helpful. So no more digressions. I just wanted to tell you, real quick, that for some reason, Abe Goldmil is the only one who seems honestly interested in Uriah Einhorn's story. He keeps nodding in sympathy, his lower lip curling over his upper one, his eyes almost tearing up when Uriah Einhorn approaches the end of his woeful tirade.

* * *

And all of a sudden I faint. I'm in another strange town, riding in a taxi to another job interview—and I faint. The taxi driver takes me to the local hospital, where I'm diagnosed with multiple system failure due to a severe state of exhaustion. I ended up staying there for two months. A team of serious-looking doctors came to see me every day. They didn't look very optimistic. And when I started getting better, I realized it was too late: I've already wasted my life looking for a sleeping job—instead of sleeping.

* * *

Hadassah Benedict comes out of her room, walking by the TV on her way to the dining hall. Amos Ashkenazi is still watching the movie, tense and rigid, determined not to repeat the mistake of abdicating his precious plastic chair. Ibrahim Ibrahim is on the verge of bankruptcy. The black guy, enraged by some racist remark pitched at him at another comics convention, draws a gun and starts shooting.

"Are you crazy?!" his friends scream at him.

"Take it easy," he laughs. "This baby here—she full of blanks."

I say nothing.

* * *

You must remember that those of us who behave in such a shameful manner reaffirm the anti-Semitic views that the Gentiles hold and encourage the nations of the world to reject us. I urge all of you who are traveling abroad to behave appropriately. Respect your hosts and their property. Act politely. Each and every one of you is an unofficial ambassador of our country. The nations of the world will judge us according to your behavior.

* * *

It's suppertime. I get up and go to the kitchen. I open the gray containers, tell them to distribute the food onto the orange plastic plates that are laid on the little metal cart, and roll the cart into the cold dining room, where I stand and watch as they pounce at the delicacies of the day: tepid chicken-noodle soup, sticky beef stew with carrots and peas, lumpy mashed potatoes, and dry sponge cake. The reason we eat on orange plates tonight is because we're having meat. It's a state hospital, so it has to be kosher, which means that we have two different sets of plastic plates: orange for meat, blue for dairy.

Supper is almost over. Ibrahim Ibrahim pulls a bag of toasted sunflower seeds out of his coat pocket, tears it open with his teeth, and places it on the table for everybody to eat. Excited about this unexpected treat, they all reach for the open bag, grabbing fistfuls of seeds, cracking them in their mouths, spitting out the shells onto their plates. Ibrahim Ibrahim offers me some, and out of courtesy, because I don't want to offend him, I take a few.

Ibrahim Ibrahim has just been transferred to our unit from a military penitentiary, where he was serving a life sentence for murder.

"Take some more," he says.

"Why does it say *Eternal* on the bag?"

"Eternal Imprisonment. The wardens wrote it on all my possessions. My mother sent these to me. I got them the day before I moved here."

Ibrahim Ibrahim has a round face, thick neck, hairy knuckles, and a hole in his leg.

"You like it better here?"

"I had friends in jail."

"You'll make new friends in the unit."

"All my friends were Eternal, just like me."

"It doesn't look like anybody here is going home any time soon."

I must admit, I feel a little uncomfortable talking to Ibrahim Ibrahim. He's new here, so I guess I should ask him some questions, but no matter how hard I try to be professional and unbiased, the fact that he killed a teenage girl makes me a little nervous.

"Where are you from?"

"Nablus. Balata, actually. I was a stone child."

"What's that?"

"I used to throw stones at the soldiers."

"How old were you when you were a stone child?"

"Eleven. Maybe twelve."

"Did you ever get caught?"

"I only did it once. My heart was not in it."

"Why?"

"I was depressed. I've always been depressed. Never saw the point of it all. Nothing made me happy, not even throwing stones at the soldiers."

"But you said you were a stone child."

"You're a stone child even if you throw stones only once. And besides, I was wounded, which automatically made me a hero."

"Wounded?"

"The soldiers shot me."

"When you were eleven?"

"Maybe twelve."

"And what happened?"

"Nothing. I just got shot in the head."

"And nothing happened?"

"It was a rubber bullet."

"What do rubber bullets do?"

"They hurt, but they won't kill you. Unless they shoot you from close range."

"Did you have to go to the hospital?"

"Yes, in Bethlehem. For a long time, actually. But it was okay. They took really good care of me. Treated me like a brave warrior. I kept telling them that I was never really into fighting for Palestine, but they didn't care. They still came to visit me, important officials from the Uprising Headquarters. It's the action that counts, they said."

"What did your mother say?"

"She was angry. She didn't think I was a hero."

"Why?"

"She didn't want me to throw any stones. She wanted me to learn Hebrew. As a persecuted minority, she said, it's important for us to know the language of our oppressors. She also wanted me to learn how to drive."

"Did you?"

"I did, but I didn't pass the test."

"When was that?"

"A few years later, when I was eighteen. Maybe nineteen. After I came back from Russia."

"You went to Russia?"

"To recover."

"From the injury?"

"Yes. First they sent me to Bethlehem, then to Moscow."

I really don't know whether or not Ibrahim Ibrahim knows what he's talking about. And assuming that the trip to Russia was real, does his current mental condition have anything to do with that head injury? He says he's always been a depressive, even before he was shot in the head, so I'm confused.

"Did your mother go to Russia with you?"

"They only had money to pay for one person."

"Who?"

"Me. Who else?"

"No, I mean—who paid for it?"

"Oh. I don't know. Some Palestinian fund."

"Did you feel honored?"

"Not really. The honor they bestowed on me only meant that I had disappointed my mother. And to make things worse, I disappointed her again when I got shot for the second time."

"Rubber bullets again?"

"No, this time it was real bullets. But that wasn't the worst part."

"What was the worst part?"

"That they didn't kill me. I'm going to bed now, with your permission."

Ibrahim Ibrahim gets up, bids me a silent farewell—a subservient nod and a half-smile—and limps to his room. Hadassah Benedict is the only one left in the dining hall, sitting by herself at the sticky table, still munching on her sponge cake. She looks at me, a faint smile on her face.

"That pill the doctor gave me—it works."

"Good," I say. "Now finish your dessert and go to bed."

"It really works," she says. "It made me dead."

CHAPTER 3

I'm with the Jerusalem Interdisciplinary Theater, playing Hamlet in a new production of the play, and we're having a rehearsal, and everything is going smoothly—I'm not sure if the ghost is real or just a figment of my imagination, all that crap—but then a group of other actors organizes a mutiny. They overthrow the director, rearrange the stage, and hand out photocopied sheets with changes in the play. It turns out my character is a nonspeaking Hamlet now. According to the new version of the dialogue, I have no lines. I go berserk. I scream and shout and go around kicking chairs and smashing glasses, but it's all an episode in a comedy act, and I'm not sure whether the nonspeaking Hamlet and my fit of anger are genuine or just a part of the show.

And now I'm in the audience, and I'm sitting beside Carmel's husband, but he's religious, and it's Friday night, and it's already dark when the play ends, which means he'll have to drive home now and desecrate the Sabbath. But he doesn't seem to mind, which I find strange. After he leaves, the play goes on, and Carmel joins me in the audience. She sits next to me, and several suitors approach her, suave and sexy, asking for her phone number. She's not interested, so, pointing at me, she says: "This is my fiancé." But when I put my arms around her, just to make it more believable, she admonishes me, letting me know that I'm just a cover.

Then an old man with a black beard approaches us, pushing a little cart, selling pairs of big metal scissors, the kind that cut through barbed wire.

"How much?" I ask.

"Two shekels," he says.

Which is very cheap, but I only have dollar bills in my wallet, so I give him two dollars, but then I realize that two dollars, because of the exchange rate, are a lot more than two shekels. So I ask him for change, but he just puts the two dollars in a little box on his cart and walks away. So I chase him, and I reach for the box to take one dollar back, but all the dollar bills are fake. Some have a picture of Ezra Pound instead of George Washington, some have a picture of Harpo Marx, and I can't find any of the real dollars that I just gave him. The man begins pushing his cart faster now. He gets out of the theater and into a next-door synagogue, but when I get there, he's gone. Instead, there's a group of soldiers sitting around a coffee table, playing backgammon. One of them says to me: "Do you hear this buzz? It drives my wife crazy. Have you ever hospitalized someone?" So I say to him: "No, I work in a hospital, but I never actually hospitalized anyone. I just take care of people that are already there." And he says: "If you're born with the buzz, you're used to it. If you grew up by the sea, the murmur of the waves doesn't bother you."

And then the phone rings.

What does she want from me so early in the morning? I'll let the machine get it. She didn't call last night, so I just drove home, listened to Celtic Frost's *Into the Pandemonium*, and went to bed.

I check my watch. It's not as early as I thought. It's just a dark morning. And cold. It's always cold in my apartment.

I stay in bed for a little while, listening to the rain coming down on the roof, imagining that Carmel somehow did come over late last night, and that she's here now, waking up next to me, getting dressed, putting on her high-heel sandals and brown slacks, or her almost-see-through summer dress, the one with the sunflowers and skulls, or the deep-red velvet dress, the one that makes her look tall, almost fragile. Or just a pair of tight jeans and her black army boots.

I wonder what she'd look like if she were in the army. I bet she would have made a cute soldier. I bet she would have looked good in uniform. Better than the way I looked when I was in the army.

Tall and thin, I always looked awkward in uniform. I was drafted when I was eighteen, fresh out of high school, and after four weeks of basic training I was sent to the Military Intelligence Academy to study Arabic. The one good thing about the army is that they teach you the language of the enemy. So if you happen to be into languages, it might actually be fun. The main problem was that it lasted four years and three months, which was a little exhausting, especially considering the fact that Elimelech, the top sergeant, was constantly threatening to fine me for putting my feet on my desk. A desk is a table, he used to say, and a table is an altar, and putting your feet on it is a sin.

Elimelech used to harass everybody, especially Tamar, the plump teleprinter girl with the red eyes and the big tits. Tamar and I used to work night shifts together, taking long coffee breaks, talking about science fiction and favorite bands. She liked *The Long Afternoon of Earth* and Faith No More.

One time, at four o'clock in the morning, after a long night of excessive translating and telecommunicating, we took a break, had some coffee, and went for a little walk on the base. We found an empty office behind the armory, went in, locked the door, and made out under a harsh florescent light, leaning on a cold iron desk. She was pale and tired, and her lips were dry, almost cracked, but her skin was warm and yielding, and she had a serious expression on her face, a strange mixture of passion and concentration. It was the first time I saw her not smiling. We kissed and touched for a long time, until we gradually got drowsy, lost interest, walked back to our offices, had some more coffee, and went back to work. We kept talking about books and records but never touched again.

One day Elimelech caught her chewing gum while using the teleprinter. He swore he would see to it that she spent at least two weeks in military prison, but before he had a chance to take disciplinary action, they computerized the division and moved her to another base, and I never saw her again.

I was lonely. I remember sitting on the bus every day, before I had the Justy, the ever-loyal walkman in my lap, listening to Slayer's *Reign in Blood*, thinking how horrible it would be if I died before they released their next album. It's a shame I didn't know Carmel back then, when I really needed her. It could have been nice to have her by my side, on the bus, with her teak-brown eyes and tasty lips, wearing a khaki shirt, khaki pants, and those black, heavy, sexy army boots.

It would have been nice to have a soldier girlfriend. The kind Ibrahim Ibrahim killed.

The phone rings again. Let me get it real quick and then I'll tell you everything I know about Ibrahim Ibrahim.

"Listen to this. How did the Israeli ambassador to the United States describe the liftoff? 'We had deep, beautiful, blue skies, and then with the smoke coming in huge bursts, it was very, very moving. After all, these are our national colors.' Of course, when you make the right choice of national colors, the world sings your glory. Ours are the colors of life itself: the sky, the clouds, the sea, the doves, the beautiful girls with the ivory skin and the indigo eyes. Theirs, on the other hand, are the colors of death: the black of the mandatory veils, the red of the spilled blood, the green of the rotting flesh."

"Tell me more about the beautiful girls with the ivory skin and the indigo eyes."

"Now listen to this. What did the proud colonel transmit down to earth before the spectacular disintegration of his spacecraft? 'I saw Jerusalem from space.' Which indeed seems to be the safest distance to look at our hometown from."

"Thanks for calling. I have to go to work now."

"You're welcome. Call me later."

"I will."

She hangs up. I get out of bed and take a shower. The water is nice and hot, but on a day like today it'll get cold very quickly, so I hurry up and get out and dry off and go back to the heated bedroom. I play *Defenders of the Faith* while I'm getting dressed, but halfway through the first song, doing my Rob Halford imitation in my underwear, there's a knock at the front door. I put my pants and shirt on.

Another bearded loiterer, a stack of papers in his hands, a pen behind his ear.

"Would you like to sign a petition against the Mormon University?"

"The Mormon University? What did they do?"

"Have you seen the monstrosity they're building on Mount Scopus?"

"Many times. It's right across the street from the Hebrew University."

"Exactly. They must be stopped."

"It's a beautiful building."

"Of course it's a beautiful building. All their buildings are nice. That's how they entice and entrap."

"Entice and entrap whom?"

"Us! Who else? That's what they came here for. To destroy us from within."

"They don't bother me."

"Are you sure? They're missionaries. You should be very concerned."

"I have strong faith in our nonaesthetic religion. They'll never be able to convert me."

"You might be strong, but what about our children? What about our younger generation, our innocent kids who don't know right from wrong?"

"What about the Arabs? The Arabs have some very beautiful mosques here."

"I'm not worried about the Arabs. If you've read the Koran, you'd know that such foolishness could not possibly come from God. My guess is that Muslims all over the world are beginning to recognize the futility of their faith."

"I've read the Koran."

"You have?"

"In high school."

"Lord have mercy. Is that what they teach Jewish students in the Jewish State? No wonder our country is in such bad shape."

"They didn't *teach* me the Koran. I majored in Arabic, so naturally, we had to read major Arabic texts."

"You studied the Koran in *Arabic*? Lord have mercy."

"We read other books in Arabic, not just the Koran. Moses Maimonides, for example."

"You read the wisdom of Moses Maimonides and the gibberish of the Koran in the same class? Dear God."

"It was an academic appreciation of Arabic texts."

"Arabic texts? I can't believe it. Do they really teach you that our great rabbi Moses Maimonides wrote his holy books in Arabic? And they call themselves the Hebrew University!"

"It was in high school."

"In high school? Even worse. We'll have to organize a petition against that too."

"What about the Mormons?"

"Forget the Mormons. You need to pray, young man, not sign petitions. Pray hard and hope for forgiveness."

I close the door. Sometimes even Carmel's phone calls don't seem so bad.

But enough about Carmel. I promised to tell you about Ibrahim Ibrahim.

In his file it says that Ibrahim Ibrahim walked all the way from his home in Balata to the Dead Sea, where he stabbed to death a nineteen-year-old female soldier. Balata is a big Palestinian refugee camp near the town of Nablus, on the West Bank of the Jordan River. I've never been there, and I've heard from some guys I used to go to high school with, who were later stationed there in the army, that it's huge and crowded and unbelievably poor and sort of medieval—but everybody knows that all those cheap, shock-value descriptions are nothing but Palestinian propagandist exaggerations. The place has been under Israeli martial law for over thirty years now, so naturally, after stabbing the girl, Ibrahim Ibrahim was tried as a terrorist before a special military court and sentenced to life imprisonment. But after a few months in jail they began to notice that something was wrong with him. He claimed that he had a snake around his neck, and that the snake was choking him, and that the only way he could get rid of it was by killing himself. It's not entirely clear why he ended up killing that poor girl instead, but it did become obvious that his place might not be in jail but in a mental institution.

So now he's in our unit, for observation, which means that Dr. Himmelblau has to decide whether he's crazy or not. She told me she'd asked for his medical file to be sent to our unit from the psychiatric hospital in Bethlehem where he'd been treated in the past, but it's a complicated procedure that requires cooperation between the Palestinian Authority, the Israeli Ministry of Health, and the army. She says that when we get the file, since I'm the only employee in the unit who knows Arabic, and since I used to do it professionally, I'll get to translate it into Hebrew.

And here's an example of a typical Celtic cleft sentence by Flann O'Brien:

Before we die of thirst, called Kelly, will you bring us three more stouts. God, he said to me, it's in the desert you'd think we were.

It has nothing to do with Ibrahim Ibrahim, but it's a wonderful cleft.

It's two o'clock now. I make myself a cup of coffee as I play Motörhead's "Killed by Death," which is a song that I particularly like, and not just because of the brilliant tautology of the title. I used to collect tautologies when I was a linguistics major, and heavy metal songs always provided me with plenty of good examples: *A Corpse Without Soul*; *Hail the*

Vindictive Avenger; Voices from the Sepulchral Grave. Other good sources are tax forms and sex sites: *The beneficial owner is the person who is the owner of the income and who beneficially owns the income. Seeing that hot sperm explode all over her face is a sight to see.* Porn sites are usually abundant in other priceless grammatical fallacies: *Asses spanked beat-red.* You beat them— that's why they're red. Makes sense.

Carmel says we should try it sometime.

But enough about Carmel. Time to go to work.

I get dressed, turn off the computer, lock the door, and drive to the hospital. The road is empty, as usual, and as soon as I walk into the unit, Abe Goldmil marches toward me with his brown notebook, and Hadassah Benedict announces that she's dead again, and Immanuel Sebastian says he can't believe Dr. Himmelblau is forcing him to take this fake new medicine, and Uriah Einhorn, still in his green *South Dakota* cap, asks me if he can borrow the newspaper to go over the want ads, and Ibrahim Ibrahim shouts in Arabic something about Adam and Eve and the serpent, and Amos Ashkenazi, purple T-shirt tucked into his sweatpants, argues with the TV, and Desta Ezra cries without a voice, and the phone rings. It's a long ring—must be Carmel—so I kick everybody out of the nurse's station and tell them to shut up or I'll have them all transferred to the acute ward, where they'll be tranquilized unconscious and electroshocked repeatedly. I pick up the phone.

But it's not Carmel. It's a man with an accent. Says his name is Reverend Joachim, and that he's with the Church of the Current Crucified, and that he was wondering if we had any Christians in our unit.

"Only one."

"Have you heard of our Cured by the Cross project?"

"Can't say that I have."

"We're visiting people in mental and correctional institutions all across the country. We offer those forced to live in social seclusion a chance to pray together."

"Sounds like an important job."

"It is. You may be ill, but not ill-fated. God will cure him whose heart is pure."

"That's nice."

"And it's not a missionary thing. We approach only those already subscribed to the Christian faith."

"No problem."

"So how many Christians did you say you had?"

"One. But he's not a real Christian."

"What do you mean?"

"He *thinks* he's Christian. His calls himself Immanuel Sebastian, but his real name is Immanuel Yerushalmi."

"Would it be okay if I came over and talked to him?"

"No problem."

"I'll be there in two, maybe three hours."

"Looking forward to it."

The threat of electroconvulsive therapy seems to have done the trick, and everybody's quiet now. I grab the newspaper and sit down in the nurse's station. I read a short piece about a memorial service in Finland commemorating the death of a group of teenagers slaughtered by an unknown murderer in 1960, and another piece, a longer one, about termites in California. Termites are not so big in Israel, but I did have some recently, when I moved to my new apartment. I didn't see them right away. They waited for me to settle in, and then, after two or three weeks, they attacked: millions of rusty-red creatures raiding my bedroom, feasting on the very foundations of my house. It would have been easier to fight them had they invaded from the outside. But what's the point of closing the window when it's from the window frame that they're hatching?

Once, when I was still living with my parents, I decided to cook myself some spaghetti Bolognese. My parents were on vacation. I was home alone. I took a chunk of ground beef from the freezer and put it in the microwave. While I was waiting for it to defrost, the phone rang. Some friends wanted to go to a movie. "Sure," I said. I put my jacket on, forgetting all about the meat in the microwave, and took the bus downtown. Three days later, when my parents returned, they opened the microwave. Inside was a white, quivering pile of worms. "The maggots ate your meat," my dad said. I didn't understand. Where did they come from? And how did they crawl into the microwave?

Abe Goldmil knocks on the open door to the nurse's station: a short, hesitant series of soft staccato taps.

"What is it?"

"May I show you something?"

"Is it something you wrote?"

"Yes."

"A poem?"

"A sonnet."

"Whatever. Have I seen it before?"

"No. I just finished it last night."

"Let me see."

He hands me his brown notebook:

Goading my pen, poor blood-tipped instrument,
To keep her entertained, my soul tormented,
I coax a scorching, scornful firmament,
Dark skies of love disdained, of pain augmented.

Unread, my rhymes lie dead, my lines lamented
By willful hands attempting to entice
A heedless pet. Mine is a mind demented,
Hers is a hardened heart—a spurn device
Designed like metal forged, like arctic ice—
To which I beg admission still in vain:
I offer this despondent sacrifice
To heavens whose neglect dooms me insane.
Yet, writing to my life, I must take pride
In my delirium, which is death to hide.

"Very nice," I say to him. "Don't forget that you're patient-on-duty today."

"I can't believe it," says Immanuel Sebastian. "Are you still writing to that silicone slut of yours?"

"She's good-looking," says Abe Goldmil, "but that doesn't automatically mean she's a slut. Take Beatrice, for example. Or Laura. Or the Dark Lady. Nobody ever called any of them a bimbo."

"Yes," says Immanuel Sebastian, "but just keep in mind that your fellow poets were all singing praise to ladies who did not have to go through plastic surgery in order to look divine."

"Natural beauty is overrated," says Abe Goldmil. "Any idiot can be born beautiful. The trick is to be able to mold your congenital ugliness into something gorgeous."

"In that case," says Immanuel Sebastian, "your desire is as artificial as its object. I don't believe in that fake passion of yours."

"You don't believe in anything."

"Yes, but at least I don't waste my time writing nonsense poems."

"I don't know if you've bothered to actually read any of my poems, but just for your information, they happen to be very meaningful."

"Oh, yeah? And may I ask what their deep meaning might be?"

"My poems are myself. My writing is who I am."

"I'll tell you who you are. You're the devil."

"Hey, Goldmil," I step out of the nurse's station. "Sorry to interrupt your scholarly debate with Mr. Sebastian over there, but I'm going over today's newspaper, and I just thought you should know: there's a Julie Strain movie coming on in five minutes on the movie channel."

"Which one?"

"*Fit to Kill.*"

"I've seen it a million times," says Abe Goldmil.

"And you're not going to watch it again?"

"Sorry."

"Suit yourself."

Too close to the TV sits Amos Ashkenazi, negotiating with the images on the screen. I click the remote behind his back, switching it to the movie channel, but he doesn't seem to mind. Or notice. Abe Goldmil throws a quick glimpse at the screen and sinks back into his conversation with Immanuel Sebastian, which, if you're interested, I'll transcribe for you in chapter 4.

The opening titles are over now, and former Playboy Playmates Dona Speir and Roberta Vasquez are skinny-dipping in a small lake by the mountains, splashing water at each other, laughing. A hummingbird is sucking honey out of a flower. Two butterflies are mating in the sun. But the pastoral sequence doesn't last too long. Speir and Vasquez get out of the lake, dry off, put on their military uniforms, arm themselves with assorted deadly weapons, shoot two guys, then run for cover when the enemy jets attack. But it turns out it's only a war game, and the two guys they just shot are actually their boyfriends, and they're not really dead.

"I'm dead," shouts Hadassah Benedict from the kitchen.

"Drink some water," I shout back.

Cut to the bad guy: Kane, son of cinema legend Roger Moore, who plans on stealing a special diamond from a high-ranking Chinese diplomat. The diamond, Kane informs his half-naked Chinese girlfriend, will enable him to take control over the entire planet. World domination, he assures her, is at hand.

"Word domination," says Immanuel Sebastian, "ultimately means world domination."

The phone rings.

"The only way to exit is going piece by piece."

"Carmel, I'm watching a movie."

"Aren't you supposed to be working?"

"I am. It's a Julie Strain movie."

"What's it about?"

"Women in uniform."

"Oh, I get it. 'They made me wear it. I can't wait to take it off.' Is that what you guys imagine a woman in uniform whispering in your ear? Is that what you men fantasize about whenever you see a nun, a nurse, a cheerleader, a waitress?"

Uriah Einhorn walks into the nurse's station, green cap under his arm, an orange plastic cup in his hand.

"Can I have some milk?"

"Wipe your glasses. I can hardly see your eyes."

"Can I?"

"Were you born yesterday? You can't have milk in an orange cup."

"Shall I get a blue one?"

"We're out of milk. Can't you see I'm on the phone?"

He puts his cap on and walks out.

"Who was that?"

"Nobody. Now listen. First of all, don't pick on *me*. I can't speak for other guys, but I, personally, do *not* fantasize about women in uniform. Second of all, I didn't *make* the movie, I'm just *watching* it. And third of all, the same is true for you girls when it comes to uniformed men: soldiers, policemen, firefighters, football players. Don't tell me you don't find them a little more attractive than regular people who have the privilege of making their own decisions regarding their choice of clothes."

"Yes, but we never see ourselves as their rescuers. You, on the other hand, assuming the role of the noble liberator, detect a hidden message which you believe all uniformed girls are trying to communicate: 'My poor naked body is trapped in this cage-like costume. Come and set it free.' As a man, you see all women in uniform as prisoners in need of your help."

"Are you saying that a uniform implies neediness?"

"Of course. And also tidiness. There's something un-equivocally titillating about the impeccable sense of clean-liness a uniform suggests. In a world marked by dirt and disarray, a meticulous uniform embodies the human desire for symmetry, perfection, and order. But at the same time, it also invites a libidinous rebellion against that order. A devoted cheerleader or a disciplined schoolgirl will always stand for innocence aching to be defiled. A pious nun or a dedicated nurse will always represent immaculacy yearning to be violated."

"Which brings us back to your favorite topic: pornography."

"Exactly," says Carmel. "A mandatory outfit divests the person wearing it of individual identity. And once a human being's identity is erased, it's easier to treat him, and especially her, as a sexual object. It's the pornographic principle of victimization through uniformization. It makes women in uniform—or mental patients, in your case—easy, toy-like targets for desire, exploitation, and abuse."

"Speaking of mental patients, I have to get back to work. I'll call you back."

And here comes the moment we've all been waiting for. Enter Julie Strain, a gigantic former Penthouse Pet of the Year, who triumphantly overshadows the entire cadre of Playmates-turned-agents. She's actually one of the bad guys, so the movie is basically about a war between Playboy and Penthouse. Special agent Cynthia Brimhall (October 1985 Playmate of the Month) teams up with Speir (March 1984) and Vasquez (November 1984) in an attempt to prevail over the mighty Penthouse monster. But Julie Strain is stronger, taller, meaner, faster, and much bigger-breasted, assets which not only help her kill most of her enemies, but also get her the best lines in the movie:

Julie Strain: *Do you have the goods?*
Motorcycle Man: *I was born with them.*
Julie Strain: *Oh, yeah? Let's see.*
Motorcycle Man (pointing at the box which contains the missile): *Open it.*
Julie Strain (examining the contents of the box): *Quite a piece of machinery you have there, flyboy.*
Motorcycle Man: *It's long.*
Julie Strain: *It's quick.*
Motorcycle Man: *It's hard.*

GILAD ELBOM

Julie Strain: *It's dangerous.*
Motorcycle Man: *It's aggressive.*
Julie Strain: *It's deadly.*
Motorcycle Man (changes the subject): *You got my money?*
Julie Strain (hands him a black Samsonite briefcase): *Almost everything you want is right here.*
Motorcycle Man (looking her up and down): *Almost.*

But this is no time for talking. Once the delightfully equivocal dialogue is over, Julie gets the action going. She kills the motorcycle man with his own missile and steals the diamond for Kane, then unscrupulously betrays Kane and sells the diamond to a secret order of black kick-boxing warriors. She then hijacks a remote-controlled miniature helicopter, seizes a destroyer, has sex with the captain of the destroyer, kills the captain of the destroyer, raises hell, spreads mayhem, wreaks havoc, kicks ass, and takes off her clothes whenever the director tells her to take off her clothes, which is very often. Kane, who dramatically confesses to being the long-lost son of the former Nazi officer who sold the diamond to the Chinese diplomat, joins the good guys for no apparent reason, assuming command over the special forces that storm Julie Strain's secret hiding place in the jungle.

The movie ends with the spectacular death of Julie Strain—blown to bits by her own miniature helicopter—and a promise to bring her back to life for the sequel, this time as a good character.

"Wait a minute," says Immanuel Sebastian. "I know what you're doing. You're putting it under your tongue, right?"

"Shush!" whispers Abe Goldmil. "He might hear you."

"And what if he does? He doesn't care anyway."

"Just in case," says Abe Goldmil.

The phone rings again.

"This is exactly what happened in the Holocaust. The Nazis used uniforms to eradicate the individual identity of not only the Jews, but also the Germans."

"Carmel, please."

"I'm serious. While the German entity had to be cleansed of any trace of individuality in order to be transformed into a unified killing machine, the Jews were forced to undergo the same process in order for their destroyers to be able to see them as raw material fit for murder and molestation."

"Carmel."

"Look at all those pictures from the death camps. You take a man—or even better, a woman or a child—you strip them naked, tattoo a number on their arm, and what do you get? Pornography. Helpless, obedient objects, with no identity or personality, ready to be humiliated and abused. People whose only purpose is to serve as nameless pieces of meat in a mad carnival of torture, faceless flesh for the gratification of the sick desires of the victimizers."

"Carmel, I'm trying to work here."

"I *am* talking about your work. You incarcerate innocent people whose only crime is that they deviate from a certain subjective norm. You demand that they adapt to an arbitrary code of conduct, and since they can't, or don't want to, you remove them from society. You claim that they suffer from a dangerous disease, you label them insane, classify them as subhumans, and lock them away."

Carmel has been raving about such theories from the moment I met her. "I'm a religious studies major," she introduced herself when we happened to share a table on a busy afternoon at the Humanities cafeteria. "I'm writing a paper about Hrotsvitha."

"Who is Hrotsvitha?"

"You don't know?"

"I don't."

"Hrotsvitha was a sadomasochistic nun-poet from Saxony who wrote sexual-religious plays in Latin."

"When was that?"

"About a thousand years ago."

"Right. And I'm writing a paper on evil aliens from outer space who travel across the galaxy to abduct overimaginative undergraduate female students who write about nonexistent nuns."

She smiled.

"And they're only looking for the very cute," I said, "so you better beware."

"Thank you," she smiled again, "but before you go on, there's something you should know about me."

"What's that?"

"I'm married."

"Oh, that's perfectly okay. Those aliens? They're not looking for meaningful relationships. They just want to have some fun."

"Do they?"

"Oh, yes. They're much more advanced than us."

"Well, then I guess it's okay. I *am* into progress."

"You are?"

"Sure. But let me also give you my phone number, just in case they can't contact me telepathically, these aliens."

I know it sounds like a bad dialogue from a cheesy teenage comedy, but that's exactly how the conversation went, which means that if I want to be honest, I can't change it, not even for the sake of this book. We talked for more than an hour, me telling her about languages and metal bands, she telling me about her husband—originally her roommate—and how he had agreed to marry her to help her get out of the army. Single Israeli women do two years of military service; married women are exempt.

We kept seeing each other almost every day, but recently we decided to keep the relationship platonic while we wait for things to get a little clearer. In other words, while we wait for her husband to die. The only problem is that every time we see each other, we somehow end up doing what we're not supposed to be doing anymore.

"Call me when your shift is over. If I don't have to go to the hospital tonight, you can come over."

Supper is served: buckwheat pie, hard-boiled eggs, lettuce-and-onion salad, and lots of bread. No dessert today, and I see Hadassah Benedict already sneaking back to her room, probably to secretly munch on some chocolate.

Hadassah Benedict is addicted to chocolate. She spends most of her social security money on chocolate bars, which she buys almost every day at the cantina. I once peeked into her room when she thought I was in the nurse's station and saw her standing on the bed, throwing pieces of chocolate to Desta Ezra, who was kneeling on the floor, naked. Desta Ezra was supposed to catch the chocolate with her mouth, but she kept missing most of the pieces, and Hadassah Benedict made her lick them off the floor without using her hands. I stood there for about thirty seconds. Neither of them saw me. Hadassah Benedict was laughing ecstatically. Desta Ezra was sweating. Her breasts were globular and full, rather big for her small body, with stiff nipples that trembled whenever she tried to catch a piece of chocolate in midair. She had little black toes and a little baby-fat belly. Her ass, shiny and round, reflected the florescent light in the room.

I turned around very quietly, walked back to the nurse's

station, sat down at the Formica desk, and shouted: "Hadassah Benedict!"

After what seemed like a minute she appeared at the door.

"Don't eat chocolate in your room."

"I'm not eating chocolate. I'm dead."

"You'll get cockroaches in your bed. Eat only in the kitchen."

Supper is over. Abe Goldmil puts on the long yellow plastic apron and begins scrubbing the dishes to the point of perfect spotlessness. Everybody else is getting ready to go to bed when a strange man appears at the door, short and scraggy, with grubby sneakers, a gray suit, yellow tie, and a horrendous comb-over, which in Hebrew we call Savings & Loans.

"Shalom," he says. "I'm Reverend Joachim."

"Are you a doctor?" Amos Ashkenazi asks him.

"No," the man smiles. "I'm Reverend Joachim."

"You should talk to the boss, then," says Amos Ashkenazi, pointing at me.

"Good evening," says Reverend Joachim. "I believe we spoke on the phone earlier today."

"I believe we did."

"It won't take long. I'll be out of here in ten minutes."

"Take your time."

"So where's our man?"

"Over there," I point at Immanuel Sebastian, who's sitting on the couch in front of the TV, picking his teeth with his pinkie.

"Hello," Reverend Joachim walks up to Immanuel Sebastian. "I'm Reverend Joachim of the Church of the Current Crucified. Will you pray with us, fellow Christian?"

"I can't play now," says Immanuel Sebastian. "Can't you see I'm busy?"

"Pray," says Reverend Joachim, "not play. Will you *pray* with us?"

"I can't. I'm sick."

"What is your illness?"

"FDD."

"May Jesus cure you."

"I don't believe in Jesus."

"You *are* Christian, aren't you?"

"Of course."

"So how come you don't believe in Jesus?"

"FDD."

"I'm sorry?"

"Faith Deficit Disorder. I don't believe in anything."

"Jesus can cure that too."

"I just told you: I don't believe in Jesus."

"Yes, but you're only saying that because you have FDD."

"The fact that I have FDD means I really don't believe in Jesus."

"But Jesus believes in you."

"Maybe he doesn't have FDD."

"I've never heard of FDD. Forgive me for asking, but is there really such a thing?"

"Look at me: I believe in nothing."

"I believe you, but you must know that some people, especially mental patients, can sometimes fake illnesses."

"Can Jesus cure fake illnesses?"

"Jesus can cure anything."

"Then what do you care if my illness is real or fake?"

"No," Reverend Joachim clears his throat, "what I mean is—well—does FDD really exist?"

"Does Jesus really exist?"

"Of course he does."

"Then let me tell you something: FDD is just as real as Jesus."

"I'm sure it is. It's just that some people, sometimes—how shall I put it—*believe* that they suffer from imaginary diseases."

"Not me," says Immanuel Sebastian. "I do not—how shall I put it—*believe* in anything."

"I'm sure your condition is authentic. But you *are* aware of the fact that, again, some people might fake a sickness in order to avoid certain duties or obligations."

"Like what?"

"Like going to church, for example."

"Yes, but those are malingerers. I, on the other hand, really don't believe in Jesus."

"And the fact that you don't believe in Jesus—is that what makes you genuinely sick?"

"Exactly."

"Still, you could just be a nonbeliever. It doesn't necessarily make you mentally ill."

"Are you kidding? Jesus died for you. You'd have to be insane not to believe in him."

"That's very true," says Reverend Joachim.

"Hence the inevitable conclusion," smiles Immanuel Sebastian: "I'm insane."

"But you seem so normal," insists Reverend Joachim. "I look at you and, frankly, I find it hard to believe you're a mental patient."

"Oh, but I am. Diagnosed, hospitalized, and medicated."

"Well," says Reverend Joachim, "all I'm saying is that it's just hard to believe."

"Maybe you just have to take a leap of faith."

CHAPTER 4

Immanuel Sebastian has never been religious. The religious one is Abe Goldmil, who comes from a strict orthodox family. He stopped practicing years ago, when he fell in love with Julie Strain and started writing poetry instead of going to the Yeshiva every day to study the Talmud. After a few years of composing sonnets to Julie Strain, locked up in his room, refusing to leave the house, his parents, following the advice of their rabbi, had him committed. Dr. Himmelblau says that one of the symptoms of his illness is that he fails to distinguish between God and his own private goddess. She also says that one of the symptoms of Immanuel Sebastian's condition is the sadistic urge to provoke and torture people who suffer from an internal conflict, which is why he's likely to harass Abe Goldmil. It's my job, therefore, to observe their behavior and record it for Dr. Himmelblau in the report, without omissions, additions, commentary, or any kind of editing, in order to provide her with as much information as possible before she makes a decision on what drugs they should be taking.

So I'm back in the nurse's station, sitting at the small Formica desk, trying to reconstruct the conversation between Immanuel Sebastian and Abe Goldmil. Reverend Joachim is gone, everybody's asleep, the rain is still tapping at the windows. I make myself a cup of tea and take it back to the nurse's station with some homemade cookies that Odelia brought to the unit the other day. We have our own cups and utensils, of course, reserved for employees only, and our own plates, made of glass, and our own kitchen, with our own little fridge. Sometimes, usually on Friday nights, I eat with the patients, just to show that I'm not above them. But normally, I just wait for them to go to bed before I go into the staff kitchen and make myself some tea and a little snack.

The phone rings. Two short rings. Must be the doctor-on-duty.

"Everything okay in rehab?"

"All quiet."

"Getting ready to go home?"

"As soon as I finish the report."

"We might need your help tonight, if you don't mind staying just a little bit longer. We have a new Arab patient at the acute ward."

"Another prisoner?"

"They're not all terrorists, you know."

"I know."

"A woman from Abu Ghosh."

"Don't they all speak Hebrew in Abu Ghosh?"

"They do, but if we could conduct the intake interview in Arabic, she might be able to give us more accurate information. Shouldn't take more than fifteen minutes."

"Okay."

She hangs up. Her name is Dr. Kagan, and she's forty-something and single and not unattractive, which is why rumors, probably just vicious rumors, say that she's sleeping with the Pharmaceutical Enterprises medical representative, sent to the hospital once a month to give the doctors promotional gifts and free samples of the latest drugs. The medical rep is not bad looking either: tall, thin, healthy-looking hair, always conditioned to perfection, perfect breasts, probably artificially augmented, perfect tan, probably artificial too. Medical reps are always overly sexy. They have to be. They have to push expensive merchandise, and I guess that complimentary pens and calendars are sometimes not enough to persuade the doctors to prescribe the right drugs.

Something strange is going on here. I thought they were all asleep, but now I think I hear some noises. Sounds like heavy breathing. And a doorknob rattling. Is it the front door? Are they finally coming? It makes no sense for them to attack our unit, but who knows. Yesterday the army demolished the house of the parents of a suspected member of the Islamic Resistance Movement, killing some stupid American protester who tried to block the bulldozers with her body, so today everybody's expecting the revenge that they vowed to unleash upon us. I don't think the patients are important enough to be chosen as targets, but what about assistant nurses? And besides, if they're desperate, they might try to slaughter anybody within knifing range.

I think I hear a door opening, but it's not the front door. And footsteps. Someone must be going to the bathroom. The footsteps are getting closer. Uriah Einhorn appears at the door.

"Don't tell me you're sleeping with your baseball cap on."

"I'm not. I just put it on."

"What for?"

"Just in case."

"Wipe your glasses. I can tell what you had for breakfast."

"I'll wipe them in the morning."

"Why aren't you in bed?"

"I'm scared."

"Of what?"

"Arabs."

"Don't be silly. There are no Arabs in the hospital."

"What about Ibrahim Ibrahim?"

"Ibrahim Ibrahim? He's not an Arab."

"He's not?"

"Of course not. Would they let him in the hospital if he were an Arab? He's a good Jew, just like all of us."

"I thought Ibrahim was an Arab name."

"It's his nickname."

"Are you sure?"

"I'm positive. And even if we had Arabs, I'm sure they wouldn't try to hurt you. They're not all terrorists, you know."

"I know."

"So go back to bed now. You have nothing to be scared of."

"Can I get some milk?"

"Can't you see I'm writing the report?"

"I can't fall asleep."

"If I give you some milk, will you promise to go straight to bed?"

"I promise."

"Okay, get a blue cup."

I get up and go to the staff kitchen. Uriah Einhorn follows me with his plastic cup in his hand. I give him half a cup, which he drinks on the spot. He puts his empty cup in the kitchen sink—their kitchen—and follows me back to the nurse's station.

"Now what?"

"Nothing. I just wanted to say thank you and good night."

"You're welcome. Now let me finish the report."

There's that noise again. What's going on here? If this is their response to the knocked-down house and the dead demonstrator, it's certainly driving me crazy. Make up your mind already: either attack or stay home. Oh, I forgot. Your home is demolished.

"What was that?"

"I don't know. Probably nothing. Go back to bed. You promised, remember?"

"Should we call the doctor-on-duty?"

"What for? I'm here, Einhorn. You have nothing to worry about."

"But you're going home in a little while."

"If anything happens when I'm gone, you can call the doctor-on-duty."

"I think I hear footsteps."

He's right. I get up. Sounds like someone bumping into the wall, then footsteps again. I put my hand on the phone. The footsteps are getting closer. Amos Ashkenazi walks into the nurse's station.

"You too? What's wrong with you guys tonight? Are you also scared?"

"Of what?"

"Arabs, jackals, monsters under your bed. You name it, we got it."

"I'm not scared. Should I be?"

"Of course you should. You're a certified paranoid, aren't you?"

"Paranoid schizophrenic. There's a difference."

"I know, I know. What do you want?"

"I think Uriah Einhorn has been kidnapped."

"Are you blind? Or did the Arabs kidnap your brain while you were sleeping?"

"Oh," Amos Ashkenazi takes two awkward steps into the nurse's station, looking at Uriah Einhorn with big eyes. "I didn't see you. What are you doing here?"

"He gave me milk."

"What are you wearing this green hat for?"

"Just in case."

"Why green?"

"It doesn't mean anything."

"Is South Dakota an Arab country?"

"I don't know."

"I think it is. Take it off."

"I will. Before I go to bed."

"Are you with us or against us?"

"Would you two be so kind as to consider postponing this fascinating conversation to a later date? Because if you don't go to bed right now, I'll have no choice but to write in the report that both of you are agitated and insomniac."

"We're going to bed."

"Good night."

As soon as they walk out of the station, the phone rings. A long one.

"Guess what? I don't have to go to the hospital tonight."

"Did he die?"

"No, but the doctors said no visits tonight. Are you coming over?"

"I can't. They need me here as an interpreter."

"Come over when you're done."

"I don't know. They said it might take a few hours."

"Can't you do it right now and get it over with?"

"I'm still writing the report."

"What's to report? Nothing ever happens in your unit."

"I'm working on this dialogue."

"What dialogue?"

"Two of the patients were having this argument earlier today."

"Who?"

"Immanuel Sebastian and Abe Goldmil. And now I have to transcribe their conversation."

"What did they argue about?"

"I think they were talking about God and Satan. Or something like that."

"Sounds interesting. What did they say?"

"I don't know. Something about human sacrifice, snakes, cannibals, monsters, demons, spiritual exercises, masters and slaves, sinful poets going blind, Walt Whitman worshipping the devil. The usual psychotic stuff—with a pseudo-academic twist."

"Yeah, right. Do you really think that mental patients are capable of having academic debates about theological approaches to literature?"

"I don't know, Carmel. All I know is that most of the time I have no control over these characters, and if you find the way they talk lacking in authenticity or believability, there's really nothing I can do about it."

* * *

Still writing to that silicone slut of yours?

She's good-looking, but that doesn't automatically mean she's a slut. Take Beatrice, for example. Or Laura. Or the Dark Lady. Nobody ever called any of them a bimbo.

Yes, but just keep in mind that your fellow poets were all singing praise to ladies who did not have to go through plastic surgery in order to look divine.

Natural beauty is overrated. Any idiot can be born beautiful. The trick is to be able to mold your congenital ugliness into something gorgeous.

In that case, your desire is as artificial as its object. I don't believe in that fake passion of yours.

You don't believe in anything.

Yes, but at least I don't waste my life writing nonsense poems.

I don't know if you've bothered to actually read any of my poems, but just for your information, they happen to be very meaningful.

Oh, yeah? And may I ask what their deep meaning might be?

My poems are myself. My writing is who I am.

I'll tell you who you are. You're the devil. You're God's enemy. And you know why? Because by writing the stuff you write you compete with God.

Me? How can I compete with God?

God is the ultimate creator, and by trying to create your own world, the imaginary world of your poems, you actually defy God. It's as if you're saying, "I'm as good a creator as God. Maybe even a better one."

I never said that.

But that's what your poems imply.

You can't prove that.

Of course I can. How do you think God created the world?

How?

You tell me. What did he use? What were his tools?

I don't know.

Words. And God said: Let there be light, and there was light.

And?

And what do *you* use to create your little made-up world? Words?

Exactly. You write. You invent your own textual reality merely by arrangement and rearrangement of words.

Like God.

Yes. God created the universe by rearrangement of chaos into order. A true master of shape, form, and design, God constructed the world using nothing but words. And you, by writing poems, aspire to do the same. You present yourself and the fake reality you construct as a new, better alternative to God and the *real* world. You may think that writing, the rearrangement of words, simply produces texts, but you have to understand that a new word order ultimately means a new world order.

I don't get it.

Let me put it this way. You and God are basically two manufacturers fighting over language, which is the means of production. Word domination ultimately means world domination.

I think you've got it all wrong. I don't *compete* with God. I try to *imitate* God.

But can't you see that by trying to imitate God you only become his rival? You were made by God. You can't attempt to outdo your maker.

I don't attempt to outdo anyone.

The very fact that you write suggests that you do. Anyone wishing to make room for himself as an artist must fight with his ultimate mentor. If you want to sound your voice as a poet, you have no choice but to wrestle with your divine precursor. And that's exactly what you do. You're a mortal man who challenges God's creative power. You're the devil.

I can't be the devil. I believe in God.

I thought you believed in Julie Strain.

Same thing.

Then why do you keep writing? If Julie Strain is your God, then your pathetic little poems don't praise her at all—they only praise your aggrandized self. Writing is a boastful act of self-assertion. Every text is always about its writer, not about God.

What about Hopkins?

Gerard Manley Hopkins?

Gerard Manley Hopkins. Every poem he wrote was a song of praise to the grandeur of God.

That's what *he* thought.

God was his inspiration.

God was his enemy. He thought he was glorifying a benevolent, protective deity, but in fact he was engaged in a lifelong war with a cruel, bloodthirsty, punitive God. The God Hopkins describes is a brutal beast. It's a God whose lion-like paws tear the poor poet to pieces, a God whose earthshaking feet crush the poet's brittle body, break his splintery spirit. It's a rough and rude God, a menacing monster whose all-seeing eyes threaten to devour his devotee, a penetrative power that forces Hopkins to undergo a series of humiliating examinations and inspections, an exhausting battery of tests and trials.

But Hopkins *loved* God.

Maybe at first. But soon he was driven almost completely insane by the notion of his competition with God.

What competition? He always tried to belittle himself. He always wanted to efface himself while stressing the greatness of God.

That's true. He did try his best to erase himself from his own texts. But he failed.

He did?

Colossally. Instead of self-effacement he succeeded only in achieving the exact opposite: a strong assertion of his individual presence in each and every poem he ever wrote. And the sad thing was that he actually knew his poetry was nothing more than sinful narcissism at the expense of God.

But you can't ignore the fact that he dedicated his poems to God. He did write in the most unequivocal manner possible: Glory be to God.

Yes, but when you look at all those special words he keeps inventing, when you examine all those idiosyncratic tricks of language Hopkins is notorious for—rhythm, meter, rhyme scheme, imagery—even though you can tell he's trying to make his poems perfect hymns to the glory and beauty of God, somehow his own presence dominates the text almost to the point of overshadowing the presence of God.

Almost. But not entirely. God is still very much present in every poem written by Hopkins. There's a purpose to that special language Hopkins invents.

And what is the purpose?

I told you: imitation. Hopkins is trying to imitate God. His poetry is an honest attempt to mime the language of the Lord.

Maybe. But it's not working. By exploring the most radical possibilities of language, Hopkins is pushing his poetic diction to a point where it challenges the Logos itself, the original divine Word. The linguistic boundaries he touches upon are like the sun that what's-his-name was trying to reach, the one with the wings made of wax.

Icarus?

Icarus. It's the point where imitation becomes defiance.

I'm not sure. Hopkins is grateful for being allowed to use the language of God. And to show his gratitude, he offers his poetic words back to the one who gave him the gift of language, back to God. He's not doing anything new. He just completes a linguistic cycle. He simply returns the human word to its divine origin.

Yes, but the language he returns is not the same language he received. It's not the original divine language God gave him but a pretentious, ostentatious version of that language. It's a highly conceited attempt to improve the language of God, which forces his poetry to become vanity and blasphemy.

On the contrary. His poetry is sacramental. Hopkins was a member of the Society of Jesus. A man who, throughout his life, strove to be in the company of Christ. In his poetry, he uses words in a way that enables him—and his readers—to be granted grace and communion with God. His poems are like spiritual exercises. They're like the Eucharist. Reading them is an act of faith. They bring you closer to God. They are transcendence, maybe even transubstantiation.

Yes, but instead of using his so-called poetical practices to glorify God, he simply abuses them to glorify himself. By making his mimetic poetry a religious act, a manifestation of divine grace, he fights with God not only over language, the source of creative energy, but also over the attention and devotion of potential readers and followers. Instead of imitating God, your heretical Hopkins proudly presents himself as an *alternative* to God. And you know who the alternative to God is, don't you?

Julie Strain?

The devil. The antichrist.

Hopkins was not the devil, and neither am I. You may argue that Hopkins did not succeed in his attempt to imitate God or identify with Christ, but I'm not Hopkins. I'm just trying to be myself.

To be yourself is to be like Satan.

Says who?

Hopkins himself. Hopkins was well aware of the fact that any kind of artistic self-expression was devilish. He never read, for example, the guy who wrote "Song of Myself."

Walt Whitman?

Walt Whitman. Hopkins knew deep in his heart that his mind was very much like Whitman's—which made him all the more desirous to read him, and all the more determined he would not.

Why?

Because he knew it was Satan's song. He knew that a work of art is always a hymn in honor of the artist himself, and that the self-celebrating quality of the act of writing is dia-bolical. Finding your own voice is clearly an imitation of Lucifer rather than God. It's man's pride in himself.

Do you really believe that the act of writing is a satanic ritual?

Well, first of all, you have to remember that I don't believe in anything. But yes, the mock sacrament Hopkins was trying to perform did turn into Satan's supper. The whole concept of transubstantiation is based on the real presence of Christ in the Eucharist, but what Hopkins does is a demonic rever-sal of this principle. There is no God in his poetry, there's only Hopkins himself. And when real presence is reduced to real absence, the holy sacrament quickly degenerates to an infernal ceremony in which the participant is tempted to feed on himself. Like a serpent with its tail in its own mouth, Hopkins is tempted to feast on despair, to taste the bitterness of his own sweating self, to yield to the lure of self-cannibalism, to eat the dead body of his own hopelessness, to succumb to the satanic pleasure of luxuriating in his own bad selfhood. He becomes something that fails to undergo transubstantiation. And that's exactly what *you* do.

Me?

Yes, you. Let's assume you have the gift of writing. But if you employ your artistic gift not in the service of your goddess but in praise of yourself, then you're a sinner.

And what if I *am* a sinner?

Then why do you keep writing? If by writing you speak and spell nobody but yourself, then why don't you resolve to remain silent? If by writing you become not a servant of the Lord but a God-defying dissident, a demigod wannabe, a rival rebel, a satanic challenger, a devilish demiurge obsessed with creating alternative worlds of which *you* are the center—then why do you insist on being a writer?

I'll tell you why. Have you heard of the parable of the talents?

The parable of what?

The talents. It's a fable.

Never heard of it.

Then let me tell you about it. A talent was an old monetary unit, a currency used in Biblical times. A lot of money, actually. One talent was worth fifteen years' wages of a worker. Anyway, the story goes like this. Once there was a master—an owner of property—who had three slaves. One day he went on a journey and entrusted his slaves with different portions of his property, each according to his individual ability. He gave the first slave five talents, the second slave two talents, and the third slave one talent. During his absence, the first and second slaves traded with their talents and collected interest: the first slave tripled his original sum, the second slave doubled it. The third slave, on the other hand, dug a hole in the ground and hid his money. When the master returned from his journey, he rewarded the first two slaves, who had been able to make profit with their talents, and punished the third slave, who had refused to employ his talent.

So what's the point?

He ordered that the third slave be cast into the darkness outside.

But what's the point?

The point is that it's a sin not to use your talent. If you have a gift, you must use it.

And that's why you write?

Exactly. My writing is myself. That's what I do. That's who I am. That's my talent. I received a gift from my goddess, a special talent from Julie Strain, a precious deposit from my mistress. It's my obligation not to neglect it, not to let it go wasted. I'm not allowed to hide it. I'm not supposed to bury it in the ground. I must not suppress it.

What would happen if you did?

I would die. Hiding your talent means death.

Says who?

What's-his-name, the blind guy.

Milton?

Milton. Milton knew he had a special talent. He knew that God had given him a gift, and he wanted to put his talent to use, to serve his master with it, to show God that he could do something with it, be creative with it. He didn't want God to come back and check on him only to find out that he had neglected his duty. But the trouble was that he was going blind. So when he realized that his eyesight was gone before he had completed even half his life on earth, and that his remarkable talent was still lodged inside him, pretty much useless, he cried: "How can God demand service when he denies light? How can he expect me to write when I can't see?"

And what did God say?

God didn't say anything.

Why?

Because it was a stupid question. God doesn't need you to do him any kind of special service. All you have to do is be yourself. Just do what you do best. God already has thousands of people rushing all over the place, trying to please him. You don't have to be one of them. All you have to do is stand and wait for your creative self to emerge and consummate. That's the best service you can offer God.

But what if by doing so you become Satan?

Doesn't matter. That shouldn't stop you. Using your creative talent can be an unpleasant experience—it might be extremely painful or diabolically sinful—but *not* using it would be even worse. It's your duty to employ your talent in any case and at any cost. Even if you're blind or desperate. Even when it brings you nothing but pain and torture. To remain silent is the ultimate sin. You must not repress your poetic creativity, no matter how satanic its implications might be.

Wait a minute. I know what you're doing. You're putting it under your tongue, right?

* * *

The phone rings. Two short ones.

"How's the report progressing?"

"I'm done."

"Very good. Whenever you're ready, come over to the acute ward."

"I'm ready."

"Good. Don't swipe out yet. We'll pay you overtime."

I put my coat on and lock the door. I walk over to the acute ward, where Dr. Kagan is already waiting for me at the double door. She lets me in and walks me over to a small room at the end of the hall, where a nurse is sitting by an iron bed to which the new patient is tied down. The nurse looks tired. I've seen her around the hospital before, but I don't know her name. She's sitting on a chair by the bed, reading a magazine with Oded Katash on the cover. We walk in. She puts the magazine on the floor, stands up, tightens the straps around the patient's wrists and ankles, and sits down again.

"Still threatening to kill herself?"

"She hasn't talked about it in the last few hours."

"Let's keep her tied tonight. Just in case."

I look at the new patient. Skinny, dark-skinned, a long mess of black, unwashed hair. Pretty face. Pimply, but pretty. Eyes open, but she keeps staring at the ceiling. Dirty pajamas. She smells. Dr. Kagan unbuttons her pajama shirt.

"I think she's pregnant. Ask her what her name is."

"What's your name?"

"Izdihar."

"Ask her if she knows where she is."

"Do you know where you are, Izdihar?"

"In Israel."

"She's in Israel."

"No, ask her if she knows what this place is."

"What is this place?"

"An insane asylum."

"She says it's an insane asylum."

"And why is she here?"

"Why are you here?"

"A test from Allah. He said unto me: You're a sinner, and because of what you did, which is unforgivable, you'll be sold to the Jews."

"She says she's being tested by God. This is some sort of punishment for her sins."

"What kind of sins?"

"What exactly did you do to deserve this?"

"Horrible things. Unforgivable. I used to be beautiful before it all happened, but they turned my hair black, my eyes brown, my body ugly. I used to have hair like the sun, eyes like the ocean, but they put stuff in my body that turned me dark. They cut my head off and replaced it with this hideous face."

"She used to have blonde hair and blue eyes, but they changed her body and gave her a new face."

"How did they do that?"

"What was that stuff you said they put in your body?"

"The seed of the misguided. They made me take a shower and they put that stuff in me, but I turned it in my body into the deliverer. A shot of white that made me black."

"I'm not sure. She had to take a shower, then they injected her with some white stuff, but somehow she managed to transform it into some sort of salvation."

"She does drugs."

"Do you do drugs?"

"Drugs are from the devil."

"She doesn't."

"Sure she doesn't. Ask her if she's pregnant."

"Are you pregnant?"

"I used to be a virgin."

"She used to be a virgin."

"And?"

"And now?"

"I'm still a virgin, but my son will save us."

"She's still a virgin, but her son will save us."

"Okay, I can see where it's going. Thank you."

"That's it?"

"That's it. You can go home now. Thank you for your help. Will you let him out, Svetlana?"

The nurse gets up and takes me back through the hall. She opens the double door for me.

"Good night."

"Good night."

The rain has stopped. It's cold. I start walking to the parking lot. My breath comes out white clouds, mingles and hangs in the air. I stop. There's someone standing by my car. Three of them. Two tall, one short. The parking lot is empty. Who are they? It's dark. One of them lights a cigarette. They're standing with their backs to me. The one with the cigarette is leaning against my Justy. I take a few steps forward. They turn around.

"Hi," says the one with the cigarette. Leather jacket, trendy stubble, stylish sideburns.

"Hi," I say.

"Where's the bus stop?"

"Right outside the gate."

"Thanks."

The short one is a girl. The other guy has glasses. They turn around and walk to the bus stop. I get in the car and warm up the engine. A light goes on in one of the windows in the unit. Is it Hadassah Benedict's room? I think it is. I turn on the radio. They're playing a song in Hebrew that I actually like: "Mind the Gap" by Inbal Perlmutter, who had a band called The Witches and a three-legged dog and drove her old Volvo into a little concrete wall on the side of the road late at night on the Jewish New Year's Eve a few years ago and died.

The light in the unit goes off. The song is over. I turn off the radio, push the choke back in, and pull out of the parking lot. The gate goes up. They're still waiting at the bus stop. I stop. They walk over to the car.

"Visitors?"

"Yep," says the girl. "Our friend came back from India and went crazy."

"Need a ride?"

"Sure."

They get in. The leather jacket guy and the girl take the back seat. The other guy, the one with the glasses, sits in the passenger seat. I think the leather jacket and the girl are boyfriend and girlfriend.

"Thanks," says the girl.

"Sure."

I'm driving down the hill, slowly. The guy in the leather jacket rolls down his window. It's windy. He throws his cigarette out, then rolls the window up again.

"So what happened to your friend?"

"Went to India and lost his mind. Didn't want to come back. His dad had to go all the way over there to get him on a plane back home."

"From India?"

"Bombay. Do you know Bombay?"

"I've never been to India."

"You've never been to India?"

"No."

"Why?"

"I don't know. I just never went there."

"So what did you do after the army?"

"Studied Welsh. Listened to heavy metal. Wrote. Did you all go to India?"

"Of course."

"Together?"

"We actually met in India," says the girl, hugging the guy in the leather jacket in the back seat.

"I've been there twice," says the guy with the glasses.

"I might go there again next year," says the leather jacket. "I just came back from America."

"America?"

"California."

"Where in California?"

"Hollywood. Have you been there?"

"I've never been to America. What's it like?"

"Hell on earth."

"Why?"

"Stupid place."

"What did you do there?"

"Nothing. Just hung out."

"With?"

"Stupid people. Brain-dead teenage alcoholics, hyper-tattooed pretend rock stars, overly pierced aspiring pimps. Terrible."

"You know what their problem is," says the guy with the glasses.

"They don't go to the army," says the leather jacket.

"Exactly," says the glasses.

"So how come so many people think America is a good place?"

"Good is a relative term," says the leather jacket. "In Los Angeles, good food means a super-greasy double chili-cheese-burger, a good time means overpriced sex with silicone-injected strangers, and good visibility means that you can see the smog."

"Don't you get used to it after a while?"

"I didn't."

"Did you have friends over there?"

"I met this American guy, a student at LMU: Loyola something University. So I thought I'd go over there, visit him on campus, check out some hot Jesuit coeds."

"And?"

"What a disappointment."

"No coeds?"

"Tons of them."

"Not very hot?"

"Sexiest girls I've ever seen."

"But?"

"They weren't Jesuit. Some of them weren't even Catholic."

"Some of them weren't even Christian," says the girl, "right?"

"Right," says the leather jacket.

"Bummer," says the glasses.

"Yeah," says the leather jacket.

"Did you go to strip clubs?" asks the glasses.

"Once," says the leather jacket.

"And?"

"Stupid girls."

"Did you go by yourself?"

"With that guy from Loyola. What a moron. Kept telling me that some of those girls were actually smart."

"Yeah, right," says the glasses.

"Said that some of them do it just to put themselves through college."

"I wonder what they major in," says the girl.

"Exactly," says the leather jacket. "Anyway, I kind of liked this one girl—a blonde, dressed like a schoolgirl—and I was throwing money at her while she was dancing on that little stage they had there, but he got all serious, told me not to throw the money on the floor."

"Yeah, I know," says the glasses. "You're supposed to put the money on the rail, otherwise the girl might slip on one of those dollar bills with her high heels, crack her head open."

"Right," says the leather jacket. "Which didn't make any sense to me. I thought the whole point was to make her pick it up from the floor, like a dog."

"Exactly," says the glasses. "What's the point if you have to be considerate? Means the place is touristy."

"That's right. He said we should go to a *real* strip joint. There's a place near the airport, he said, where they have three-hundred-pound Mexican girls. And he starts giving me directions—take the Hollywood Freeway, then the Harbor Freeway, then the Century Freeway—something like that. But I never went there."

"Why?"

"I realized I had to get a girlfriend."

"Right."

"Not for the sex, of course. For the carpool lane."

The road is wet, but it's not raining. We pass by the kibbutz. Smells like cows. The darkness is getting thicker now. I switch my high beams on. A porcupine disappears into the bushes on the side of the road, black and white.

"Same thing happened to me in Amsterdam," says the glasses.

"What's Amsterdam like?"

"Amsterdam is a good place," says the leather jacket. "I'd like to go to Amsterdam."

"Amsterdam is one disgusting place," says the glasses. "Cold and filthy and nothing to do but look at tulips and ugly people on bicycles."

"What about the Red Light District?" says the leather jacket.

"Yeah, that's true. They have the Red Light District."

"And the coffee shops," says the leather jacket.

"And the coffee shops," says the glasses.

The girl laughs.

"But other than that," says the glasses, "nothing. Just tulips and bicycles."

"Stupid," says the girl.

"There's nowhere to go," says the leather jacket.

"Believe me," says the girl, "we live in the best place in the world."

"I've been to London," I say.

"London is an amazing place," says the glasses.

"London sucks," says the leather jacket.

"Good record stores," I say.

"Bad food, cold weather, cold girls," says the leather jacket. "And the people are just unbelievably square."

"I'd like to live in London for a while," says the glasses.

"London is dead," says the leather jacket. "New York is the place to be."

"New York is even colder than London," says the girl.

"Not in the summer," says the leather jacket.

"In the summer it's hotter than Tel Aviv," says the girl.

"So where would you go?"

"Paris," says the girl.

"Paris?"

"Paris is the most beautiful city."

"Have you ever been there?"

"No," says the girl. "I want to go."

"I've been to Paris," says the leather jacket. "Believe me, you don't want to go there."

"Why?"

"I'm sitting in a restaurant, eating some French fries. I can't finish my fries. I ask for a box. The waiter is not very happy about it, but he brings me the box. I put the fries in the box, pay him, tip him, everything. I go out. Just outside the restaurant, on the sidewalk, I meet a friend of mine from the army, another Israeli in Paris. I open the box, offer him some fries, we start walking—and who comes storming out of the restaurant, chasing us down the boulevard, snatching the fries out of my hand?"

"The waiter."

"The waiter. Can you believe it?"

"They're insane," says the glasses.

"I'm telling you," says the girl, "this is the best place. No need to go anywhere."

"This is as far as I go," I say.

"You live here?"

"Yes."

"Thanks," says the leather jacket. "We can catch a bus from here."

They get out. The leather jacket lights a cigarette. They walk to the bus stop, laughing. I park the car and walk in. My apartment is cold. I turn the heater on, play side A of Manowar's *Battle Hymns*, make myself a cup of tea, turn the computer on.

But I'm tired, and I can't concentrate, and for some reason, I don't know why, I'm thinking about Nathan Cook, who was one of the seven soldiers I shared a room with in the army, and who later claimed his fifteen minutes of fame when he appeared on TV as a national hero, telling the interviewer and the audience at home about his trip to Japan and how he had discovered a pay phone in Nagoya from which, due to some strange technical malfunction, you could make long-distance calls without depositing any money, and how he had informed all the Israelis in Nagoya about it, and how they all called Israel and talked to their families and girlfriends and boyfriends for hours—for free.

I give up. I turn the computer off, finish up my tea, wait for Eric Adams to scream the last notes of "Shell Shock," turn the heater off, and go to bed.

CHAPTER 5

Remember I told you I had a bachelor's degree in compara-tive literature and linguistics? Well, it's not exactly true. I'm still missing two credits. To be precise, I owe a paper. It's for one of my literature classes, and next week is the last date to turn it in without having to pay for those credits again.

I play *Countdown to Extinction* while I'm making myself breakfast. I like Megadeth. No embarrassing orchestral maneu-vers, no megalomaniacal lawsuits, no premature dinosaur sta-tus. It's not quite as good as *Rust in Peace*, but they're still aging a little more gracefully than, say, Dave Mustaine's old band. I like the deliciously prolonged guitar solos, the angry, snarling vocals, the constant shift from the stormy-fast to the pensive-mellow, from the personal to the political, from the wild and rampant to the slick and poppy.

Another quiet morning, but I don't care anymore. My breakfast is ready: a cheese omelet, sliced cucumber with cilantro and dill, black olives, and buttered toast. I lay it all on the kitchen table and sit down with my pocket edition of *Robinson Crusoe.* I've always liked to read while eating. Which always made my mother angry. She used to snatch the book out of my hands, especially at breakfast, and when I would resort to reading the cereal box, she would take that away too. Maybe she didn't want me to be late for school. My mother actually likes books, so maybe she considered reading a semi-sacred act that should never be practiced at the kitchen table. I don't know. In any case, now that I'm living in my own apartment, I find it very refreshing to be able to read while I'm eating. Although I must admit that I still feel a little guilty.

A knock on the door. My next-door neighbor. Her eyes are puffy. They always are.

"I have to ask question."

"Go ahead."

"Moroccan people, they don't talk—they shout. And I heard there is machine make silence."

"Machine gun?"

"No. Noise—machine make quiet. Neighbors shout—machine help."

I think I know what she's talking about. I saw an ad for it in the newspaper the other day: a little battery-operated device that reduces noise level in your apartment. I don't know exactly how it works, but it's supposed to be able to detect noises coming from outside, identify the wavelength of the undesirable sound, and transmit a silent counterwave to eliminate it.

"I want to call, order machine. You will help me?"

"Now?"

"No, not now. First I have money, then I call. You help me."

"Okay."

"Difficult to live with animal people. Very difficult. You know."

"I know."

"No culture. Not like you."

"Thank you."

"A friend in need is a friend indeed. Spasiba."

"You're welcome."

Two o'clock. I put *Robinson Crusoe* in my backpack. I'll read it in the unit. Hopefully it'll be a quiet shift. I lock the door and get in the car.

It's a fast and easy drive today, but when I get to the unit, instead of being quiet, they're all up and awake, active and talkative again. So I throw them out of the nurse's station and take *Robinson Crusoe* out of my backpack, but before I even get a chance to open it, the phone rings.

"You think by killing me tonight my powers will not rise?"

"Carmel, I'm trying to work here."

"You're paying more attention to your patients than your girlfriend."

"Not true. I just kicked everybody out."

"You kick the whole world out of your life, then you run away to this bedlam of yours—only to kick its residents out of your life as well? That makes no sense."

"It's not my fault that reality makes no sense."

Ibrahim Ibrahim is at the door.

"Are you coming over tonight?"

"I'll call you later."

I hang up.

"What is it?"

"Do I have a snake on my chest?"

"Not that I can see."

"You're not saying that just to make me feel better, are you?"

"Why would I want to make you feel better?"

"Can I ask you a question?"

"Sure."

"Do you have a driver's license?"

"Why do you ask?"

"Did you know that my mother made me take driving lessons?"

"Yes, you told me."

"It was rare for a camp boy to take driving lessons. My mother had saved for years."

"But you didn't pass the test."

"That's right. I used to take the bus to Jerusalem every week to go to my driving lessons. I used to get off at the central bus station, cross the big square to the other side, then walk over to the parking lot of the Hilton, where my driving instructor used to wait for me in his car."

"And why are you telling me this?"

"Have you ever been to the Hilton?"

"I've never been inside, but I know where it is."

"Usually there were other students there, either arriving with me at the Hilton or already in the car, and we would take turns driving around the city. They knew I was from Nablus, but they didn't care."

I try to flick through *Robinson Crusoe* while listening to teenage Arab reminiscences, but it looks like it's going to be another one of Ibrahim Ibrahim's soliloquies, in which case the best thing to do is just pretend like you're listening and hope that he'll soon get tired of his own story and leave you alone. I put the book aside.

"One day I was on the bus to Jerusalem, running late for my driving lesson. When the bus stopped at the central bus station, I got off and started running over to the Hilton. As always, there were lots of soldiers on the bus, and one of them, a girl, as soon as she saw me getting off the bus, as soon as she saw me running, she got off the bus and started chasing me."

"The girl you later killed?"

"I'm talking about five years ago."

"Right. Sorry. Go on."

"I guess I looked suspicious jumping out of my seat as soon as we stopped, looking as if I had planted a bomb on the bus or something. Which, of course, I didn't."

"Of course you didn't."

"I was just running late. That's all."

"Of course."

"So I'm crossing the big square, running to my instructor's car, and the soldier girl is running after me. About my age, only half my size—but she had a gun, so even though I knew I hadn't done anything, I began to run faster, hoping she'd realize there was no reason to chase me. But when I look over my shoulder, she's on my tail. So I'm increasing my speed, and so is she. And I'm crossing the street, and so is she. And I'm running across the square, and so is she. And everybody's looking at me, and I'm thinking, Run, run, all I need to do is get to my student driver car, my driving instructor will tell her that I'm okay, he knows me, he knows I'm not a terrorist, he'll tell her to leave me alone."

"Did he?"

"Well, the funny thing was that when I finally got to the parking lot at the Hilton, I couldn't say anything."

"Why?"

"I don't know. Maybe because I was out of breath. I don't know. Maybe I was too terrified to speak. Or maybe I was afraid that he might not stick his neck out for me. What if he turns me in instead of telling her that I'm okay? So I'm standing there in front of him, ready to faint from panic and from running like a madman, and after ten seconds, the girl gets there, and she's standing next to me, and I'm thinking, That's it, my life is over now, and she says to my instructor, Sorry we're late, traffic was so bad, it took the bus forever to get to the central station. And he says, Well, hurry up and get in, you two, I was just about to give up and drive away. And she says to him, Thanks for waiting for us, and then she turns to me, and she says, This is one lesson I wouldn't want to miss, I'm taking the driving test tomorrow."

"Did she pass?"

"I don't know. I know I didn't."

"Yes, you told me."

"May I be excused now?"

"Sure."

"Thank you," says Ibrahim Ibrahim, leaving the nurse's station with an almost invisible bow.

Thank God for the snake that doesn't let him carry a conversation for more than five minutes. Or maybe he just remembered something important he had to say to himself. Who knows. In any case, I guess it's my chance to do some reading now.

I open the book, and for five minutes, maybe even ten, I actually manage to get some reading done, but then, as if detecting that the assistant nurse is busy attending to matters more important than some nutty purple patient, Amos Ashkenazi wanders in, blue cup in his yellow-fingered, shaky hands. His purple shirt smells like he's been sleeping in it for the past three weeks.

"Do we have milk today?"

"I'm trying to read here."

"Oh. Sorry."

He walks out, leaving behind a malodorous afterpresence that makes it even harder for me to concentrate. I open the window, then the book again.

In the first place, I was removed from all the wickedness of the world here. I had neither the lust of the flesh, the lust of the eye or the pride of life. I had nothing to covet; for I had all that I was now capable of enjoying. I was lord of the whole manor; or if I pleased, I might call myself king, or emperor over the whole country which I had possession of. There were no rivals. I had no competitor, none to dispute sovereignty or command with me.

Amos Ashkenazi walks into the nurse's station again.

"What are you reading? If I may ask."

"We don't have milk."

"I'm not thirsty anymore."

"Have you heard of Robinson Crusoe?"

"From *The Bold and the Beautiful*?"

"No, from the book."

"What book?"

"*Robinson Crusoe.*"

"Oh. Sure."

"You've read the book?"

"Sure."

"What did you think?"

"About the book?"

"About Robinson Crusoe."

"Was he the one with the slave?"

"Yes, Friday."

"When?"

"No, Friday. The slave."

"Right, right," says Amos Ashkenazi. "Friday. He was a good guy."

"What do you mean?"

"I mean, if he was black, I guess it would be okay for him to be a slave. But the fact that he was white, and in spite of it agreed to become a slave, that was a magnanimous act."

"Yes, but he wasn't white."

"Are you sure?"

"Trust me. Friday was black."

"Friday?"

"Yes, Friday. That's the whole point."

"What point?"

"The point of view of Robinson Crusoe, who thinks that it's natural for Friday to be a slave just because he's black."

"Does the book say Friday was black?"

"Of course it does."

"I don't remember that part."

"Do you think it would be possible for an eighteenth-century English writer to imagine a situation where a white man would willingly become another white man's slave?"

"What white man?"

"Robinson Crusoe."

"Robinson Crusoe was white?"

Sometimes it's hard to tell whether Amos Ashkenazi actually takes part in the conversation or is still engaged in another dialogue with an imaginary interlocutor. And if he does have a good command of the language, he very rarely demonstrates it. Once, when I asked him about his allegedly big vocabulary, he said he used to memorize challenging words as a teenager. When I asked him why, he said: "To impress girls. Girls like a guy with a big vocabulary."

I open the book again, which Amos Ashkenazi, wisely, takes as a sign for him to leave.

It would have made a stoic smile to have seen me and my little family sit down to dinner; there was my majesty, the prince and lord of the whole island; I had the lives of all my subjects at my absolute command. I could hang, draw, give liberty, and take it away, and no rebels among all my subjects.

Hadassah Benedict peeks into the nurse's station.

"Now what?"

"I need your protection."

"From what?"

"From the Arab. He's harassing me."

"Ibrahim Ibrahim?"

"Yes."

"What's he doing?"

"He says he'll revive me."

"He's just teasing you. He's harmless."

"I heard that he killed somebody."

"He's heavily medicated, just like you. He wouldn't hurt a fly."

"He says he's some kind of Arab saint who can make the dead come alive."

"So he says he's an Arab saint who can make the dead come alive. Who cares?"

"I do."

"You shouldn't. Just ignore him."

"How can I ignore him when he's intimidating me all the time?"

"He's not intimidating you, he just has his own problems. What do you care if he believes he's an Arab saint? Leave him alone."

"I can't. He says he can wake the dead."

"Does he actively threaten you?"

"He speaks in general terms, but I feel scared. You have to protect me."

"Go get him."

"What do you mean?"

"I want to talk to him."

"Shall I call him?"

"Yes."

"Ibrahim!" Hadassah Benedict screams across the unit.

"Don't yell like you're in the marketplace! I could have yelled myself!"

"Here he is."

"Yes?" says Ibrahim Ibrahim. "Did someone call me?"

"Hadassah Benedict says you're talking about waking the dead."

"I was just telling her about the Reviver of the Female Infants Buried Alive."

"Who?"

"Did you know that back in the Age of Ignorance, before Islam, people used to bury their newborn females in the ground?"

"I didn't know that."

"They did."

"Why?"

"Because of the drought and the poverty and the fact that girls were always a burden and could never go to work and only caused the family more expenses."

"So they just killed them?"

"Yes, by burying them alive. Until the Reviver of the Female Infants Buried Alive came."

"And what did he do?"

"He redeemed the girls. He would approach the father and say, 'I heard that your wife recently had a female baby, and that you were planning on burying it alive. Would you consider selling me the baby?' And the father would say, 'With pleasure.' And then the Reviver of the Female Infants Buried Alive would pay the ransom and save the girl. They say that by the time Islam came, he had already redeemed three hundred girls, maybe even four hundred."

"And what did he do with them?"

"I have no idea."

"And why does Hadassah Benedict feel threatened?"

"I have no idea. It's just a story."

"You heard him, Hadassah Benedict. It's just a story."

"He's torturing me."

"Don't be such a scream queen."

"He's making my life a living hell."

"I thought you were dead."

"I am. So why can't he leave me in peace?"

"I'll tell him to leave you in peace. Now if you two would be so kind as to remove yourselves from my station, maybe I could finally go back to my reading."

First of all, I gave him a pair of linen drawers, which I found in the wreck; and which with a little alteration fitted him very well; then I made him a jerkin of goat's skin, as well as my skill would allow, and I was now grown a tolerable good tailor; and I gave him a cap, which I had made of a hare-skin, very convenient and fashionable enough; and thus he was clothed for the present tolerably well; and was mighty well pleased to see himself almost as well clothed as his master.

"What are you reading?"

Abe Goldmil. Standing at the door, holding a book in one hand, his brown notebook in the other. Behind him stands Immanuel Sebastian, an unlit cigarette hanging from his lips, an overflowing ashtray cupped in his hands.

"What are *you* reading?" I ask Abe Goldmil.

"*The Dharma Bums.*"

"Kerouac?"

"Yes."

"Why?"

"Why am I reading it?"

"Yes, why?"

"Research. I'm working on a new sonnet to Julie Strain."

"What does *she* have to do with the Dharma Bums?"

"Well, she's from California, right? And the book, *The Dharma Bums*, takes place in California, right? So I figured, if I could evoke in my poetry images she can relate to, maybe she'd respond."

"She'll never respond," interjects Immanuel Sebastian from behind Abe Goldmil's back.

Abe Goldmil steps into the station and sits down across the desk from me. Immanuel Sebastian moves forward and takes Abe Goldmil's place at the threshold.

"Why do you think she'll never respond?" I ask Immanuel Sebastian.

"Because his poems suck. They're all like, 'Oh, I'm so lonely and miserable, you're my goddess, I worship you, I want to be your doormat.' That's stupid. Be a man." He turns to Abe Goldmil. "Be aggressive. She doesn't want a wimp. She doesn't want you to be her slave. She wants you to be her master."

"Speaking of masters and slaves," I say, "have you guys read *Robinson Crusoe*?"

"Gregory Corso?" asks Abe Goldmil.

"No, *Robinson Crusoe*."

"Oh, Robinson Crusoe. Yes, of course. Robinson Crusoe. The third guy. The one who climbs the mountain with Jack and Japhy."

"Who?"

"Yes, I remember him. He's in the book."

"What book?"

"*The Dharma Bums*."

"I'm talking about *Robinson Crusoe*."

"Yes, Robinson Crusoe. But that's not his real name, you know. They all use fake names in *The Dharma Bums*."

There's definitely something weird about Abe Goldmil today: barging into the station, sitting down uninvited, talking about the beats. I might have to call Dr. Himmelblau.

"Forget *The Dharma Bums*. Have you read *Robinson Crusoe*?"

"Sure. I like his poems."

"No, no. Listen to me: have you ever read a book called *Robinson Crusoe*?"

"By Kerouac?"

"No, by Defoe."

"By the what?"

"Defoe. Daniel Defoe."

"Was he the one who wrote *Moll Flanders*?"

"Exactly. And *Robinson Crusoe*."

"They wrote it together?"

This is obviously going nowhere.

"Have *you* read *Robinson Crusoe*?" I turn to Immanuel Sebastian.

"Sure."

"Is he in *The Dharma Bums*?"

"Sure. They're all there: Robinson Corso, Japhy Snyder, Allen Goldberg, Philip Warren. They were great poets."

"You're right," says Abe Goldmil to Immanuel Sebastian. "I should be a man, write like Jack and Japhy."

What's wrong with Abe Goldmil? He's much too hyper today. If he doesn't calm down in, say, twenty minutes, I'm calling Dr. Himmelblau.

"You're patient-on-duty today," I say to Abe Goldmil, "aren't you?"

"No, I was patient-on-duty yesterday."

"So go set the table in the dining hall."

"Okay."

After I had been two or three days returned to my castle, I thought that, in order to bring Friday off from his horrid way of feeding and from the relish of a cannibal's stomach, I ought to let him taste other flesh; so I took him out with me one morning to the woods. I went, indeed, intending to kill a kid out of my own flock and bring him home and dress it. But as I was going, I saw a she-goat lying down in the shade and two young kids sitting by her; I catched hold of Friday. "Hold," says I, "stand still"; and made signs to him not to stir; immediately I presented my piece, shot and killed one of the kids. The poor creature, who had at a distance, indeed, seen me kill the savage, his enemy, but did not know or could imagine how it was done, was sensibly surprised, trembled and shook, and looked so amazed that I thought he would have sunk down. He did not see the kid I had shot at, or perceived I had killed it, but ripped up his waistcoat to feel if he was not wounded, and, as I found presently, thought I was resolved to kill him; for he came and kneeled down to me and, embracing my knees, said a great many things I did not understand; but I could easily see that the meaning was to pray me not to kill him.

Ibrahim Ibrahim is now pacing up and down the unit, appearing, disappearing, and reappearing in front of the door to the nurse's station, delivering a passionate sermon to himself, half in Arabic, half in Hebrew. When he sees me, he freezes and smiles an embarrassed, idiotic smile.

"Come here," I call out to him. "I want to ask you some questions."

"About the Reviver of the Female Infants Buried Alive?"

"No, about literature."

"What do I know about literature?"

"It's about a famous book. Perhaps you've read it."

"The book you were asking Goldmil and Sebastian about?"

"I thought you were talking to yourself."

"I was. But I thought maybe you were giving them a test."

"A test?"

"To see if they're really crazy."

"Do you think they're not really crazy?"

"Oh, they are. Goldmil—he's completely insane."

"What makes you say that?"

"All those poems he writes to that girl—what does he want from her?"

"I don't get it. If you believe they're genuinely crazy, why did you think I was giving them a test?"

"I thought maybe *you* thought they weren't crazy."

"Why would I think that?"

"You're in charge of us. It's your job to suspect us."

"Do you *want* me to suspect you?"

"No, but you'd be neglecting your duty if you didn't."

"What do you care if I neglect my duty?"

"You're right. I'm a patient, not a client, so why would you bother to make sure I'm a satisfied customer?"

"What are you trying to say?"

"That I really shouldn't care whether the service here is good or bad, because I'm not paying for it. The state is. And it's not even *my* state."

"What do you mean, not your state? You were born and raised here, weren't you?"

"Yes, but I'm not a citizen. I'm a Palestinian."

"Listen, I didn't call you over to talk about politics. I wanted to ask you about literature."

"Okay. Ask me about literature."

"Have you read *Robinson Crusoe*?"

"No, but I've heard about him. He was a famous Jew."

"Robinson Crusoe was Jewish?"

"Of course."

"Who told you that?"

"Everybody knows that."

"That Robinson Crusoe was a Jew?"

"Yes. And that Friday was an Arab."

"I thought this wasn't going to be about politics."

"That's what I thought too."

"What do you mean?"

"When I first came here, I thought I was being treated as a regular patient. But soon I found out that they only put me here for observation, to determine whether I'm a terrorist or a madman."

"And which one are you?"

"Neither. I'm just a killer."

"You killed a Jewish girl."

"Yes, but I didn't kill her because she was Jewish."

"Why *did* you kill her?"

"Because I wanted to die. My motive was not political. It was personal."

"You knew her?"

"Of course not."

"So what do you mean, personal?"

"Personal in the sense that it served a personal purpose, not a political purpose."

"And what was your personal purpose?"

"I told you: I wanted to die."

"So why didn't you just commit suicide?"

"I was afraid. I wanted someone to suicide me, and I knew that if I killed that girl in front of the soldiers, they would shoot me dead."

"So why a Jewish girl? Why didn't you kill an Arab girl?"

"If killed an Arab girl, who would bother to shoot me?"

"Hold it, hold it. I told you: I don't want this to be political."

"It's going to be political whether you like it or not. The very fact that I'm alive is political."

"Yes, how come you're still alive?"

"Because they shot me in the leg. They didn't want to kill me, because then I would be just a crazy dead murderer. They wanted me alive. They wanted to keep me as a symbol of Arab terror, as living proof that all we want to do is kill as many innocent Jews as we possibly can."

"Yes, but now you're here, and the whole beauty of this place is that you're all equally insane here, no matter who you are."

"Do you really think that just because this place is removed from society it isn't political? Take Robinson Crusoe, for example. You can spend almost a lifetime on a desert island, all alone, thinking that you're free from political ideologies and power structures and social conflicts, but the moment you discover so little as an innocent footprint, it becomes, in your mind, the footprint of your enemy. The footprint of a cannibal."

"But Friday *was* a cannibal."

"Only in *your* mind. He killed to eat, that's all. But you call him a cannibal. You claim he's a threat to humanity. You interpret his personal drive as political."

"I keep telling you: I'm trying to avoid the political."

"You can't, because you do the same to me. I killed to get killed, but you call me a terrorist. You claim I'm a threat to your country. You translate my private cause into a political one."

"I never called you a terrorist. I treat you as a madman, just like I treat anybody else here. And as long as you're in this hospital, I don't care what you did or why you did it. As far as I'm concerned, you're all mental patients, regardless of your actions or motives."

"Yes, but the difference is that I'm not a real patient. I'm just here for observation."

"Trust me, you're going to stay here."

"And what would you do if they put me back in jail?"

"How can they put you in jail? You're insane."

"Suppose they decide, at the end of my observation period, that I'm a regular terrorist. What would you do?"

"Don't worry, I'll tell them you're crazy."

"And what good would your word be? You're just an assistant nurse."

"So what do you want me to do?"

"You won't be able to do anything. When they take me away, you'll just stand and watch."

What does Ibrahim Ibrahim want from me? Why can't he talk pure nonsense, like a normal mental patient?

"I thought you said you didn't read the book."

"I didn't."

"But now you're saying that you're Friday."

"I'm not Friday. I'm the bear."

"Ibrahim Ibrahim, you're neither Friday nor a bear. You are you. And one of the things you'll learn here, in rehab, is how to rebuild your fragmented self."

"I'm the bear."

"There is no bear in the book. Robinson Crusoe has a dog, a cat, a parrot, and goats. No bear."

"I'm the bear."

"Okay, now go get ready for supper."

"Okay."

Just as I'm about to get up and go to the dining hall, to check on whoever is patient-on-duty today—and, more importantly, to get rid of Ibrahim Ibrahim—Abe Goldmil steps into the nurse's station, shoving his notebook in my face.

"Here," he says to me, "read this."

Hitchhiking up, crisscrossing your terrain,
My karma boots caressed your granite crest.
I was the muster-monk of your domain,
I stood & watched you push your snowy breast
Into my sturdy, furry hoof. I pressed
My Zen-drunk lips under your fecund hood.
I climbed where eagles & coyotes nest,
& cooked myself a bowl of dirt-cheap food.
I said: "I'd love to touch your greenest wood,
& levitate above your steepest peak."
You said: "Oh, quit the Buddha-babble, dude,
And dig your dharma deep into my creek."
I said: "Goodbye, I'm going to Tibet.
You'll wait for me, won't you?" You said: "You bet."

I page Dr. Himmelblau, who comes down to the unit and gives Abe Goldmil an extra dose of Tegretol. "Don't worry," she says, "I anticipated it. I noticed he's been down lately, so I increased his antidepressant dosage. But apparently, it's making him high. We'll balance him with some mood stabilizers, and please let me know if he continues to be manic."

"I will."

They say I'm evil, but Dr. Himmelblau says that we really have to keep an eye on them. She leaves the unit just as the food arrives: oil-soaked fried eggs, canned sardines, over-cooked pasta again, and lots of bread. Whenever they don't have enough food in the main kitchen, they send lots of bread. And the patients love it. If they could—that is, if I let them—they would chew on bread all day. They say I'm starving them, but Dr. Himmelblau says they have to learn the meaning of the word *boundaries*, and that it's our responsibility to restrict them.

After supper I try to locate the ones that haven't bugged me about Robinson Crusoe yet, see if they're still alive. Desta Ezra wouldn't talk anyway. Hadassah Benedict is in the kitchen, washing the dishes. Uriah Einhorn is in his room, probably sleeping. Should I wake him up? Should I ask him about Robinson Crusoe? Probably not. I'm going to have to wake him up at eight for his meds, and there's no point in going through the whole ordeal of reviving a narcoleptic twice. I might as well try to talk to the necromimetic.

Hadassah Benedict is stooped in front of the kitchen sink, wrapped in the long yellow plastic apron, soaping up the dishes in slow, circular motions.

"How's it going?"

"Good. I'm feeling better today. Much better."

"You are?"

"Yes. I think I'm ready to go."

"Go where?"

"Home."

"Home? You don't have a home. You've been here for how long?"

"Six years."

"And you think that after six years you can just leave the hospital and go home?"

"I'm not talking about right now. In the future. Maybe next week."

"Next week? Two hours ago you said you were dead."

"That was two hours ago. I think it's over now."

"What's over?"

"The death."

"The death is over?"

"Yes. I think I'm ready to be released."

"Why don't you talk about it with Dr. Himmelblau. She's the one who decides, not me."

Poor Hadassah Benedict. This is a state hospital, which means that she'll probably stay here for as long as the state exists. Her family got rid of her ages ago, when she began to talk about being dead, and after many years of wandering between all kinds of shelters and institutions, she landed here, in our rehab unit.

"Good idea," says Hadassah Benedict, "I'll talk to Dr. Himmelblau. She'll let me go, she's a good woman."

"Okay, now listen. I want to ask you a question."

"Okay."

"Have you read *The Dharma Bums*?"

"*The Dharma Bums*?"

"No, I'm sorry. My mistake. *Robinson Crusoe*."

"*Robinson Crusoe*?"

"Yes, *Robinson Crusoe*."

"So why did you say *The Dharma Bums*?"

"I got confused, I'm sorry. I meant *Robinson Crusoe*."

"Yes, I've read *The Dharma Bums*."

"No, I'm not interested in *The Dharma Bums*. I just got confused. And it's all your fault, all of you. You and your nonsense about the Dharma Bums."

"Well," says Hadassah Benedict, scrubbing the pale-blue plastic plates with a grimy, worn-out, almost soap-free sponge, "both stories are about slaves, so I guess they're easy to confuse."

"Slaves?"

"Yes. Robinson Crusoe has Friday, and the Dharma Bums have Princess."

"Princess? Who's Princess?"

"The girl. The girl they gang-rape at the beginning of the book."

"Gang-rape?"

"Yes. They bring her to their apartment and force her to have sex with them. All three of them. First this guy Japhy makes her happy, so to speak. Then this other guy, Alvah, has a turn, so to speak. And then she's crying on the floor as all three of them are working on her—so to speak."

"She was crying?"

"Well, she was crying *and* laughing, which means that it must have been very traumatic for her. I think."

"Maybe she was bipolar."

"I guess she was," says Hadassah Benedict, "because they actually admit that she was a little off her nut, so to speak. But they didn't care. They had their way with her and left her lying on the floor in a fetal position, violated and abused. And they even tell her that from now on they'll be doing it to her every week. They assumed she liked it."

"Didn't she?"

"I don't think so. They took advantage of a helpless mental patient and called it Buddhism. They decided she needed this kind of guidance. They believed she actually wanted it."

"Okay," I say, "now finish cleaning up the kitchen—and when you're done, come to the nurse's station and I'll give you your pills."

"Okay," says Hadassah Benedict, probably unaware of the fact that I've completely lost my patience for her psychotic babble.

After they all take their meds and go to bed, I sit in the nurse's station and read a few more passages from *Robinson Crusoe*. Everybody's asleep now, so I drop the book and write the stupid report—as if something interesting will ever happen, as if all of a sudden there will be a dramatic improvement in their condition and they'll be ready to start a new life of good health, hard work, and social dignity—then I pick up the book again, but after ten minutes I put it aside and start doodling on some scratch paper, killing time.

It's ten o'clock now—my shift is over—but just as I'm about to leave, Carmel calls.

"Are you coming over?"

"I can't. I have a paper to write."

"What about?"

"Robinson Crusoe."

"Come over and I'll write it for you."

"I don't think so."

"Don't worry, I'll write you a good paper. What class is it for?"

"Eighteenth Century Literature."

"And what exactly do you have to write about?"

"Representations of subjectivity."

"No problem. I'll do it for you."

"Without talking about psychiatry being a sinister form of tyranny disguised as scientific compassion?"

"But it is."

"I know you think it is, but can you write a paper without mentioning it?"

"Sure."

"Promise?"

"I promise I'll do my best."

So I turn off the lights, and I swipe my card and walk to the parking lot, and I start the car and look for something interesting on the radio, but all the stations are playing sad, late-night, wintertime music, so I push Cradle of Filth's *The Principle of Evil Made Flesh* into the tape player, and I start driving. The road is dark and slippery, and I'm cold inside my car, and as I approach Carmel's house, it's beginning to rain again, and all I want to do is call the whole thing off and go home and start writing the paper, or just crawl into bed, far away from all these people. What do they want from me? Why do they keep beleaguering me? And how can they expect me to perform sexually in this kind of weather? Who knows what Carmel has in mind for tonight. Maybe I'll just tell her that I can't stay, that I really have to go home and start working on my paper.

But when she opens the door in blue shorts and a white undershirt, I forget all about my escape plans. She smiles, and the heat from her apartment feels good on my face, thawing my ears and nose. I hug her, and I walk inside, and she makes me a cup of tea, and I begin to feel a little hot and sweaty, but in a nice and soothing way.

"You want to play Robinson Crusoe and Friday?" she asks, her face very close to mine, her mint-and-honey breath warm in my nostrils.

"How do you play Robinson Crusoe and Friday?"

"Oh," she says, "it's very simple. I have to be naked, and you save my life, and I put your foot on my head, and then you do me in the butt."

"Okay," I say, and we play Robinson Crusoe and Friday, and when we're done, she tells me to go ahead and take a shower while she starts working on my paper.

"You're not going to write it *now*, are you?"

"Why not?" she says. "Do you have the book with you?"

"*Robinson Crusoe?*"

"Yeah. I might need to quote from it."

"Sure," I say, and I pull the book out of my backpack and put it on her desk. I kiss her on the cheek and grab a towel from the closet and take a long hot shower, and when I come out of the bathroom, she's sitting in front of the computer, in her shorts and undershirt again, typing.

"How's it coming along?"

"Good," she says, her eyes on the monitor. "Listen, I'm going to take a quick shower too. But don't read it yet. It's not finished."

"Okay," I say, and she goes into the bathroom, and of course I read it as soon as I hear the water running:

Shipwrecked on a desert island, Robinson Crusoe finds himself with no one to supply him with a sense of superiority, no dependent inhabitants to reinstitute him into his natural role as governor and caretaker. In the absence of women, children, Blacks, Jews, or Moors, Robinson Crusoe is unable to dominate and subjugate the inferior strangers so vital to his survival as the crown of creation. His first and most important task on the island, therefore, is to invent an imaginary other.

As a self-proclaimed member of the master race, Robinson Crusoe sets out to concoct a lesser human being in order to maintain his own sense of supremacy. Thus, the absent islanders become an imaginary swarm of menacing cannibals, heathen savages threatening to eat poor Robinson Crusoe alive. The threat, however, is entirely spurious. During his twenty-eight years on the island, Robinson Crusoe has not been disturbed by a single so-called savage. The danger of being devoured, attacked, or even spotted by the locals is utterly fabricated. In fact, the real peril lies in the nonexistence of the islanders. It is the very absence of the other that poses the greatest threat to Robinson Crusoe.

For without the weak and lowly, how can we ascertain our own sense of preponderance? We need the fantastic savages to define ourselves as civilized. We need the fictitious sick to continuously feed the illusion of our own health. We need the imaginary needy to confirm our remarkable generosity.

And in the absence of human beings, animals will do. Robinson Crusoe's notion of mastery and control is sustained by the dependency and loyalty of his companions: his dogs, cats, goats, and parrot. However, these are mere prefigurations of the ultimate pet: Friday.

By assigning to Friday the attributes of a fallen beast in dire need of guidance, protection, domestication, and salvation, Robinson Crusoe conveniently makes himself a benefactor, protector, savior, and creator. The local brute has to be given a name; he needs to be taught how to eat, dress, and speak; he requires spiritual direction and a set of rules for proper conduct. A master's work is never done.

But it is not just the archetypes of tame animals—the obedient dog, the language-acquiring parrot, the useful goats—that herald the inevitable appearance of the easily housebroken man-slave. The land itself, raped and exploited, foreshadows the arrival of the ever-docile Friday. "He let me know," says Robinson Crusoe, "that he would work the harder for me, if I would tell him what to do."

Friday is required—and, according to Robinson Crusoe, is eager and happy—to forsake his former self for the sake of ascending to a much higher sphere. It is only natural, Robinson Crusoe believes, for Friday to relinquish his family, homeland, culture, religion and language to win the greatest reward of all: becoming a loyal servant to the Lord of the Island. However, *even after doing so, Friday still remains dangerous. Robinson Crusoe, in order to be able to justify acts of aggression as self-defense, needs to maintain an imaginary threat.*

For the vile other serves not only as proof of our righteousness, but also as a highly effective and much-needed conscience purifier. By calling the islanders savages, Crusoe, the epitome of enslavement and oppression, manages to cleanse himself of his own barbarity. By accusing women of witchery, the male inquisitors were able to justify the persecution of the helpless as a holy mission. By imagining that the Jews conspired to take over the universe, the Germans could pave their guilt-free way to world domination. By calling our neighbors terrorists, we legitimize our own malevolent practices of abduction, imprisonment, torture, murder, senseless bombing and systematic starvation. By diagnosing physically healthy people as insane, we grant ourselves the right to incarcerate and torment the weak and poor under the guise of medical treatment.

Thus, the pseudo-compassionate psychiatrist becomes an agent of cruelty and oppression. He needs the constant presence of his patients in order to be able to construct his own perception of himself. He surrounds himself with allegedly crazy people in order to feel compos mentis. He needs the powerless in order to feel competent. And if there are no sick, helpless people around, he goes looking for them. He diagnoses miserable creatures as dangerous monsters in order to assert himself as strong, smart, and benevolent. And if he cannot find miserable creatures, he simply creates them. The ultimate goal of the psychiatrist's search for the lowly other, therefore, is to turn ordinary people into wretched freaks.

I hear Carmel opening the bathroom door. I quickly move away from the computer and lie on the bed, closing my eyes, pretending to be thinking about subjects and predicates. In the following example, the grammatical subject

Ibrahim Ibrahim can also be, like any of the other three elements in the sentence, the psychological predicate: *Ibrahim Ibrahim drives tomorrow to Berlin.*

Carmel walks into the room. I open my eyes. She smiles, a not-so-big towel wrapped around her body, covering her breasts but only half her ass.

"Isn't it nice to take a hot shower when it's so cold outside?"

"Yeah," she says, "but the water got cold halfway through. I had to make it real quick."

"Oh, I'm sorry," I rub her knee. "Next time you go first."

"Did you read it?" she asks.

"Of course not."

"Good. When is it due?"

"The day after tomorrow."

"Are you going to sleep over?"

"I'd love to, but I don't think I should. I have a morning shift tomorrow. Have to be at the hospital at seven."

Which, of course, is not entirely accurate. I have to be at the hospital at three, as usual. But I do intend to wake up early.

CHAPTER 6

The sun is up, but everything is still colorless. Jerusalem can sometimes feel like the North Pole, dreary and dismal for weeks, with thick rain coming down from dark clouds, no signs of warmth or light. Not that I've ever been to the North Pole, but this is what the weather should be like up there, not in the Mediterranean Basin. The Mediterranean Basin is supposed to be hot and sensual, with honey and olive oil dripping from every corner, pomegranates and figs growing on big trees, succulent and wild, greens and reds glittering in the sun.

I'm sitting in front of the computer, showered and dressed, drinking my second cup of tea, listening to Diamond Head's *Lightning to the Nations*. I woke up early today, determined to be productive and efficient, two words that my mother is very fond of. I hate waking up early. Which is why I always do the three o'clock shift at the hospital. Everybody else hates the three o'clock shift. Odelia, Dr. Himmelblau, all the nurses and doctors at the other wards, all the psychologists, social workers, occupational therapists, art therapists, psychodrama therapists. They wake up early anyway, probably because they have kids, and if they did the three o'clock shift, they would have nothing to do at home until three, probably because they don't listen to heavy metal or write papers about Robinson Crusoe. And they probably hate coming home late at night, tired, to tired spouses, with nobody waiting up for them with a cup of hot mint-and-honey tea and detailed plans for active interpretation of key scenes from the great myths of Western civilization. So they always ask me if I wouldn't mind doing all three o'clock shifts again next week, never realizing that I actually like the three o'clock shifts. Because if you do the morning shift, you have to be there at seven, and at eight o'clock you have to start waking up Hadassah Benedict and Immanuel Sebastian and Uriah Einhorn and Abe Goldmil and Amos Ashkenazi and Ibrahim Ibrahim and Desta Ezra, and then Uriah Einhorn again, and then everybody all over again, which is always much harder than making sure they go to bed at night.

We don't have a night shift at the unit. Other wards have night shifts, and everybody loves them—you get paid more—but Dr. Himmelblau decided that in order to help the patients move out of institutionalization and into independence, they must overcome their fears and anxieties and get acquainted with the harsh reality of having to sleep unattended. They have a special phone in the dining hall, which they can use to call the doctor-on-duty in case of an emergency, but so far there hasn't been an emergency.

In the army, when I had to do guard duty, I always preferred the night shift. And not because I got paid more. In the army you don't get paid at all, which is why everybody hated the night shift. They only give you a small allowance, enough for a pack of cigarettes every other day and a movie once a week—if you get the weekend off—so you might as well do your best to avoid walking up and down along the fence with your M-16 for six hours in the middle of the night.

But I liked it. Everybody thought I was crazy, but I didn't care. I liked rising in the dead of night, watching the little hours go by, peering into the darkness, into nothingness, looking for invaders that never came, humming entire records from beginning to end, pacing endlessly, pretending to be walking somewhere, somewhere quiet and spacious, even cold, I didn't mind. Somewhere like the North Pole, where a night shift lasts six months.

Sometimes I would even whistle out loud. I knew it was dangerous—I was making myself an easy target for the enemy—but I didn't care.

The closest I've been to the North Pole was when I flew to London to see Danielle Dax and Raymond Watts. It was my first and only time out of Israel, and the shows were good, very good, but what really excited me were the record stores. Splendid palaces with literally millions of discs, and flocks of guilt-free people openly listening to what will forever be considered underground music in my hometown. I saw the British Museum and Buckingham Palace and the Tate Gallery and Hyde Park and everything, but Shades was by far my favorite place in London. Just a little alcove on an elusive alley in the heart of the city—the exact opposite of the colossal HMV shop on Oxford Street—but entirely devoted to heavy metal. At first I was confused. I couldn't find the metal section. Then I realized that there was no metal section. It was all metal.

The phone rings. It can't be Carmel. She's never up so early. Unless her husband died. Must have kicked the bucket last night while the two of us were playing master and servant. Or bought the farm, or checked out, or whatever stupid idiom they use in this ridiculous language.

It's Dr. Himmelblau.

"I have a special job for you. I want you to drive to Tel Aviv to get our patient's file."

"Ibrahim Ibrahim's?"

"Yes. I called the army this morning. The file is ready, but we have to collect it in person. The hospital will reimburse you for the gas, of course, and you'll be paid double your regular hourly rate."

"What about my shift?"

"Odelia will fill in for you."

"When do I have to be there?"

"As soon as you can. Go straight to the liaison unit at the Central Headquarters. You know where that is, don't you?"

"Of course."

"I gave them your name and hospital employee number."

If I'm lucky—and quick—I might have time to check out two or three record stores in Tel Aviv. There's no Shades or HMV there, but they still have better stores than Jerusalem. When I was in high school, I used to pretend I was sick, get a note from my mother, skip school, and take the bus to Tel Aviv to go on a record-hunting expedition, which usually yielded at least one or two items I could never get in Jerusalem.

At first I used to actually become ill. I used to stay in bed for three or four days—asthma, sinus problems, angina, things that are easy to produce even when you're healthy—then take an extra day for my convalescent sally. But after a while I started skipping the sickness part. "You're a good student," my mother would say to me, "you deserve a day off. Go buy yourself a record so you have something new to play when you're doing your homework." Then she would write notes to my teachers, simply saying that I was unable to come to school. If the teachers wanted details, they had to call her. Which they never did.

I lock the front door and get in the car. I warm up the engine for a minute or two, then start making my way out of the city and onto the Tel Aviv Highway. On the side of the road they placed burnt armored vehicles from 1948, mostly troop carriers that were attacked on their way to free the besieged Jerusalem. Usually I don't notice them—I've seen them so many times—but today they're being refurbished by men in orange vests. Repainted, actually. Rust paint. I slow down to take a look, but the car behind me honks, so I speed up. They burnt us in Europe, and when we ran away, they burnt us here. And here's the proof, in rust-proof rust.

I stop for gas at a little gas station where they have a big Elvis statue standing outside a gift shop that sells Elvis memorabilia and paraphernalia, including photomontage postcards that show Elvis visiting the Wailing Wall, the Dead Sea, the Golan Heights.

"Hey. Can I catch a ride to Tel Aviv with you?"

I'm pumping gas, and standing next to me is a man of about forty, maybe forty-five, slightly balding, shorter than me, wearing dirty boots, a dirty pair of jeans, a blue sweatshirt tied around his belly, and a clean white T-shirt with four little red silhouettes on the front: an ant, a spider, a praying mantis, and a dung beetle.

"You're going to some army facility, right?"

"How did you know?"

"I can tell."

"Are you a soldier?"

"Me? No."

"Reservist?"

"I'm an exterminator."

I replace the nozzle.

"I'll pay you. I just can't afford to wait for the bus."

"You don't have to pay me. But I'm going to Central Headquarters," I say. Which is what I usually say to unwanted hitchhikers, hoping they'll think I'm some undercover officer driving to a military base on a secret mission, so secret that it prevents me from giving them a ride.

"That's exactly where I have to be. Thank you."

He gets in. I always feel uncomfortable with hitchhikers, I don't know why. I always feel as if I have to apologize for something: for owning a car, for driving to Tel Aviv like I'm on vacation, for not being fat or short. I push Anvil's *Metal on Metal* into the tape player, turning up the volume a little louder than necessary, but halfway through the first song he starts talking, forcing me to turn it down.

"What?"

"They drafted my car."

"Who?"

"The army, who else?"

"But you said you're not a soldier."

"They didn't draft me, they drafted my car. My new van, the one I use for my job. And I just got it, which means that the bastards must have records of all the new vans that are being bought in the country."

"Your exterminator's van?"

"My one and only. I got people waiting for me in houses full of rats. What am I supposed to tell them? That the army took my van away?"

"Why did they take it away?"

"Some big maneuver, they said. They didn't have enough four-wheel-drive vehicles. Have you ever heard such crap?"

"Maybe they did have a big maneuver."

"Big maneuver my ass."

"They're not necessarily lying. Maybe they really had a shortage of vehicles."

"Don't make me laugh."

"Is it legal?"

"Of course it's legal. They can do whatever they want. They can draft your wife if they happen to decide that there's a shortage of women in the maneuver."

"So what are you going to do?"

"What can you do? Nothing. They've had it for two weeks, and today they called and said I could come pick it up at Central Headquarters."

"Don't they provide some sort of transportation? For you to get there?"

"Don't make me laugh. It's an army, not a welfare service."

We pass through Abu Ghosh, one of the few Arab villages that were spared after 1948. They have good restaurants in Abu Ghosh, and sometimes I go there to eat, hoping to get a chance to practice my Arabic, but the Arabs always talk to me in Hebrew.

"Do you like your job?"

"Sure."

"Do you ever feel sorry for the bugs you kill?"

"You're driving to Tel Aviv. Do you feel sorry for the gas you're burning?"

"The gas is not a living creature."

"I don't care if they're living creatures. They bug you, I kill them."

I turn up the volume again. "March of the Crabs." We leave the Judean Mountains and enter the Inner Plains, where it's slightly warmer. The rain has stopped, and I speed through unripe green fields, placid argent reservoirs, and a chain of little ready-made towns. It only takes fifty minutes to get to Tel Aviv, but since it's on the Mediterranean, on the other side of the country, and since Jerusalem is high up in the mountains, close to the Jordanian border, it always feels as if you're traveling an incredibly great distance.

"What do *you* do?"

"I'm a student."

"Do you have a degree?"

"No, not yet. I still have a paper to write before they let me graduate."

"What do you study?"

"Literature."

"So you read books?"

"Sometimes."

"Can I ask you a question?"

"Sure."

"There's this one story that I never understood."

"A short story?"

"It didn't seem that short to me. Have you read the one about the guy who turns into a cockroach?"

"Of course."

"So please explain to me, if you can, why his family doesn't spray him."

We pass Ben-Gurion International Airport, which means that we're getting close to Tel Aviv. I look at him, and I notice that he's not wearing his seat belt. He's looking at me as if he knows that in spite of—or maybe even because of—all my education, I'm going to say the stupidest thing now about humans and insects. Why did I have to pick up an exterminator? Why couldn't I get a guitar player, or a structural linguist, or a lingerie model?

"He's their son."

"That's ridiculous. If cockroaches invaded your house and said they were related to you, would you let them stay?"

"Maybe."

"They're dirty creatures."

"But they write beautiful stories."

"I don't think it's such a great story. I think they should have gotten rid of him right away."

"But he didn't do anything."

"That was exactly the problem. He was a parasite."

"I thought *they* were the parasites."

"I can see why you never graduated."

Next to the airport there's the dump, and then the suburbs, and then Tel Aviv. It's raining again, and everything is gray and slow. We're almost there, but as usual, there's a traffic jam that starts almost ten miles before the city.

The worst traffic jam I ever got stuck in was in Jerusalem, the day I moved into my new apartment. The place I had in the Greek Colony, close to the trendy Ghost Valley Street, was getting too expensive for me, and I moved to my present apartment, a smaller place in a cheaper neighborhood, where strangers knock on your door every morning, and you can never take a nap in the afternoon either, because in the summer, a guy with a megaphone and a pickup truck full of watermelons drives up and down the street screaming *Watermelons*, and in the winter, another guy, an Arab with a megaphone and a pickup full of second-hand junk, drives up and down the street screaming *Alte Sachen*. At first I thought it was interesting that an Arab would scream in Yiddish. I thought that the way the watermelon man used the conditional was also interesting, and I even toyed with the idea of writing a paper about it: *no red, no sweet—no money*. But then

I decided it was more annoying than interesting, and I started cursing them and turning up the volume on the stereo. Then I started working three o'clock shifts.

The day I moved in, I got sick. Really sick, not record-shopping sick. Fever, chills, nausea, weakness in my bones. It was in the spring, so I can't remember if it was the watermelons or the old things, but I remember that I couldn't sleep. My mattress was on the floor, in the middle of the living room, no bed, and I just lay there, shivering, surrounded by unpacked cardboard boxes. I had hooked up the stereo system, but the place still looked strange, and I knew that something was missing.

Piccadilly was the best record store in Jerusalem at the time. I drove there very slowly, pressing my fingers against my forehead, blowing my nose into a tissue every few seconds. When I got there, I could barely stand up. My heart was beating frighteningly fast as I searched the metal section. I had a hard time deciding between Enslaved and Dark Funeral. Enslaved is dark, punishing, unpredictable, with multilayered songs that are usually long and ominous. The best music to recuperate to. Dark Funeral is fast, tight, and brutal, with a white-noise kind of heaviness that leaves you exhausted. Could be perfect for driving the flu away.

I got both. And felt guilty. And took it as a warning against avarice when the police blocked half the roads in the city due to a false Suspicious Object alarm. I spent more than two hours in the car, on the verge of fainting, cursing myself and my headache and the police and all the suspicious objects in the world, forced to watch the clumsy little police robot dismantling an innocent briefcase that some absent-minded jerk had left at a bus stop.

When I finally got home, I collapsed on the mattress, in my clothes, unable to move. I played Enslaved and Dark

Funeral alternately for three days in a row—didn't shower, didn't shave, didn't open any of the boxes—until true Scandinavian black metal finally defeated the germs.

I check my watch. It's almost ten. The highway is still jammed. We've been crawling-and-stopping for the past twenty minutes, but now we're not moving at all. I stare at the bumper sticker on the car ahead of us: ISRAEL IS REAL. Tel Aviv looks far away, even though you can already see its skyscrapers.

"So how did you know I was going to Central Headquarters?"

"Premonition."

"Really?"

"Of course not. What do I look like, the Messiah?"

"So how did you know?"

"Statistics. If a Jerusalemite goes down to Tel Aviv, chances are he has some army business to take care of: pick up a drafted car, get permission to go abroad, postpone reserve duty."

"Sometimes I go to Tel Aviv to buy records."

"You wouldn't need all those records if you didn't have to go to the army."

But I'm not paying attention to my exterminator anymore. We're moving now, and I crank up the volume again, fumigating the remains of his sentence with a thick cloud of guitars and growls. I thought I could have a nice, quiet drive, with some time to myself. I was wrong.

Never mind. We're almost there.

"You can drop me off in front of the main gate."

"No problem."

"And if you ever have cockroaches, here's my card."

"I once had termites."

"And did you let them stay in your house?"

"Not really."

"There you go. I'll see you around."

He gets out, and I drive on to the parking lot, where I park the Justy under a big eucalyptus and walk to the liaison unit. I like going to military bases as a civilian. Not that I get many chances to do it, but when I do, it always feels good to walk free among the soldiers. They probably think I'm a good-for-nothing deserter, a turncoat, a parasite, a cockroach. But I don't care.

The guard at the main gate takes my identification card. He picks up the phone and reads my number into the receiver, then hangs up.

"They'll call me right back," he says.

I'm waiting. I look at the other people waiting to get in. Drafted cars? Permits to travel to India? Deferment of a three-week reserve duty stint in the refugee camps of the Gaza Strip until the wife and baby are released from the hospital? Maybe they're just outside contractors. Does the army have a pest control unit?

The phone rings. The guard says it's okay, I can go ahead and take the main path all the way to Building 6, Floor 3, where they'll have me fill out some forms before I'm admitted to the liaison unit. He keeps my ID and gives me a visitor's pass, and I walk through the gate and into the base, where everybody is moving with speed and importance, even the privates who sweep the paths and paint the fences, as if the fate and future of Zionism is resting on their uniformed shoulders. I walk slowly, looking around, scanning the faces attached to the insignia, checking their feet. Those who shine their boots are good soldiers. Those who don't are even better. They're out there, in the battlefield, running in the dust, chasing the enemy, protecting our country, too busy to pay attention to such trivialities as military discipline.

I pass by a handwritten sign, one of many posted along the path:

Do not try to compete with the sun
Turn off all the lights when your work is done.

And another one:

The gun is your friend in times of dismay
Clean it and oil it every day.

And another one:

The Israeli soldier is not a mutt
Keep your hair clean and cut.

"Can I help you?"

I must look suspicious, strolling down the main path in civilian dress. I look at the soldier blocking my way: a short captain with sleek black hair braided into a long pigtail, thick legs in a straight khaki skirt, and black glasses resting a little too low on an aquiline nose.

"No, thanks. I'm fine."

"Can I see your visitor's pass?"

I show her my visitor's pass.

"Where are you headed?"

"The liaison unit."

"Building 6, Floor 3."

"Thank you."

She walks away, her pigtail dancing on her back. I walk a little faster. At the entrance to Building 6 I have to state my business and show my pass to another guard. He lets me in, and I take the stairs to Floor 3, where a teenage sergeant tells me to have a seat and fill out a form in which I promise not to examine the contents of the documents about to be handed to me while they are in transit and without proper authorization from the Israeli Defense Forces, the Ministry of Health, or an official plenipotentiary.

And another form, in which I promise that, if granted permission to inspect the file, I will not, under any circumstances, disclose its contents or part thereof to commercial agents, hostile elements, or anyone not authorized by the Israeli Defense Forces, the Ministry of Health, or an official plenipotentiary.

And another one, where I have to supply information about my military medical profile, rank at time of demobilization, current occupation, marital status, and recent visits to foreign countries.

All the forms are filled out and signed now, and the teenage sergeant says that Dan Ron, the second in command, will see me now. She opens the door for me, letting me into his office.

"You're here for Ibrahim Ibrahim's file."

"Yes."

"We don't have the file."

Dan Ron is a major, broad-shouldered, with a five o'clock shadow at noon, probably tall—but I can't really tell because he's sitting behind a big desk covered with telephones and internal communication equipment and pictures of him and his girlfriend vacationing in different pretty places in Israel and abroad. There's a big map of Israel on the wall behind his desk, a framed picture of the chief of staff on the wall opposite the desk, and a big window overlooking the privates painting the fence.

"You don't have the file?"

"The division didn't send it."

"So what do I do?"

"I don't know. You can go get it from the division."

"Where is that?"

"Netanya."

"Netanya?"

"I happen to have someone from the division here. You don't mind giving him a ride back to Netanya, do you?"

He gets up. He is tall.

"Lunchtime. The sergeant will give you directions."

He grabs his gun from his desk, stuffs it into his pants—holsters are for dorks—and storms out of his own office in a way that communicates both military determination and urgent hunger. The teenage sergeant escorts me out of the office and into her little reception space, where she draws a map for me on the back of a blank DERF, Damaged Equipment Report Form, with detailed instructions on how to get to the division. If I'm fast enough, I might be able to do one or two record stores.

"But don't go yet," she says. "Let me get Oz."

She dials the number where he's supposed to be, but he's out to lunch, of course.

"You can wait for him here."

"Can I make a phone call?"

"Who are you calling?"

"My girlfriend."

"There's a pay phone downstairs. Floor 1."

I go down to the first floor, but Carmel is not home. Or she's not picking up the phone. I try again. No answer. Three soldiers are standing in line behind me. I let the first one make his phone call, then the second one, then I try her one more time, but there's still no answer.

I climb back to the third floor. Oz is a captain, and he's already waiting for me. He looks as if he's slightly angry, but he doesn't say anything. We walk to the Justy. Traffic is slow, and it takes us a long time to get out of Tel Aviv and onto the Coastal Highway. This time, instead of playing my music, trying to avoid being harassed by my hitchhiker, I'll simply initiate the conversation, which will hopefully allow me more control of the dialogue.

"So what do you do in the division?"

"I prefer not to talk about it."

"Classified information?"

"You got it."

"So where exactly are we going? How far is the division from downtown Netanya?"

"I prefer not to discuss the location of the division."

I push *Transilvanian Hunger* into the tape player. The title track begins, with Fenriz shrieking about the cold mountains and the cruel hands and the shadow of the morbid palace and the eternal embrace of daylight slumber, but my passenger's face is not registering any change. His jaw is tight and stern, his mouth frozen in fortitude, his eyes locked on an imaginary target down the road.

"So what's it like up there? Is there any action in Netanya? Interesting places to go?"

"I'd rather not answer any questions."

We drive in silence for a few minutes, listening to the rest of the album. The title track is in English, but most of the other songs are in Norwegian. We pass through the northern suburbs of Tel Aviv, then a long stretch of sand dunes, then a row of villages that haven't decided if they're happy being affluent and relatively close to both the sea and the city, or miserable because they're dead. The Coastal Highway can sometimes be beautiful, but today it's foggy and congested, and the sea to our left is as muddy as the sky. I open the glove compartment.

"Have a mint."

"I'd prefer not to at the moment. Thank you."

I turn up the volume. I like it when the music reaches a point where it becomes a blur, all the instruments bleeding into each other to create a cacophonous wall of sound in which hardcore fans can trace melodies that might not be there. Four of the songs were written by the guy who killed Euronymous. That was what Yoram Yizraeli wrote his last piece for *The Capital* about. But I'll have to tell you about Yoram Yizraeli some other time. The last song is over, and I let the sharp contrast of the sudden silence achieve its full impact before my next attempt at verbal contact with Oz.

"Black metal," I explain.

No answer.

"Some people can't stand it."

No answer.

"The squealing guitars, the butchered-banshee vocals, the cement-mixer bass, the super-fast drums, the cheesy key-boards. Some find it absolutely intolerable. Do you like it?"

"I'm not particular."

We pass by the Wingate Institute of Physical Education, which means that we're getting close to Netanya. Netanya used to be a cool town, known for its beautiful beaches, beautiful girls, beautiful tourists, and superior soccer team. But now it's just another grim place between Tel Aviv and Haifa, characterless and creepy. Back in its glory days, when Maccabi Netanya dominated the National League, before David Pizanti left to play for Brighton, England, the newspapers revealed, not without a hint of pride, that the striker's lovemaking routine included the application of hummus to the private parts of his European supermodel bedmates, as well as to his own member, followed by the inevitable mutual licking of this popular oriental dish.

We get into town, and I slowly make my way to the division, following the instructions on the back of the DERF. Oz doesn't say anything, but that's okay. The instructions are clear, and I can already see the antennas and watchtowers by the seashore. I stop at the gate, and Oz releases his safety belt and opens the door before I even get a chance to come to a full stop.

"You don't happen to know who can help me with the file here, do you?"

He spreads the palms of his hands on both sides of his body, gets out of the car, and walks past the guard and into the base. The guard salutes him, then walks over to my car.

"Park it outside the gate."

"I need to pick up a medical file for the Tranquil Haven Mental Health Center in Jerusalem."

"Park it outside the gate."

I park the Justy outside the gate and walk over to the guard's booth.

"I need to pick up a medical file for the Tranquil Haven Mental Health Center in Jerusalem."

"Show me your ID."

I reach inside my pocket, but it's not there. Where is it? Oh, no. I gave it to the guard at Central Headquarters. Great. Now I'll have to stop by that stupid place again on my way home.

"Are you going to show me your ID?"

"I just realized: I left it at Central Headquarters. But I have my hospital employee card with me."

"You have to have your official ID."

"It's a picture ID."

"Not good enough."

"I have my visitor's pass from Central Headquarters."

"You have to give it back to Central Headquarters."

"I know. I will. But if I have it, doesn't it mean that I was okayed by Central Headquarters?"

"The Central Headquarters is the Central Headquarters. This is the division."

"So what do I do?"

"I know what you *can't* do. You can't go in."

"Could you get somebody to meet me here? At the gate? They just need to bring me the file."

"I'll see what I can do."

He calls somebody on the red phone, which is not an emergency phone, just a regular tone-dial phone. It's red to distinguish it from pulse-dial phones, which until a few years ago were the only option in Israel. The first time I used a tone-dial phone was in the army. Before that, I used to think it was ridiculous when people on American TV shows—*Dallas*, for example, or *Dynasty*, or *Three's Company*—would pick up the phone, push a few buttons, and start talking right away. I thought it was just another one of those TV conventions that required the suspension of disbelief. Just like actors and actresses who woke up in the morning clean-shaven and made-up. It took me eighteen years to learn that the ability to start talking on the phone two seconds after you finished dialing was not something that happened only in the movies. It was reality. A reality that existed only in America and in the army.

Somebody is approaching the gate. A soldier. Of course a soldier, what else? I would describe him to you, but there's really nothing distinct about him. Army boots, shined but not overshined; fatigues, a bit too baggy but not exactly slipshod; a round face, tired; glasses; a top sergeant, with shiny top-sergeant buttons on his collar.

"I'm here to pick up a medical file for the Tranquil Haven Mental Health Center in Jerusalem."

"Yes, I know. We can't give you the file."

"I'm coming from Central Headquarters. I filled out all the forms, signed all the documents. Unfortunately, I forgot my ID over there, but I have my hospital employee card."

"We don't have the file."

"What?"

"It got stuck in the brigade."

"You can't be serious."

"I just called them. They couldn't send it over today. But you're welcome to pick it up over there, if you want."

"Right. And when I get there, they'll tell me that it's being held up at the regiment."

"I don't know what they'll tell you. All I know is what they told me: they were unable to send it, and you can go pick it up from there."

"From where?"

"Caesarea."

I check my watch. It's two-thirty. One record store is better than none. I can make it.

"Okay. I'll go there."

"Good. It's just before the old city, right by the amphitheater. You'll have no problem finding it."

"What amphitheater?"

"The Roman amphitheater. The stadium."

"I don't think I've ever been there."

"Hold on. Our quartermaster needs to be there for a four o'clock gas mask inspection. He was going to try and hitch a ride, but since you're here, let me go get him. You don't mind giving him a ride, do you? He knows all about Caesarea. He'll tell you everything you want to know."

"Can I make a phone call?"

"Sure. Here, you can use my cell phone."

I can use his cell phone? That's not a good sign. My new hitchhiker must be exceptionally obnoxious.

I call Carmel again, but she's still not home. I wonder where she is. Oncology? Intensive care? The morgue?

Here comes the quartermaster, with a purple beret tucked under his epaulet.

"Hey. Who's taking me to Caesarea?"

"That would be me."

"Fabulous. Let's go. You know how to get to the brigade, don't you?"

"I don't think I do. You're supposed to help me."

"Then help you I will, my friend. Fear not the road to King Herod's palace, for I am with you."

I hate him already.

"And I also need your help to get into the base. I left my ID at the Central Headquarters."

"Permission to enter the palace will be granted to you, my friend. Fear not. Let's go."

The main attraction north of Tel Aviv is Cinema City, a brand new twenty-one-movie theater complex that boasts what the promoters claim to be the biggest silver screen in the Middle East, a four-dimensional fighter-jet flight simulator, an interactive multimedia show about the Jewish underground militias and their contribution to the Zionist effort to drive the British out of Palestine, and free parking.

The main attraction north of Netanya is the big power plant. Its Babylon-like chimneys, forever resting on a flickering cloud of lights, are visible from far away, like guiding pillars of smoke that always go ahead of you. There's considerably less traffic on this section of the Coastal Highway, and we speed again through little nowhere places that, apart from the occasional ancient billboard on the side of the road, show no signs of life.

"So what do you want to know about Caesarea, my friend?"

"Is it an interesting place?"

"I don't know much about the modern city. It's mostly for rich people. But I can tell you about the old city."

"That's okay. You don't have to."

"I'd love to."

"I don't want to impose on you."

"Perish the thought. It would be my pleasure. Did you know that the city was founded by King Herod?"

"I didn't know that."

"First century. Before Christ. Actually, it's named after King Herod's patron, Augustus Caesar. It was the largest harbor on the eastern Mediterranean coast."

"What's in it?"

"In the old city? Oh, Herod was a compulsive builder. He built aqueducts, baths, theaters, stadiums, a palace for himself, a temple for the emperor, all kinds of public buildings, private dwellings, gardens, religious shrines, entertainment facilities. And a harbor, of course."

"Of course."

"Saint Paul was imprisoned in Caesarea, and from there sent to Rome for trial. But when the Roman Empire embraced Christianity, the city became a Christian center, with famous churches, a Christian academy, and even a library, with more than thirty thousand early Christian manuscripts."

I could go into a long aside now about the word *manuscript* and how manuscripts are not really manuscripts these days, because nobody writes by hand anymore—but who

cares. I could also go off on a tangent about these old billboards and how they might have been relevant five years
ago, maybe even give a few ironic examples—"Israel is Waiting for Rabin" or "Netanyahu. It's Good for the Jews"—but
who cares.

"Then the Arabs took it, then the crusaders, who suppos-
edly found the Holy Grail somewhere in the city, then the
Arabs again, then Richard the Lion Heart, then the Arabs
again."

"That's very interesting."

"It is. What else do you want to know?"

"Are there good record stores over there?"

"That I don't know."

"Object in initial position. I like it."

"Excuse me?"

"Nothing. Go on."

"That's it. We're almost there. Here's the wall. And the
fortifications."

"Of the brigade?"

"No, of Caesarea. The brigade is over there—see those
tanks?"

I slow down. Everything is wet. There's a little dirt road
that takes us to the brigade, sludgy and wobbly, and I'm hoping that the poor little Justy doesn't get stuck here, right in
front of the tanks and the baths and the holy grails. I'm holding the steering wheel very tightly, trying to keep a steady
pace, avoiding using the brakes.

And here's the gate.

"Come with me, I'll make sure you get in."

"Thanks."

We get out of the car. Stubborn rain. I try to somehow
keep my shoes from getting dirty, but it's no use. I'll just
have to clean them when I get home.

"He's with me," says the quartermaster to the guard.

"Go ahead," says the guard.

"I assume you need the orderly officer," says the quartermaster.

"If you say so."

"He's in charge of your case. You're the medical file guy, right? Let me go get him for you."

I wait under a little awning in front of the orderly officer quarters. It's almost four. The shops in Tel Aviv close at seven. Fuzz is the closest to the Central Headquarters. I usually go to Allegro on Allenby Street, then to the House of Records, then to the Third Ear, then to the Black Hole on King Solomon Boulevard—but I probably won't have time for any of them today. If they give me the file right away, with no additional forms or examinations, I'll jump in the Justy, zip back to the Central Headquarters, grab my ID, and shoot straight to Fuzz.

I'm beginning to get a little hungry, but that's okay. I'll grab something on the way. Or maybe after I check out Fuzz. They have a good Yemenite fast-food place right around the corner from Fuzz. Or maybe a hamburger, which I usually have only when I go to Tel Aviv. I guess you could call it tradition. When I was in high school, the only American burger place in Israel was Wendy's in Tel Aviv. We had our local imitations, of course—McDavid's, King Donald, Burger Ranch, Gulliver's Burgers—but Wendy's was the real thing. So real that when American soldiers were stationed here to help us operate the Patriot missiles, they could eat there for free. They didn't have anything with bacon or ham, of course. And no cheeseburgers. But I would stop there every time I skipped school for one of my record-store missions, to get the kind of hamburger that wasn't available in Jerusalem.

"The orderly officer will see you now," says the quarter-master. "You can go in."

"Thanks."

It's dark inside, and I can't figure out if it's the orderly officer's office or living quarters. There's a folding bed next to what looks like a desk, but the yellowish light coming from a little desk lamp that rests on the floor is so pale that I can only see the left side of his face: stubble, glasses, a uni-brow, receding hairline. I think I smell motor oil, but I'm not sure.

"Hi."

"Sit down."

"Do you have the file?"

"We do."

"I came to pick it up."

"It'll be sent directly to the hospital."

"That's what I came here for. To pick it up and take it to the hospital."

"It'll be delivered directly to Jerusalem."

"I'm going straight back to Jerusalem."

"It'll be delivered to Jerusalem by Army Post tomorrow."

"Then what am I doing here?"

"I'm sorry. These are the orders we have."

"Dr. Himmelblau is expecting it today."

"She'll receive it tomorrow."

His voice is weird. Raspy and soft at the same time. And clear, but also distant, as if it's not coming out of his body. Or maybe it is coming out of his body, but not out of his mouth. As if his vocal cords have been replaced by some gadget that imitates human speech.

"So you have it, but you won't give it to me. Is that what you're saying?"

"That's exactly what I'm saying."

"So what am I supposed to do now?"

"You said you were going back to Jerusalem."

"I am."

"That's a long drive. You better get going."

"And I suppose you'll want me to take a few hitchhikers with me, won't you? Or are your hitchhikers also delivered by Army Post?"

"Actually, there *is* someone here who could use a ride back to the division."

"Only one? Why don't you let me take your entire cavalry unit with me? I have plenty of room in my car."

"Could you please wait outside?"

"The horses and swords will be safe in the trunk, don't worry."

"Could you please wait outside?"

"Can I make a phone call?"

"Who are you calling?"

"Dr. Himmelblau."

"She's been notified."

I don't slam the door—it wouldn't be wise to slam the door of an officer who's in charge of several dozen tanks— but I'm angry. If I smoked, I would need a cigarette. But I don't smoke, so I just stand under the awning again, watching the drizzle, planning my next move.

I have no next move. I just need to calm down and drive home. Alone. No more strangers in my car. My freeloading soldier will probably show up in a few seconds, but I'll just tell him to get lost. I don't care if you have no other way of getting out of here. I don't care if you need to inspect the elasticity of the newly purchased shoelaces in the division, or if you have an urgent mess-tin steering committee meeting at the platoon, or if it's your first night off in two months and your garrison girlfriend is waiting for you at the squadron.

"They told me you might be able to give me a ride back to the division. If it's not out of your way."

I turn around. She's almost as tall as I am.

"I could just take the six o'clock bus," she smiles. "If it's inconvenient."

"No. Not at all. I could use some company."

"Are you sure?"

"Of course. Let me help you with that kitbag."

"Thank you."

I carry her kitbag to the car. She yawns. A cute little yawn. I put the kitbag in the trunk. She yawns again. She gets in. We drive.

"I'm tired," she smiles.

"I know what you mean. I was chronically exhausted when I was in the army. They marched us into the Study Zone at six in the morning and pumped our brains full of Arabic for eighteen hours a day, six days a week, for six months. You couldn't leave the classroom before midnight."

She yawns again.

"I need to get some gas."

I pull into a gas station, fill up, put the receipt in my wallet, and walk inside to get something to drink. And two candy bars.

When I get in the car, her head is resting on the window, her neck long and sculpted, her hands clutching the Uzi in her lap.

"I got you a candy bar."

No answer.

"Would you like a candy bar?"

She's sleeping.

I start the engine, but she's not waking up. I get back on the road. I eat my candy bar. The rain has stopped and we zoom down the highway, past little intersections dotted with soldiers trying to get home, past the old billboards, past the power plant. The sea to our right is foaming in the dusk. She's still sleeping.

I turn on the radio. A professor of literature at the University of Haifa is talking about the Prioress's Tale and the tradition of the blood libel. On Army Radio Two they're playing "Smoke on the Water." On Army Radio One they have a comedian who says that Switzerland must be the most boring country in the world. Israel is where the action is, whereas a typical front-page headline in a Swiss newspaper would be: COW SAT ON TRACKS; TRAIN DELAYED THREE HOURS.

"I have a soft spot for Deep Purple."

She's still sleeping.

"Of course, they were never as heavy as Black Sabbath. And they had those funny folk music undertones, which I always found a little distracting. But *Machine Head* was a truly monumental album. Paved the way for metal legends such as Judas Priest and Slayer. And probably most of the thrash metal, death metal, and maybe even black metal bands of today."

Still sleeping.

"What they did is they came up with the ideal formula that defined heavy metal, the definitive *modus operandi* that was later perfected by much faster, much heavier bands: verse, chorus, keyboard solo, verse, chorus, guitar solo, verse, chorus, the end. Sometimes they switched between the keyboards and the guitar, like in 'Pictures of Home,' which is my absolute favorite Deep Purple song of all time. And sometimes they skipped the last verse and chorus, just to make it shorter. There were variations. But basically, that was the structure."

Sleeping.

"Then came Judas Priest, who took the exact same formula, replaced the keyboards with a second lead guitar, and sped up the whole thing. What Deep Purple did in six minutes, Judas Priest could do in four or five."

My very own Sleeping Beauty. Too sublime for words. Am I doomed to talk only to exterminators and crusaders?

"And then came Slayer, who did it all in two minutes, with an incredible mixture of raw intensity and vicious accuracy that all the bands before them—and most bands after— could only dream of."

What was that? What did you say? Oh, okay. I'll just shut up and drive. No problem. Holler if you need anything. And please try not to drool on my car. I really like that sweet saliva of yours—wouldn't mind tasting it if it were still in your mouth—but please try not to get it on the upholstery. I'll have enough trouble selling it as it is, what with the scratch and everything. And point that gun of yours the other way, will you? I know I may sound like my mother, but what if you have a bad dream and start twitching in your sleep with your cute little finger on the trigger? Or just give it to me, I'll put it in the back seat. I like the wooden stock. So warm and smooth. Was it custom-made especially for you? How much are you asking for it?

Never mind. We're almost in Netanya. Time flies when you're having a good conversation, doesn't it? I can already see the antennas and watchtowers. We're almost there. It's been a pleasure. You've made this trip a most enjoyable one, Little Miss Martial Beauty. Here's the division. Thank you. Hope we meet again.

I stop the car in front of the gate. She wakes up.

"I must have fallen asleep," she smiles. "I'm sorry."

"That's okay. You were tired."

"Yes, I guess I was. Thanks for the ride. Could you get my stuff for me?"

"Sure."

I keep the motor running, get out of the car, open the trunk, hand her the kitbag, and drive off.

At the next gas station I stop, get a cup of cappuccino from the coffee vending machine, and call Carmel. I let it ring three times, and I'm just about ready to give up, hang up—when all of a sudden I hear her voice.

"Hello?"

"Carmel."

"Where are you?"

"Netanya."

"I thought you had a morning shift."

"I had to drive to the army to pick up a medical file."

"Did you say the army?"

"Ibrahim Ibrahim's file."

"Who?"

"The Arab."

"The one with the snake?"

"The one with the snake."

"And did you get it?"

"The file? Of course not."

"Why?"

"Long story. I'll tell you when I get back."

"Are you okay?"

"I think so. What have you been up to?"

"I liked what you wrote about Metallica."

"What?"

"Although you must admit that you can't dismiss them completely. They should have broken up after the black album, I agree. But they were an important band."

"Wait. Where were you all day?"

"In your apartment."

"Did you read my book?"

"Only what you have so far."

"Carmel!"

"What?"

"Who gave you permission to read my stuff?"

"Since when do I need permission to read about myself?"

"What were you doing in my apartment?"

"I came to see you."

"I told you I had a morning shift."

"I wanted to make sure."

"You thought I was lying?"

"I just thought you might be there."

"How did you get in?"

"With the extra key you gave me."

"That was for an emergency!"

"I wanted to see you."

"You wanted to see me or my book?"

"It was there."

It's getting cold. I take a sip of my cappuccino. It has a slight aftertaste. I take another sip. I think it smells like gasoline, but maybe it's just the air here. A white Mitsubishi, which in Hebrew we call Mitsibushi, stops under the red-and-green sign that says *Delek*. A little blond boy comes out of the back seat and operates the pump by himself, his parents waiting in the car. He lifts the nozzle with both hands. "Nu," his mother sticks her neck out of the window, "hurry up already."

"So what did you think?"

"I liked what you wrote about Metallica."

"What about the rest?"

"I wasn't too impressed with the rest."

"Why?"

"It's entirely artificial. You're using the patients as literary fodder instead of presenting them as real human beings."

"Don't start again, Carmel."

"Okay, forget the patients. What about me?"

"What about you?"

"Same thing. You're making me into a character, not a real person."

"You *are* a character."

"I'm not even a character. I'm a caricature. I'm didactic, argumentative, moralistic. I'm boring."

"Didactic and boring? I thought you were wild and exciting."

"How can I be exciting when there's no action?"

"What do you mean?"

"Do something. Make things happen."

"Like what?"

"I don't know. Kill my husband."

"Maybe I will."

"Forget it. It won't help."

"Why not?"

"Because I could never be interesting when all you care about is this private little world you've created for yourself."

"What's wrong with my private world?"

"Nothing. You seem to be very happy in it, so why do you even bother calling me? Just stay there, with your patients and records and words, and don't ever come out."

"I don't get it. What do you want me to do? Revise it? Rewrite it? Change the whole thing?"

"It's your book. Do whatever you want. Obviously, it's more important."

"More important than what?"

"Forget it. Just do whatever you want."

It's almost six. There are no cars in the gas station now. The janitor is whistling "The Flower of the Cities."

"It's getting dark, Carmel. I'll call you tomorrow."

"Aren't you coming over tonight?"

"Do you want me to?"

"Only if we can play officer and tenderfoot."

"It's a deal. I'll see you in a couple hours."

"Drive carefully."

I have to stop in Tel Aviv, of course. Which means that I'd better hurry. Great. Now I'll have to drive by all those desperate hitchhikers outside the gas station, which means that I'll probably have no choice but to stop for another annoying soldier. But there's only one person standing here, and he's not a soldier.

"Tel Aviv," I say.

"Perfect. Where in Tel Aviv?"

"Central Headquarters."

"Perfect. I can catch a bus from there."

He gets in. A black suit, smells of dust. White shirt, no tie. Black fedora. Trimmed beard, pasty hands tapping on a hard-cover copy of Psalms. Must be in his forties, looks younger.

"Thanks for stopping for me."

"No problem."

"So what do you say?"

"About what?"

"About the situation."

"It's a tough situation."

"And it will get tougher. If we don't stop giving them everything we have."

"What did we give them?"

"Only the Sinai Peninsula."

"The Sinai Peninsula? That was twenty years ago."

"And it still hurts. I died the day we gave back the Sinai Peninsula to those worshippers of stars and constellations. For me, that was the end. We showed too much mercy where we should have shown no mercy at all. We should have eaten them alive. God gave us all these people to devour, and what do we do instead? Hand them our promised patrimony on a silver platter."

"Show no mercy."

"Exactly. If we only did what we were told to do, if we only obeyed our own commandments and laws, we could easily get rid of all of them. All their maladies and abominations, all the diseases of Egypt, all that blasphemy and infertility and sterility. But no, we had to be smarter than that."

"We always think we're smarter."

"Exactly. So what do we say? Oh, there are so many of them, how can we ever wipe them out? Right? Wrong. Remember the Pharaoh? Remember the hand of God? Same thing with these nations we're so foolishly afraid of. The wasps will kill them all. And those who somehow survive? Don't worry. We'll figure something out. Little by little. We don't want to get rid of them all at once. Because then there would be more lions and tigers here than people. You know that we used to have lions and tigers here, don't you?"

"Of course."

"And where are they now?"

"Gone."

"Exactly. All those people? Gone. Their kings? Destroyed. Their names? Erased. Their idols? Burnt. But don't take any of their silver or gold. We don't loot. That's what makes us who we are. No looting, no robbing, no raping. Purity of arms."

"Pull out their arms?"

"Their tongues. Assyrian, Sumerian, Hittite, Moabite. Gone. No such languages under the heavens anymore."

"I studied Welsh."

"Gone. You can forget it. Dead. You'll never use it. But don't forget what happened in the desert. For forty years we were tortured and starved. But not as a vicious king would torture his enemy. No. As a loving father would discipline his son. And we had a destination: an old-new land, a land where underground water springs out of the valleys and the hills, a land where you would never have to slave for a loaf of bread, a land where there would never be a shortage of anything, a land where the stones are made of iron and the mountains yield copper."

"Do you like heavy metal?"

"The leader of the underground. How could he? His heart must have been heavy, heavy as mercury, when he gave it away. And to whom? To the best snake? Crush its skull, I say."

"Would you like a candy bar?"

"No, thanks. And why? Because we forgot. Our hearts are haughty, not heavy. High and mighty. Good food, good houses, plenty of everything. And who took us out of Egypt? We forget. We used to be slaves. You know that, don't you? Of course you do. So let me ask you a question. Who freed us? Who led us through the desert, the terrible desert, with the snake and the scorpion and the thirst?"

"God?"

"And when we were thirsty, who made a solid rock yield water?"

"God?"

"We forget. We think we performed all those miracles ourselves. With our own hands, with our own strength. And what happens when we forget? We vanish, just like the nations we're supposed to destroy. And don't think that these nations are easy to destroy. No, sir. They're giants. Walls and fortresses. Cities in the sky. And who will destroy them for us? Who will burn them alive?"

"The army?"

"God. Only God. But not because we're good. It's not because of our decency that we're getting their land. It's because of their wickedness. That's all. We're not that great. We're bad. We're bad and stubborn, and we always make God angry. Remember the Ten Commandments? Remember the Golden Calf? Remember the Graves of Lust? I'm sure you remember. We're sinners. We're a nation of evil sinners. So evil that when God tells us that we can go ahead and take the land, we don't even believe him. We're bad, and the only reason God hasn't abandoned us or killed us all a long time ago is because he didn't want the Egyptians to say: Hey, look at these losers. Their God hates them so much that instead of letting them into the Promised Land like he promised, he left them to die in the desert."

"Is it okay if I play some music?"

"Go ahead. So what does God ask of you? Two simple things: to circumcise your penis and to circumcise your heart. That's all. And why? Because that's your job. You do your job, he'll do his. He'll give you the first and last rain right on time. He has no problem doing that. He owns not only the heavens, but also the heavens of the heavens, and the earth, and everything on earth. God of gods, Lord of lords. Big, brave, dreadful. Can't be bought, can't be bribed. Loves the widow, the orphan, the foreigner, the stranger.

Gives them food and clothing. And so should we. We must always love the oppressed. We must. We used to be an oppressed minority ourselves. In Egypt. And all over the world. You know that, don't you?"

"Of course."

"Now let me give you an example."

"Okay."

"Pick a country. Any country."

"Israel."

"A foreign country. But don't tell me."

"Okay."

"Did you pick a country?"

"I picked a country."

"A foreign country?"

"A foreign country."

"Good. Now what do they do in foreign countries?"

"I don't know. What do they do?"

"I'll tell you what they do. First they sow, right?"

"Right."

"And then what do they do?"

"They reap?"

"No. They irrigate."

"Makes sense."

"But how do they irrigate?"

"I don't know. How?"

"By foot. They go out to the field, and it's a huge field, and they irrigate the whole damn thing by foot, as if it was a giant vegetable garden. See what I'm saying?"

"Yes."

"That's it. That's what it's all about."

"Right."

"So why did we forget?"

"We're almost in Tel Aviv."

"I'll make it quick. The bottom line. No problem with the Gentiles. Our role is to inherit their land, their role is to disappear. Make room for those to whom the place was promised. We set foot in a place—it's ours. And they know that. From Egypt to Lebanon, from the Euphrates to the Mediterranean. We must strike terror in their hearts, not the other way around. Don't you agree? I'm sure you agree."

"We're almost at the Central Headquarters."

"Already? So tell me about yourself. What do you do?"

"Me? I'm a writer."

"Really? What are you writing about?"

"I'm thinking of writing about the anti-eraser."

"Bad idea."

"Why?"

"They'll never believe you."

"Who?"

"The Gentiles."

"Why not?"

"Trust me. I went to America last year. Met with Christians who support our cause. Good people. Anyway, we drank. Started telling funny stories. I told them about the anti-eraser."

"And?"

"They didn't believe me. Thought I was lying."

"That's ridiculous. Everybody knows about the anti-eraser."

"Not in America. They said it was technically impossible. They thought I was making it up."

I pull into the parking lot next to Central Headquarters. Six-forty.

"Raphael Ben-Baruch. From Ariel. Thank you for the ride."

"My pleasure."

"Good luck with the book. Send me a copy when you get it published, will you?"

"It's in English."

"In English? The whole book?"

"Yes."

"Why?"

"I don't know. I'm just writing it in English."

"See what I mean? Everything is forgotten."

"Still, I'd be happy to send you a copy."

"Never mind. Thanks for the ride."

He gets out. I hurry up to the guard's booth and hand him back my visitor's pass. He looks at me for a few seconds, as if trying to remember something, then gives me back my ID. I stick it in my wallet and rush back to the car. Six-forty-five. Quick. Fuzz closes in fifteen minutes. Left on Arlozorov, left again on Bloch, past City Hall onto Frishman, into Masaryk Square. There must be parking somewhere on Zamenhof. There we go. The perfect spot. Six-fifty. Perfect. Ten minutes is a sea of time, as they say in the army.

And speaking of the anti-eraser, here's something utterly nonsensical, though perfectly grammatical: *Ibrahim Ibrahim's colorless green ideas sleep furiously.*

I run over to Fuzz, but it's closed. I try the door again. It's closed.

"They closed."

I turn around. Someone's sitting Indian-style on the sidewalk. Looks a little older than me, but just a little. Back leaning against the storefront window, a legal pad and a pack of menthol cigarettes on the sidewalk next to her, sunken cheeks, big eyes, short black hair under a brown beanie, a long black wool sweater that goes all the way down to a dilapidated pair of cowboy boots, brown corduroys, skinny legs, skinny arms, matchstick fingers holding a pen and a cigarette.

"It's only ten-to-seven," I say.

"I know. There are no records inside."

"Are you serious?"

"I came here all the way from Jerusalem," she says, "but it looks like they're closed for good."

I put my hands around my face and peer inside. The glass is dirty. The place is dark and empty. No records, no posters on the walls, no cash register. Just empty racks. I look back at her. She gets up.

"How long have you been sitting here?"

"About two hours. But the store looks deserted. I think I'll go home now."

"You live in Jerusalem?"

"Yes."

"Me too."

"Really? Where?"

"In the Greek Colony. Well, actually, I moved. I live in Kiryat Menachem now."

"I live in Kiryat Yovel."

"I grew up in Kiryat Yovel. What street?"

"Guatemala."

"I used to live on Bolivia. You need a ride?"

"That would be great. Thanks."

We walk back to Zamenhof Street. I'm tired. Traffic is slow again. It'll be faster once we get on the highway.

"Thanks for giving me a ride. I'm Molli. Molli Badge. I hope I'm not being a burden."

"You're not a burden, Molli Badge."

"People are usually afraid of me. They don't want me in their cars."

"Why?"

"Because of the way I look."

"What's wrong with the way you look?"

"People don't like skeletons. People like people who show they're willing to fight for access to pleasures."

Which reminds me. I forgot all about the Yemenite food. And the hamburger. Never mind. I'll just eat at home. It's raining again, but there's not much traffic on the highway, just like I predicted, so I'm driving fairly fast. I push *Tools of the Trade* into the tape player.

"Is this Carcass?"

"How did you know?"

"I love Carcass," she says. "I went to see them when they came here."

"You went to the show?"

"Yes. Did you?"

"Of course," I say. "I interviewed them for *The Capital*."

"Really?"

"I was on the road with them for a while," I say. "I played air guitar with Michael Amott, listening to King Diamond on the tour bus."

"Wow," she says. "What's your favorite Carcass song?"

" 'Exhume to Consume.' Yours?"

" 'Swarming Vulgar Mass of Infected Virulency.' "

Typical. Girls always like "Swarming Vulgar Mass of Infected Virulency."

"They're cool guys," I say. "Did you get a chance to talk to them?"

"Not really. I was trying to be a groupie. I wanted to sleep with Bill Steer, but I couldn't compete with all those teenage swimsuit models from Tel Aviv. I got him to autograph my copy of *Necroticism*, and I told him I was a poet from Jerusalem, but he was not impressed."

"From what I saw, I don't think he was impressed with the swimsuit models either. He was very much into the music. Very serious about it."

"Bill Steer?"

"Oh, yes. Ken Owen told me that sometimes Bill would concentrate so hard on playing the guitar that he would forget his own chords. He would go blank, and Ken or Michael would have to remind him where to put his fingers."

"Well," she says, "maybe he just wasn't in the mood for poetry."

"Are you really a poet?"

"I published my first book last year."

"What's it called?"

"*The Badge of Honorexia.* I think I have a copy somewhere in my purse."

Great. Now I'll have to listen to her recite her own poetry.

"Can I smoke?"

"Sure."

Scratches, bullet-holes, slobber, smoke. I don't care anymore. I'll be home in forty minutes, away from this incessant swarm of hitchhiking flies that God has whistled over from the rivers of Egypt and Assyria to unleash upon me. Why do I have to be the national designated driver? Why can't I be at home already, in bed, with a cup of tea and my Xeroxed copy of *Outline of Glossematics* and the new Morbid Angel?

Never mind. Forty minutes.

"I'm a writer myself."

"You are?"

"I'm working on my first book."

"Fiction?"

"Yes."

"What's it about?"

"A mental institution."

"I sometimes write stories too."

"Short stories?"

"No. Just stories."

Okay, so now I'm going to listen to a story. Wonderful. Just what I needed. Maybe I could drop her off at the next gas station, exchange her for one of those mute soldiers.

Never mind. Forty minutes. If she starts telling me one of her stories, I'll just play along, pretend as if I'm listening. I'll use the three asterisks again and zone out. I'll think about Uldall and Hjelmslev and Carmel's undershirt and mint-and-honey tea and ass. Forty minutes.

"Would you like to hear a story?"

"That you wrote?"

"Yes. Today."

"Okay."

You see? I told you. There's no escape from these people. You spend your whole life avoiding their stories, so what do they do? Invade your car. Never mind. Forget it. Forty minutes. Here it is.

* * *

Once upon a time, in a land far away, there lived, side by side, three enemy countries. The land the three countries shared was a good land, a land where the sun is as warm as the touch of a secret lover, the sea as clear as the eyes of a newborn babe, the arms of the men as strong as mountains of granite, and the breasts of the women as lovely as fawns grazing in the lilies, a land where lush trees yield the sweetest fruit all year long, a land rich in laughter and poor in misery. Three good kings reigned wisely over the three little enemy countries, and noble people from all over the world, hard-working and pure of heart, upon hearing of the wonders of that heavenly land and its blissful shores, resolved to leave their old homes in the dark realms of frost and wind, travel many miles through icicles and frozen wilderness, and start their lives afresh in one of those three wonderful countries. So strong-minded and brave were the citizens of those countries, so determined and fearless, that each of the three little kingdoms was in a permanent state of war with the other two. So ferocious was the trilateral dispute, so uncompromising was the mutual animosity, that it precluded any kind of communication, let alone agreement, among the three great nations. Therefore, neither boundaries nor frontiers were ever set between them, and the three rival countries were forced to live together in the same good land, three sworn enemies with no separation or demarcation, three hostile nations with no lines or limits, sharing the same space while fighting devotedly, each in its own special ways, to eliminate its neighbors.

The land was good but small, and in its center towered an old city, pronounced by each of the three honorable kings the beating heart and everlasting cradle of his kingdom, divine symbol of his absolute sovereignty, majestic emblem of his overwhelming grandeur. Each of the three countries claimed infinite and irrevocable possession over the ancient city, its towers, streets, alleys, and beautiful girls. Each of the three kings decreed, by royal edict, moral statutes, and municipal bylaws, that citizens of the two rival countries should not be allowed in the splendid city, lest they profane it. Holy and forbidden, the city remained barren and desolate, a sacrosanct metropolis of glorious dereliction, a pallid palace devoid of vim, verve or vigor, a putrefying pile of silent stones and rigid rules, where trees of rotting roots bore fetid fruit, tongues of fire licked eternal fields of thorns, and empty houses sheltered carrion. The only people permitted to dwell in the hallowed city were official members of the three institutes of government and administration that conducted the affairs of their countries.

The official institute of government and administration conducting the affairs of the first country was called Army. The official institute of government and administration conducting the affairs of the second country was called Militia. And the official institute of government and administration conducting the affairs of the third country was called Police. Each of the three institutes was entrusted with the performance of three major tasks, all of a continuous nature and of equal importance: to train loyal citizens to attack the citizens of the other two countries; to arrest dissident citizens that refused to attack the citizens of the other two countries, and to arrest loyal citizens trained and eager to attack the citizens of the other two countries, thus appearing to condemn senseless and cowardly attacks on the innocent citizens of the other two countries.

One day, when no more beauty was left in the land, when sweet perfume had been replaced with pungent stench, lucid lakes with seas of muck, delicious food with sour vomit, fancy clothes with ropes and tatters, glowing locks with hairless heads, when rivulets of red had melted the mountains, and streams of marrow raked the rocks, the three wise kings decided to convene in a gallant attempt to save the good land. However, for fear that willingness to negotiate with the enemy inside the holy capital might be construed as a sign of weakness and desperation, the three kings cleverly decided that their conference of reconciliation would be held far away from the wonderful land, on foreign soil, in one of the frozen countries of the dark wilderness. Armed with the best available resources to protect them from the cold and the enemy, the kings set forth to cross the endless fields of snow, making their way through arctic icicles and frosty air, each taking a separate course, each accompanied by a royal retinue of dukes, lords, earls, bishops, counselors, advisors, officers of government and administration, and beautiful girls.

Upon their arrival at the designated location of the meeting, in the court of the king of the cold country, the three wise kings, seeking rest from the taxing journey through the snow, retired to their regal quarters, leaving their skillful dukes and counselors to conduct the auspicious conference. At the commencement of the conference, high-ranking Army, Militia, and Police officials exchanged elaborate propositions for the disentanglement of the perpetual bloody battle between the three countries.

The proposition submitted by the first country consisted of a solemn promise to spare the lives of the citizens of the second country, on condition that they pledged allegiance to the first country, became its loyal citizens, and joined the fight for the just elimination of the third country. The proposition submitted by the second country granted half the citizens of the third country permission to leave the good land unharmed, provided that the remaining half agreed to sacrifice their lives as human bombs in the service of the second country, helping it slay the tyrannical king of the first country and crown the benevolent king of the second country emperor of all the good land. The proposition submitted by the third country consisted of a sincere plea to the Army of the first country, asking it to arm and coach the Police of the third country so it would be better equipped not only to obliterate the Militia of the second country, but also to extirpate rebellious elements within the third country itself with increased efficiency, swiftness, and cruelty.

For three days and three nights they sat in the court of the king of the cold country, exchanging propositions, revised propositions, and amended propositions, forming treaties and alliances, contriving plots and subterfuges, contravening pacts and deals. Finally, when the conference approached its conclusion and no agreement had been reached, the high-ranking officials decided that, although the war must continue, a magnificent monument would be erected in the godly land, a marvelous edifice to commemorate the pioneer conference, an illustrious parlor to illustrate the future peace to which the three great nations were committed. In this parlor, merry men of all three countries would convene before they killed each other, imbibe the best of beverages before they set to butchering one another, consume the most delicious foods before they massacred their brothers. Happy games would be played in the parlor, coins of gold would be given away to the fortunate winners, and the most beautiful women, lavishly clad yet always eager to disrobe, would entertain the guests.

* * *

"Go on. I'm listening."

"That's it."

"That's it? Where's the rest of it?"

"There is no rest."

"What do you mean? No ending?"

"I don't have it yet."

"How come?"

"I told you: I just wrote it. Today. While I was waiting by the record store."

"You can't do that. You can't tell a story without the ending."

"Look who cares all of a sudden. You didn't seem very interested a minute ago."

"Of course I was interested."

"Sure you were. Don't you think I know a Black Sabbath song when I hear somebody humming it while I'm reading a story?"

"Okay, so I wasn't paying attention. But had I known it would be an incomplete story, I wouldn't have started transcribing it in the first place. I have a responsibility. I have readers waiting to hear how it ends."

"Tell them it doesn't end."

"They wouldn't like that."

CHAPTER 7

Children of Bodom, the new melodic death gods from Finland, have just released they're selftitled debut album in Europe and United States. The story which lurks behind the name of the band is a Finnish murder case, what isn't solved even in nowadays. Bodom Lake is a small lake in Finland about 20 kilometers north from Helsinki. In the year 1960 on the 5th of June this lake gave a estrade to a very scary murder case. Four teenagers, two 15 year old girls and two 18 year old guys, camped at this lake, when an insane one came and killed all teenagers but one with an axe. The one who survived, went crazy afterwards, and spends his time still in psychiatric treatment. Some years later one old man said, that he is murderer, but police proofed, that he could not have been it. So the murder was never solved.

I should move to Finland. They have unsolved murders from almost forty years ago, which I find comforting. Unlike Jerusalem, where you can't get killed without two or three paramilitary organizations fighting to take credit for your death. And you, as a good citizen, must die. And if you don't die, then the least you can do is feel guilty. Guilty for wanting to go to Scandinavia, for watching TV on a Saturday morning, for drinking beer during the seven days of Passover, for accidentally smiling on the day commemorating the destruction of our temple by the evil Romans two thousand years ago, for buying a heavy metal magazine instead of an Uzi magazine. Don't be a traitor. You have to be responsible.

My mother also thinks that I should be more responsible. Working in the hospital is bad because it's what I want to do. Individual will is always a sign of treacherous selfishness.

Which is why I think that Finland might be a good place for me. A place where even if you want to be held responsible, even if you come forward and say, "I did it," all they say to you is: "It's okay. You don't have to feel guilty if you didn't really do anything. Go home."

The phone rings.

"What are you up to?"

"I'm writing."

"I hear music."

"It helps me concentrate."

"What is it?"

"*Bark at the Moon.*"

"Ozzy?"

"Yeah."

"The big traitor."

"Why?"

"He's a hypocrite. Look at his lyrics from thirty years ago—you'd think the man was a genuine dissident, a real rock-and-roll rebel. But when the entertainment industry offers him a small pot of gold to do a mindless family TV show, to keep the masses in the dark, to take our minds off the real war pigs, the real children of the grave, the real electric funerals—he happily agrees to serve as the national acrobat, dancing to the flute of the men with the missiles and the money."

"I don't know. I still like him."

"Well. Anyway. I bet you have to go now."

"I do."

"I guess I'll see you later."

I still have some time before I have to go to work, but I log off—I'll check out the rest of the new releases later—and I'm thinking maybe I should get a haircut on my way to the hospital. If I can't die in a terror attack, getting a haircut is probably the closest I can get to being responsible.

So I take a shower and drive to the city, to downtown Jerusalem, which I'd be happy to describe to you some other time, when I'm not in a hurry. Everybody's in a hurry in downtown Jerusalem, especially on a cold day like today. In the summertime, when it's sunny and hot, and the sky is blue, and all the people seem to move with energy and vitality, the city can give a false impression of beauty and charm. But it's in the winter that the true lifeless nature of the town is revealed. It's then that you realize that all those people running up and down the grimy, gloomy streets are not full of energy. They're just in a hurry, eager to make it to their destination as quickly as they can: before the shops close, before the clerk goes home, before the end of the month, before the Sabbath comes. In a place where everybody has to meet a deadline, no wonder no one looks alive.

Segev is a small, dimly lit shop, located in an old stone building on a narrow side street, sooty and cold. When I walk in, a woman—early twenties, slender, pretty face, pale complexion—is getting her hair trimmed, dyed ash-blonde, and blown-out straight. The owner's name is Segev, which in Hebrew means *sublime*. He barks, but he's a good hairdresser. I don't know what it is. Must be some kind of a speech disorder or mental irregularity. At first I found it disturbing, but after a while I got used to it.

Segev is telling the pale woman about a vacation in Egypt he just returned from. He's putting the finishing touches on her new haircut, breathing volume into his creation with fast fingers and a complacent smile.

"Did you see the pyramids?"

"You bet."

"Didn't we build those for them?"

"You bet. It's in the Bible."

"Leviticus, right?"

"Woof. I think Numbers."

"So legally, they're ours."

"You bet they are."

"Historically, I mean."

"You bet. You built it, you own it."

"You think we'll get them back some day?"

"With the help of the Name."

"Did you see the tiger?"

"What tiger?"

"The one without the nose. Made of stone."

"The Sphinx?"

"The Sphinx."

"What an ugly thing."

"They have no taste."

"Arabs."

The woman nods contentedly at her own reflection.

"We're done," says Segev.

The woman pays him with four crisp fifty shekel bills. Out of a white plastic bag she pulls a short brown wig and puts it on her head, adjusting it to her scalp in front of the mirror, tucking her newly done hair underneath it.

"I'll see you next month," he says.

"With the help of the Name," says the woman. "Goodbye."

"Bow wow."

The woman folds the plastic bag into her purse, stretches her hand to touch the mezuzah, kisses her fingertips, and marches into the street. Looking into the long mirror inside, pretending to check out my own reflection, I watch her disappear in the foggy alley, her long skirt blowing in the wind.

Being into heavy metal, I used to hate getting my hair cut. I used to wear it long in high school, down to my shoulders. But the army made me cut it, and now I find it hard to go back to wearing it long. One of the first steps of induction, even before you get your uniform, is the haircut. They call it upkeep, a form of male maintenance. If you get your hair cut regularly, it shows you're responsible. If you don't—you go to military jail.

I remember waiting for four years for the day when I wouldn't have to get a haircut every month anymore. But when that day finally came, my hair didn't grow back the way I wanted it to. It's not thinning or anything, but when it's long, it looks a little out of place. Maybe my mother is right. Maybe I'm too old to be a headbanger.

I should check out Children of Bodom, though. I'm almost sure that website was written by someone whose native tongue is a Slavic language: the use of *what* as a relative pronoun, the occasional absence of the definite article, the mandatory comma before restrictive clauses. Maybe Polish?

Polish was one of the languages I studied in the Department of Linguistics at the Hebrew University. It wasn't an official requirement for the degree, but I wanted to read my favorite writer, Stanislaw Lem, in the original. It was hard—seven cases, five grammatical genders, impossible tenses, agonizing pronunciation, no fixed word order, and everything conjugates, not just verbs—but I liked it. And after two years, I was able to read short stories by Stanislaw Lem. My mother, of course, thought it was stupid. Why waste so much time on a useless, extracurricular language when I should stay focused on working toward a higher degree that will secure me a job in a prestigious academic institution? She also thought it was stupid because Stanislaw Lem writes mostly science fiction, and science fiction, like heavy metal, was making me dumb.

Segev is done now. I pay him—mine is only fifty—and I get out and walk to my car. I drive to the hospital, but then I remember that today I'm taking them to their monthly outing, which means I'll have to be downtown again in just a few hours.

This is part of a new program Dr. Himmelblau is trying to introduce. Or, to put it in more accurate terms, force the patients to comply with. The idea is to integrate them back into normal society by gradual exposure to life outside the hospital. Last month we went to the movies; the month before we did Yad Vashem; and the month before that, when the weather was still nice—picnic in the park. Today we're going to a restaurant.

I drive into the hospital, and I park in the little parking lot, and as soon as I set foot in the unit, Immanuel Sebastian comes up to me and informs me that he won't be joining us on our downtown excursion today because he's in the process of being switched to a new drug that makes his behavior unpredictable, and Abe Goldmil says that he can't go because there's another Julie Strain movie on TV today, and Amos Ashkenazi says that he can't go out because he's run out of clean purple T-shirts, and Uriah Einhorn says that he'd love to join us but he's tired, and Ibrahim Ibrahim says he's never been to a restaurant but they won't let him out because he's a public enemy, and Hadassah Benedict says that she can't leave the hospital because she's dead, and Desta Ezra looks at me with big blank eyes and says nothing.

"Listen," I say to them. "I already called the main kitchen, and I said to them, 'We're going out to a restaurant, so don't send supper to our unit tonight.' So if you want to stay, stay. Just keep in mind that you won't be fed until tomorrow morning."

So they all put their coats on, except for Immanuel Sebastian, who still says that he won't go until Dr. Himmelblau reverses her decision to make him take this new drug. So I page Dr. Himmelblau, who comes down to the unit and gives him an extra dose of the new drug.

"He'll be okay now," she says. "He won't give you any trouble."

They say I'm heartless, but Dr. Himmelblau tells me that I must learn to exert delegated power. So I collect all seven of them, and we're just about to walk out when Dr. Himmelblau says that Ibrahim Ibrahim can't leave the hospital. So I tell him to take his coat off and stay, and I take the rest of them to the bus stop.

The bus is new and slick, red and white, air-conditioned, with guardrails that separate the driver from the passengers. They don't look happy. They'd rather be at the hospital, sleeping or watching TV or playing Monopoly, safe in the comfort of the unit, protected from the horrors of public transportation and streets with no nurses. They're all stiff and silent, looking like they expect their names to be on the radio this afternoon, eyes out of focus, hands planted deep inside their coat pockets. They're not even looking out the windows.

A few years ago, before the Justy, a strange terror attack took place on the bus going from Tel Aviv to Jerusalem. I had often taken that bus, both as a high school student and as a soldier, but it so happened that the strange attack took place while I was safe at home, in Jerusalem—so I wasn't even close to being there. It would be a lot more dramatic, of course, if I could say that I was in Tel Aviv, trying to get home, and traffic to the central bus station in Tel Aviv was particularly heavy that day, and I got there a little late, and I saw my bus pulling out of the station, and I ran to it, trying to catch it, but the driver had already closed the doors and driven away, and I cursed him and my bad luck and all the buses in the world, knowing that now I would have to wait for the next bus, not knowing that it actually saved my life— but this is not what happened. And even though I could, of course, take the liberty of changing it—in the name of art, in the name of literature—I feel that I must tell the truth: I was nowhere near that bus that day.

Anyway, as the bus was working its way up to Jerusalem, climbing the road along the mountainside, next to a steep ravine, a young Arab got up from the back of the bus, walked up to the driver, and pulled the steering wheel all the way to the right, forcing the bus off the road, driving it downhill, into the abyss. More than twenty passengers were killed, including the Arab.

A week later, my friend Yoram was taking the bus from Tel Aviv to Jerusalem late at night, coming back from a punk-rock show he was reviewing for *The Capital*. Yoram was the one who actually got me the job at *The Capital*, and even though it was the crummiest of publications and we both hated it, I was very excited at the time. It was my first big break, my first job as a writer, and it was Yoram who gave it to me.

And I'm not just saying it because he's dead. He died of lung cancer a few years ago, but even before that, before he even became ill, I knew that I owed him.

I remember the last time I saw him. It was after chemotherapy hadn't worked. I bought him a present: the new Emperor CD, the now classic *In the Nightside Eclipse*. He had moved back in with his parents and was spending most of his time watching TV in his room, puffing on his oxygen mask. When I came over with the CD, he was really happy about it but said that it would make more sense if I kept it.

"I thought Emperor was your favorite band."

"They are."

"So what's the problem?"

"No problem. Let's play it, and then you can keep it."

"Forget it. I got you a present, you can do whatever you want with it. You can throw it out the window the moment I walk out, I don't care. It's yours."

"Thanks," he said.

He closed his eyes and reached for the oxygen again. I thought I saw tears rolling down his cheeks, but maybe it was just steam inside the plastic mask. We played Emperor and were amazed at how much they'd progressed from the first album and how fast and sharp and heavy they sounded. Then we played it again, and I went home. He died three days later.

But anyway, back to Tel Aviv. Not thinking ahead, he'd had a few beers at the show he was reviewing, shortly before he boarded the bus back to Jerusalem, and sitting through the fifty-minute express ride, he had no choice but to hold it in. He managed to be brave for about thirty minutes, but his bladder kept pressing, and he finally cracked and, despite his embarrassment, stepped forward to the front of the bus to ask the driver if it would be possible to make a quick stop so he could take an emergency leak on the side of the road.

Unfortunately, the spot where Yoram finally decided to approach the driver was very close to the spot where, a week earlier, the infamous and unprecedented terror attack had taken place. So naturally, when the other passengers saw Yoram approaching the driver, they jumped on him, grabbed him by the throat, and started beating him up. One guy strangled him with remarkable persistence while another one punched him repeatedly in the stomach. A third man pulled a gun, and when Yoram screamed that he was not an Arab, just a punk-rock kid who desperately needed to pee, the man pressed the gun to Yoram's head and released the safety catch with a threatening click, because everybody knows that Arabs who dress like Jewish punk-rock kids and speak fluent Hebrew are the worst kind of terrorists.

Finally he managed to tell them that he had his ID in his denim jacket pocket, and when they pulled it out and saw that it was blue, they let him go. If you're an Arab, you get an orange ID.

We're approaching our destination downtown, a neon-lit sandwich bar called Shalom Snack. We get off the bus and march into the restaurant, and I must admit that they seem a little more relaxed now, maybe because of the proximity of food. We all sit down around a big plastic table, and when the waitress appears—a girl of about eighteen, slightly pimpled, wearing a red shirt, yellow apron, white sneakers, and an aim-to-please smile—they all smile back and order right away. Immanuel Sebastian orders a tuna sandwich and coffee, Abe Goldmil a mozzarella-and-basil sandwich and coffee, Amos Ashkenazi a big mushroom-and-caper omelet sandwich and coffee, Uriah Einhorn pasta primavera and milk, Desta Ezra, pointing to a picture in the menu, just hot chocolate, and Hadassah Benedict just water.

"Check it out," mumbles Immanuel Sebastian, elbowing Abe Goldmil and ogling the waitress as she makes her way back toward the kitchen. "Isn't she amazing?"

"She's ugly," says Abe Goldmil.

"Are you nuts? She's blonde!"

"I don't like blondes."

"What's wrong with you? She's gorgeous!"

"I beg to differ," says Abe Goldmil.

"Go differ yourself," spits Immanuel Sebastian. "Why don't you just stick to your imaginary girlfriend, I'm sure she'll make you happy."

"If you two don't knock it off," I intervene, "we're all going back to the hospital. We're here to have a good time, so please, if you don't mind, behave yourselves."

"I must talk to her," says Immanuel Sebastian.

"You can't," says Hadassah Benedict.

"Why not?"

"She's a girl."

"So?"

"You can't talk to girls."

"I'm talking to *you*."

"I'm a patient."

"And a girl."

"I'm not a girl. I'm a female patient."

"I think I liked you better when you were dead," says Immanuel Sebastian.

"Here she comes," whispers Amos Ashkenazi.

"Just don't be rude to her," says Abe Goldmil.

"Why would I be rude to her?" says Immanuel Sebastian. "Trust me, I know how to talk to beautiful girls."

"Here are your sandwiches and drinks," the waitress announces with simulated gaiety. She lays everything on our table in quick, precise motions. "Anything else I can get you?"

"That'll be all," I say to her. "Thank you."

"Enjoy," she says.

"Wait a minute," calls Immanuel Sebastian. "Can I ask you a question?"

"Sure," she smiles.

"Is that a zit coming out on your forehead or are you wearing one of those Indian red dots to indicate the number of brain cells currently switched on in your head?"

"I'm here to take orders, sir, not insults," the waitress says with what sounds to me now like a slight Russian accent. "I'd appreciate it if you kept your observations to yourself."

"Cranky, are we?" smirks Immanuel Sebastian. "Okay, so now I know what that little dot is. It's a punctuation mark. You're obviously having troubles with your period."

"Speaking of punctuation," says the waitress, "I did notice a funny smell when I came over to your table: you must be having trouble with your colon."

"Well, well," Immanuel Sebastian rubs his hands. "If it isn't the revenge of the teenage vampire waitress. I bet you're thinking of driving a wooden stake through my heart now, aren't you?"

"I'm thinking lots of things right now, but—believe it or not—I have no intention of sharing any of them with you."

"And I have no intention of asking you to, because you know what you get when you offer a blonde a penny for her thoughts, don't you?"

"I'm not sure that I do."

"Change."

"Oh?" the waitress raises her eyebrows. "But how would *you* know? You look like the kind of man who would have to pay a lot more than a penny to get something from a blonde. Or from any girl, for that matter."

"Matter? Surely you don't mean *gray* matter," squints Immanuel Sebastian, "because I see no evidence of its existence underneath that ridiculous yellow mane of yours."

"Wait a minute. Are you attracted to me because I'm dumb or because I'm blonde?"

"Who said I was attracted to you? All I'm saying is that somehow you don't strike me as a very bright girl."

"You behave well, mister, and I won't have to strike you at all."

"Oh, I get it. It's the sequel: the vampire waitress strikes back."

"And speaking of striking back, I've already asked you once: enough with the butler's revenge. I can't breathe here."

"Butler, huh? Well, in case you haven't noticed—"

"Immanuel Sebastian!" I decide it's time for another intervention. "Enough already!"

"She started it," says Immanuel Sebastian.

"I don't care," I bang my hand on the table. "This kind of behavior is uncalled for."

"Then tell her to leave me alone."

"Yes," says Hadassah Benedict, "tell her to leave him alone. And can you also tell Julie Strain to leave Goldmil alone? He's driving us crazy with all those poems about her."

"Speaking of Julie Strain," says Abe Goldmil, reaching inside his coat pocket, "would you like to read something?"

"Not the brown notebook again," I sigh.

"It's not my notebook," says Abe Goldmil, "it's this paper I found on the doctor's desk."

"On Dr. Himmelblau's desk?"

"Yes."

"How did you get in there?"

"She wanted to see me in her office last week. After I'd pulled my pants down in front of Desta Ezra."

"And you just took a paper from her desk?"

"Yes."

"Why?"

"I don't know."

"Are you diagnosed as a kleptomaniac?"

"Not that I know of."

"Does she know you took it?"

"I don't know. I guess not."

"Let me see."

One of the most prominent psychopathological symptoms of this typical case of obsessive admiration is the issue of control. Tormented by the feeling that his own life lacks direction, the patient admires his idol primarily for what he believes is her ability to be in complete command of her life. Leading a life so hopelessly passive, the patient tries to live vicariously through his omnipotent idol.

"Is it okay for me to get another glass of milk?" asks Uriah Einhorn.

"Can't you see I'm reading?"

Another major theme pervading almost all of the patient's poems is the religious aspect of his devotion to his idol. Referring to Julie Strain as a benevolent angel capable of saving loyal followers, he expresses his admiration in terms of uncompromising religious zeal. However, it is not unlikely that the patient's reference to the actress as a divine entity originates from Julie Strain's own per-ception of herself. "I think the work I do," says Strain in an inter-view published in an American adult magazine, of which two copies were found among the patient's possessions upon his arrival at the hospital, "doesn't conflict with what God wants me to do. He gave me all these gifts, and he has let all these magical things happen to me, and maybe he's going to use me down the road as a guide to these people I've gathered as my fans" (Leg Show, vol. 13, no. 12, April 1996, p. 52).

"Can I get more water?" asks Hadassah Benedict.
"Why don't you get something to eat?"
"My body's rotting from the inside. I can't have any food."
"Get whatever you want."

Longing to be touched by the hand of his goddess, the patient devotes most of his time and energy to writing songs of praise to Julie Strain. Upon a close examination of these poems, two dif-ferent yet closely interrelated stories unfold. One is a story of a goddess, the other—of a worshipper. Julie Strain's is a tale of fame and fortune, glamour and glory, stardom and success. The patient's obsessive-compulsive sequence of sonnets is a narrative dominated by hopelessness and humiliation, anguish and aggra-vation, desolation and despair.

"So?" says Abe Goldmil, eyes shining with pride. "What do you think?"
"I don't think you were supposed to read this."
"It was on her desk."
"And you just took it?"
"Yes. And I also took something for you, Immanuel."

GILAD ELBOM

"What is it?" asks Immanuel Sebastian.

"She's making you take this new medicine, right? So I found this other thing on her desk, which I think you might want to read," says Abe Goldmil, pulling from his coat pocket another folded piece of paper.

"I'll take that," I snatch the paper out of his hand, "thank you very much. If Dr. Himmelblau finds out you've been stealing documents from her office, you're dead."

"*I'm* dead," says Hadassah Benedict.

"I once *thought* I was dead," says Uriah Einhorn.

"I once thought I was the Messiah," says Immanuel Sebastian.

"Eat your sandwiches," I say.

It's dark already, but we still have some time to kill before I can take them back to the hospital and go home. I try to talk to Amos Ashkenazi, see if I can get him to say something, maybe trick him into using some of the impressive vocabulary he's supposed to have—but he's too busy trying to wipe a mustard stain off his purple T-shirt, so I glance at the other paper Abe Goldmil stole from Dr. Himmelblau, and just because I have nothing better to do, I start reading it, hoping that by the time I'm done, it'll be late enough for us to leave.

Credoline, a new belief-stimulating agent for the clinical treatment of moderate and severe cases of faith deficit disorder (FDD), is a low-milligram high-potency compound with a preferential antagonist activity at dopamine receptors. Marking a vast improvement in both safety and efficacy, Credoline has a reduced side effect profile compared to traditional belief-stimulating drugs (antiskeptics), as well as substantially higher remission rates in acute and chronic FDD.

The TV is on. The European Basketball League. Maccabi Tel Aviv against Panathinaikos Athens. Maccabi Tel Aviv are opening with Oded Katash and four black players. What the coach and management do is fly to the United States, buy African-American players, convert them to Judaism—sometimes even give them new, Hebrew names—and bring them over to Israel. According to Israeli law, every Jew in the world is automatically entitled to Israeli citizenship, which makes it fairly easy for Maccabi to turn a bunch of former NBA players into a very strong Israeli team.

Introducing a unique pharmacological formula that drastically improves the benefit/risk ratio of treating FDD, Credoline has a considerably minimized scope of undesirable polytriangular side effects. The radically troublesome, often irreversible polytriangular symptoms (PTS) have often led to critical problems in case management and patient compliance. These motor and mental side effects were inextricably linked to the antiskeptic effect, and much effort has been made over the past three decades to identify and develop new belief-stimulating agents with a more favorable adverse effect profile.

Hadassah Benedict seems to be following the game, as do two teenage soldiers who sit on the other side of the restaurant.

"Remember in the seventies," Abe Goldmil turns to Hadassah Benedict, "when we only had one channel, and everything was in black-and-white?"

"I was dead in the seventies," says Hadassah Benedict. "Why was everything in black-and-white?"

"Because they erased the colors," explains Abe Goldmil. "The Broadcasting Authority used to buy American films, erase the color out of them, and show them in black-and-white."

Antiskeptic-induced PTS produce a wide range of motor (objective) and mental (subjective) disabilities. Motor symptoms of hyperblinking, suggestive winking, and fricopalma (constant rubbing of the hands) are usually accompanied by mental symptoms such as irritability, compulsive mockery, and disputoperdia (a tendency to engage in long arguments). These symptoms can also masquerade as secondary FDD symptoms that restrict the clinical benefit potentially available from traditional antiskeptics.

"Why did they do that?"

"To discourage people from buying color television sets," says Abe Goldmil. "That way, even if you had a color TV, you couldn't see anything in color."

"But why?"

"They said it was for economic reasons. Official government policy at the time was not to encourage people to buy color TVs, which were a lot more expensive than black-and-white TVs, so that inflation rates would stay low."

"Makes sense," says Hadassah Benedict.

"No," says Abe Goldmil. "No. That was just an excuse."

Credoline is the first new-wave, nontraditional agent to clearly demonstrate a low PTS profile while maintaining a high level of potency. Its safety and efficacy have been tested and proved in a series of clinical studies in Europe and the United States. A double-blind, parallel-group, placebo-controlled, randomized, 28-day, multicenter study was conducted to compare the effects of 400 mg of a conventional belief-stimulating agent (Tenetrone) and single daily doses of 4 mg and 8 mg of Credoline in 248 patients with FDD. Clinical improvement at endpoint was reported in significantly more patients in the Credoline 4 mg group (65%) and 8 mg group (76%) than in the Tenetrone group (47%) and the placebo group (39%). Safety data for patients treated with Credoline were essentially more encouraging than those receiving standard belief-stimulating drugs, with patients in the Credoline groups reporting less subjective polytriangular side effects than the traditional antiskeptic group. Patients receiving Credoline were also observed to show notable relief of core FDD symptoms such as cynicism, sarcastic behavior, refusal to identify with any religious denomination, or difficulty subscribing to other, nonreligious (or even antireligious) doctrines. These primary FDD symptoms are, of course, not to be confused with NPD (nihilistic personality disorder); FDD patients show no inclination to embrace any doctrine at all, not even nihilism.

"The truth is that they didn't want us to live in a multicolored world. Variety is always dangerous. It's much safer when everything is either black or white. Less confusion. Us and them, right and wrong, good and bad. It's much clearer when you don't have colors."

The Greeks are winning. The soldiers are getting ready to leave. The Russian waitress wipes the table next to us. Immanuel Sebastian is checking out her ass. Hadassah Benedict is looking at Abe Goldmil.

"For years we were prisoners. Prisoners of controlled vision, myopic subjects held hostage by rulers who wanted us to live in mandatory blindness."

"So what did you do?"

"We tricked them. We had the anti-eraser."

Immediate candidates for switching to Credoline, therefore, are patients who respond only partially to their current antiskeptic or are unable to tolerate polytriangular side effects at therapeutic antiskeptic doses. However, whether changing from a traditional antiskeptic to Credoline or introducing it as initial treatment, a major obstacle the clinician must overcome prior to the commencement of treatment is the patient's pathological suspicion and distrust. Paradoxically, the very symptoms that the proposed antiskeptic is designed to control make it impossible for the patient to comply with antiskeptic treatment. In other words, a common response on the part of the patient when offered a belief-stimulating drug to alleviate symptoms of FDD is: "I do not believe in drugs."

"The antidepressant?"

"The anti-eraser. A sophisticated electronic device. Small—and not cheap—but very effective. You plugged it into your color TV and it would restore the colors."

"How?"

"Technically? I don't know. But it worked. It would cancel the erasure the government was applying and make your world polychromatic again."

"What's polychromatic?"

"Like a rainbow."

"Oh," says Hadassah Benedict. "Wow."

Fortunately, this potentially treatment-limiting paradox is not insoluble. If the patient refuses to take Credoline because of skeptic symptoms, the clinician may use the double negativity rationale (DNR). In the subjective perception of the nonbelieving patient, all faith-related parameters are based on active negation of existing conceptions. Or, to put it in psychopathological terms, abnormal neurotransmitter activity causes the patient to uncontrollably invalidate all cognitive notions, abstract or real. However, FDD negativistic parameters do no necessarily repudiate negative notions. When the negativistic mechanism negates an

*affirmative notion, the nonbelieving patient inescapably
"believes" in the corresponding negative idea. In other words, the
patient's nonbelief in (the affirmative concept of) taking drugs
automatically implies a firm belief in (the negative concept of) the
nontaking of drugs. However, in order for the patient to demonstrate primary FDD symptoms of active nonbelief, he or she must
actively not believe in anything, including in the nontaking of
drugs, and therefore must take the drug.*

"At first they made the anti-eraser illegal. It had to be
smuggled into the country and sold on the black market. But
then they gave up and abolished erasure, and everybody
went out and bought a color TV."

Hadassah Benedict is smiling.

*In conclusion, since the introduction of Credoline into clinical
practice, more FDD patients now face the chance of significant
improvement in symptom relief and possible restoration of hith-
erto shattered lives. Its enhanced efficacy, high tolerability, and
lower propensity to polytriangular side effects make Credoline a
novel drug that should now be considered as a first-line option.*

I look at my watch. Nine o'clock. I call the waitress over,
ask for the bill, and tell the patients to pay. They're all a little stingy with the tip, but what do I care. They put on their
coats, wave goodbye to the waitress, and march out of the
restaurant. It's cold and windy and dark, looks like it's going
to rain again, and they're staggering down the empty streets,
silent and sad. We get to the bus stop, and all six of them
huddle on the plastic bench, which I think is a little wet, but
none of them seems to care. The streets look crude and colorless. The bus stop smells like the typical Jerusalem mixture of dry urine and barbecued meat. The Broadcasting

Authority may have abolished erasure, but they still have this major stronghold of murk, this dull, lackluster, bland city, praised by generations of clueless admirers as if it were the most exciting, most inspiring place in the world.

Carmel says that our sex life is also in danger of becoming bland. She also says that the phrase *sex life* is a contradiction in terms. She says that in order to avoid falling into a dreary routine, we have to keep inventing sexual fantasies.

After we storm the castle and free the slaves, we assemble them all in the main hall to decide about their future. While some of them say that they want to put an end to this nightmare and go home, others prefer to stay. They're afraid that liberation would not allow them to taste the intoxicating, death-like vortex of sexual ecstasy ever again. Dreading the insipid equilibrium of freedom, they request that Carmel and I, as the new masters, maintain their enslavement as sexual playthings.

Desta Ezra is the only one who stares into the darkness, actively waiting for the bus. The rest of them seem half-asleep now. They twist and fidget on the bench, eyes closed, chins pinned to their chests.

Carmel and I step out to the courtyard, where lie the fresh corpses of the less fortunate teenage boys and girls. The blinding sight of blood and nakedness arouses in us an uncontrollable urge to feast on this dazzling display of raped and rotting flesh, revel in the nauseating evidence of lust and violence. By devouring the dead we would be giving them new life inside our bodies. By consuming the cold, stiffening carcasses we would be animating them, reviving them.

I undress and lie motionless on the blood-soaked ground, blending with the smoothness of lifeless youth. Carmel removes her clothes, kneels down in front of my body, spreads my legs apart, and takes my penis in her mouth. I lie still, not moving a muscle, while she licks my cock to a full erection. She slides it up and down her palate, inserting its entire length all the way to the back of her throat, swallowing it in voracious frenzy. The tip of my cock pounds her uvula repeatedly, and I come in her larynx just as she gags and vomits. A gush of puke and semen spurts from her mouth as she collapses next to me, coughing. We both lie there for a while, the sweet stench of Carmel's regurgitated bile mingling with the smell of putrefying flesh.

Uriah Einhorn picks his nose, then wipes his finger on his pants, eyes still closed. Amos Ashkenazi rocks his knees in fast, self-soothing motions, head shrouded in the hood of his coat. An automatic neon light goes off in an empty hardware store across the street. Immanuel Sebastian lets out a short, sharp snore, then a little moan, then falls silent again. Desta Ezra is almost invisible in the dark. A police car zooms by, washing her face in flickering blue. She stands up, probably thinking that the bus is coming, then sits down again.

After we rise and get dressed, we summon the remaining boys and girls and order them to start digging a big grave in the far corner of the backyard. While they're busy digging, we walk back to the castle to examine the bodies of a maidservant and a soldier, both shot dead by the previous owners of the place. The soldier's corpse, perforated by multiple gunshot wounds in the chest and stomach, is useless. But the girl's body is still intact: young and skinny, long-limbed and smooth, coal-black skin, small breasts, a flat, almost concave stomach. She's sitting on the floor, naked, as if alive, leaning against the big armchair behind which she was trying to find shelter from her murderers. Her head is resting on her right shoulder, a thin line of dark, coagulated blood streaking her face, all the way from the left temple, across her cheek and neck, down to the protruding clavicle.

"I'm getting wet," Carmel whispers in my ear. "Are you getting hard?"

"I am."

"So let's do something."

"To her?"

"Why not?"

"That would be necrophilia."

"It would be sex," says Carmel.

"Sex with someone who happens to be dead."

"What's wrong with that?"

"It's sick."

"It's not," Carmel says. "It was only after it had been categorized and labeled by legislators and psychiatrists as illegal and pathological that this harmless form of human sexuality became a taboo. The desire to sleep with the dead has always existed. But the moment you condemn it as necrophilia, you label all those who practice it, or even fantasize about it, perverts."

"But isn't it against nature?"

"The fact that such a form of sexuality is even possible means that it's not, and could never be, against nature. If nature allows it, it's not a deviation. Nature doesn't care if you have sex with a man, a woman, an animal, or a corpse. And it makes no difference to the dead girl if she's consumed by worms or fucked by human beings."

"So why the taboo?"

"The fact that there is a taboo on sex with the dead means, first of all, that sex with the dead exists. And in order for it to exist, the taboo must be violated. Necrophilia is prescribed by the very law which prohibits it."

"So how come there's punishment for those who violate the prohibition?"

"The punishment is there to strengthen the desire, just as the taboo is there to reinforce the transgression."

"So what you're saying is that the law actually produces the infringement."

"Exactly. Perversion is not a natural crime. It's manufactured by social powers that encroach on innocent bodies and their harmless pleasures."

I'm not sure I agree with Carmel, let alone understand what she's talking about, but since the dead girl is indeed irresistible, I decide to cooperate. We lift the body and place it prone on the bed, face down and spread-eagle. Carmel runs her fingers over the sleek back, all the way along the visible spinal cord, down to the round, hard behind. She grabs the black buttocks with both hands, spits inside the dead girl's anus, and commands me to penetrate it. I do as she says, convulsing the corpse underneath me in such a violent manner that it appears to be alive. Fingering herself to a wild orgasm as she watches me rape the dead girl, Carmel responds with screams of simulated pain every time my penis pierces the cadaver's rectum. Carmel says that merging with the murdered maid brings us closer to death and to each other, just as it brings the dead girl herself a little closer to life.

Two teenage girls are approaching the bus stop. They giggle. They walk slowly, deliberately, almost showily. One of them reads the street sign aloud—*Jaffa Road*—and bursts out laughing. The other pretends to be pushing her friend into the road—and bursts out laughing. They stand close to me— too close, I think—but when they realize that I'm with the six dark figures sitting on the bench, they move a few steps away and start whispering. Desta Ezra turns her head to look at them, then at me, then back at the empty road.

We carry the dead girl and her butchered lover to the big, freshly dug hole in the backyard. The boys and girls have already piled up almost all the other bodies inside. We throw the remaining corpses into the tomb, and Carmel orders the male slaves to step forward. When they're all lined up around the edges of the grave, she strips, descends into the sepulcher, lies on her back on top of the pile of bodies, and commands the young boys to urinate on her. They hold their members in their hands and piss into the open grave, flooding Carmel and the bodies underneath her with a warm, golden torrent. When they're done, she asks them to masturbate. They all rub their penises strenuously, and within a few minutes Carmel's body is besmeared with the thick, sticky emissions of more than ten young men. She then instructs all of us to grab our shovels and cover the grave. Dust and mud hit her face and body as she closes her eyes and fingers herself again with rapid, circular motions. She comes just as her entire body is covered with dirt. She remains motionless inside the grave for a few more seconds, holding her breath, then exhumes herself out to the open air. She stands on the damp ground for a while, panting, then puts her arm around my waist as we slowly walk back to the castle to take a shower.

And here comes the bus.

I wake them up and make sure they all climb inside, and since it's late at night and all the streets are empty, the ride out of the city and back to the Haven is fast and smooth. The only other passenger beside the giggling girls, who both get off at the neighboring kibbutz, is an old woman with four or five plastic bags filled to the brim with market groceries, who stays on the bus when the seven of us get off at the hospital.

When we get to the unit, a sleepy Ibrahim Ibrahim greets us at the door, asking his fellow inmates about the trip. He insists on hearing all the details, and they mumble something about the sandwiches and the coffee, and he asks them if they had any dessert, but I break up their conversation and give them their medicines and send them all to bed, then quickly write the report, swipe out, and lock the door behind me.

It's good to be out of there. Actually, I spent most of the day outside the hospital—which might explain why I'm so exhausted. I should try to relax with some nice linguistic thoughts, but I'm too tired to think of syntactic analysis right now. So I'll just give you a simple declarative sentence with a nonspecific subject, a transitive verb, and two objects, the first direct, the second indirect: *They gave Ibrahim Ibrahim life*.

I walk to the parking lot, where I sit in my car for a few minutes, warming up the engine, trying to find something interesting on the radio. But there isn't anything, so I push a Judas Priest tape—*Screaming for Vengeance*—into the tape player, and I drive home.

CHAPTER 8

The first one to greet me when I enter the unit is Amos Ashkenazi, purple T-shirt exceptionally wrinkled, nicotine-stained lips trembling as he pulls the sleeve of my coat, urging me to follow him to the game room.

"Please tell Goldmil to stop," he says.

"What's he doing?"

"I'm trying to watch TV, but he's out of control. All he talks about is Julie Strain."

"What's on TV?"

"*The Young and the Restless.*"

"And who's Goldmil talking to?"

"Himself," says Amos Ashkenazi, "but they're all sitting there, listening."

"So he's not talking to himself."

"They're listening to him talking to himself."

I don't know why I let Amos Ashkenazi drag me into the game room before I even have a chance to sit down in the nurse's station, relax a little, go over the newspaper, make myself a cup of coffee. Maybe it's because tomorrow is my day off.

In the center of the game room stands Abe Goldmil, perched on one of the white plastic chairs, lecturing in a slow, steady voice. Around him sit Immanuel Sebastian, who nods in agreement to almost every word; Hadassah Benedict, who smiles at nobody as if she's very happy; Uriah Einhorn, who keeps yawning without covering his mouth; Desta Ezra, who looks terrified for no reason; and Ibrahim Ibrahim, who looks at Desta Ezra.

"Julie Strain is a heaven-sent female messiah," pronounces Abe Goldmil, "an angel whose mission on earth is to teach us all the true power of devotion, dedication, and faith."

"You see?" says Amos Ashkenazi.

"What do you care? Let him talk about Julie Strain. That's what he always does."

"But I want to watch TV."

"Watch TV later."

"Julie Strain is not only a supreme being incarnated as the most beautiful creature alive," declares Abe Goldmil, "but also the epitome of willpower. She wasn't born famous. She wasn't born gorgeous. She wasn't born glorious. But she worked her way from an anonymous little girl to the most ravishing sex diva ever, building herself a magical career with her own bare hands."

"And bare boobs," interjects Immanuel Sebastian, still nodding.

"Julie Strain," continues Abe Goldmil, ignoring Immanuel Sebastian's heckling, "serves as living proof to us all that if we just learn to do two simple things—love ourselves and believe in our dreams—there will be absolutely nothing beyond our power."

"Tell him to stop," says Amos Ashkenazi. "He's going crazy."

"Look who's talking."

"You can't let him be the king of the unit," says Amos Ashkenazi. "Please."

"But first," Abe Goldmil informs his audience, "she had to be put to a test. Before her mission could be accomplished, she had to go through a long period of hibernation. Like a butterfly yearning to blossom out of its cocoon, she spent almost three decades just sitting at home, cooped up in a prison-like small town, forced to pretend she was content with the dull life of a meek housewife. Yet she never forgot what she came to this planet for. She never forgot she had a task to perform. She always remained devoted to the goals she had set for herself, never losing faith in her ability to burst out of her solitary confinement and take the world by storm."

"You see? He's acting like a maniac. Aren't you going to do something about it?"

"What do you want me to do?"

"Call the doctor."

"What's wrong with you? Quit acting like a baby. If I call the doctor, it'll be for *you*."

I walk away from Amos Ashkenazi and the rest of them and sit in the nurse's station. I try to glance through some stupid stories in the newspaper, but all I can hear is Abe Goldmil's voice coming from the game room, interfering with my attempts to read an article about the Egyptian Coptic Church.

"Julie Strain's most prominent characteristic is, of course, her courage. Her courage to take complete control over her life, change the course of her existence, choose to be all she can be, shape and mold her own self-being in perfect accordance with her dreams and desires, recreate herself as an invincible deity, transform herself into an eternal, immortal queen. It is no wonder, therefore, that we, her fans, don't just admire her. We worship her."

"We?" I hear Immanuel Sebastian interrupting Abe Goldmil again. "You never told us you had multiple personality."

I get up and step into the game room again. Everybody's still there, including Amos Ashkenazi, who's now sitting on the couch, listening to Abe Goldmil.

"We worship her because she does what deep in our hearts we all want to do—but are just too afraid to. We worship her because she dares to love herself, free herself, express herself, expose herself, touch herself."

"Touch herself?" slobbers Immanuel Sebastian.

"Yes, touch herself," says Abe Goldmil. "I can see her now," he closes his eyes, wearing a dramatic, trance-like expression on his face, "standing in a golden wheat field on a hot summer day, her smooth skin glistening in the sun, her long, lithe hands caressing her cornucopian breasts, running down her bronzed stomach, stroking her perfectly-shaped hips, cupping the downy rectangle between her thighs. She tilts her head back in barely restrained ecstasy, a blazing crest of ebony locks cascading down her supple back as she brings herself to a wild, teeth-clenching climax."

Amos Ashkenazi gets up from the couch and hurries toward me.

"It's TV that I want to watch," he spits in my face.

"What?"

"It's TV that I want to watch, but it's Julie Strain that Goldmil can't stop talking about."

"What's wrong with you?"

"It's losing my mind that I'll soon be. Please, do something."

"Okay, relax. I'll call Dr. Himmelblau."

I go back to the nurse's station, and I'm about to call Dr. Himmelblau, but just as I put my hand on the receiver, the phone rings. One long ring.

"It's your day off tomorrow, right? Let's do something. How about you and me go somewhere?"

"I'll call you right back, Carmel. I have to call the doctor."

"What's wrong?"

"I don't know. This stupid patient. Always passive, almost subcatatonic, and all of a sudden he decides that today he's going to be difficult."

"What does he want?"

"To watch TV."

"Dear God! A patient with a will of his own? Call the doctor immediately!"

"Carmel, please."

"Does he also want to eat, the little pig?"

"Carmel, you don't know what's going on here. And also the way he talks—makes no sense."

"Wants things *and* talks funny? That's outrageous. Let's shove some drugs down his throat, that'll teach him to make no sense."

"Carmel, you don't know what you're talking about. I'm having an emergency here. Let me call you back."

I hang up and call Dr. Himmelblau. She picks up and puts me on hold, making me sit with the phone pressed to my ear like a moron for far too long, listening to Abe Goldmil raving about his idol in the other room.

"However, Julie Strain possesses much more than overwhelming sexuality. Of course, she reeks of pure carnal passion, but—perhaps paradoxically—she's also an emblem of innocence and purity. A starry-eyed girl encased within the stunning physique of a bodacious woman, Julie Strain has a unique way of combining outrageously provocative eroticism with natural exuberance and child-like honesty."

Finally she clicks over.

"What is it?"

"I'm having a bit of a problem with Amos Ashkenazi. He's acting a little pushy."

"Pushy?"

"Impatient. Aggressive. And his syntax is all mixed up. He's not making any sense."

"I'll be right there."

I hang up and walk back to the game room, where Amos Ashkenazi is waiting for me, all tense and edgy.

"Did you call the doctor?"

"I did."

"Is she going to make him stop?"

"Of course she is. Don't worry. You go to your room now and try to relax. She'll be here in no time."

"Thanks," says Amos Ashkenazi. "I appreciate it."

"No problem."

He goes to his room and closes the door. I walk back into the nurse's station and pull out *Robinson Crusoe* from my backpack, but before I have a chance to open it, Carmel calls again.

"You said you'd call."

"I'm waiting for the doctor."

"Have you been to the casino in Jericho?"

"Let me call you back, Carmel."

"Let's go there."

"Tomorrow?"

"Why not?"

"I have to write my paper."

"I thought I wrote it for you."

"I need to tweak it a little."

"Do it tonight."

"It seems almost inconceivable that only a few years ago nobody knew who Julie Strain was," I hear Abe Goldmil saying.

"Let me just get this thing over with," I say. "I'll call you right back."

"What thing?"

"But once she had become the almighty princess of light she always knew she would be, there was just no escape from the brilliant splendor she began to spread upon the earth."

"I told you: there's this patient here who's going nuts over this other patient talking about Julie Strain."

"Julie Strain is everywhere you look: films, videos, books, magazines, TV shows, computer games, trading cards, post-cards, posters—everywhere. The whole world has become a huge shrine to Julie Strain, a temple of reverence celebrating her universal glory."

"Julie who?"

"Strain. She's an actress. Let me call you back."

As soon as I hang up, Dr. Himmelblau walks in.

"What on earth is going on here?"

"We should consider ourselves extremely fortunate to have been given the opportunity to be among those who have seen the rise to stardom of Julie Strain."

"It's okay," I tell her, "that's just Abe Goldmil. I think there's something wrong with Amos Ashkenazi. He—"

"No, it's not okay," she cuts me off.

"We are lucky to be able to witness the birth of a supreme being and be touched and blessed by the benevolent hand of the ultimate goddess of love and beauty."

"He's just talking about Julie Strain. The problem is with Amos Ashkenazi. He—"

"Just talking about Julie Strain? Listen to him. He's psy-chotic like he's never been before."

"We should be forever grateful for having the privilege to offer Julie Strain our endless veneration—and in return experience her infinite divine grace."

"The reason I called you is because Amos Ashkenazi was acting weird."

"Amos Ashkenazi? Where is he?"

"In his room."

Abe Goldmil sees Dr. Himmelblau now. He steps down from his chair, bringing his little sermon to an untimely end. Dr. Himmelblau walks over to Amos Ashkenazi's room, knocks on the door, opens it without waiting for an answer, peers inside, then closes the door with a bang and walks back to me.

"I see no problem with Amos Ashkenazi."

"He was giving me some trouble before."

"This is very irresponsible of you. I'm counting on you to be smart enough to report to me immediately if Abe Goldmil or anyone else is showing any signs of instability."

"Okay," I nod, wishing I were somewhere else already, far away, in Jericho, gambling my head off, or in Finland, swimming in the lake, or in Aberystwyth, reading the *Mabinogi*, practicing lenitions and nasalizations and aspirations and palatalizations.

Dr. Himmelblau gives Abe Goldmil an extra dose of Clopixol and sends him to bed. She takes a look around, scanning the rest of the unit, deliberately avoiding my eyes—and walks out. Amos Ashkenazi comes out of his room and thanks me again.

"I knew I could count on you," he says. "You're a good man. Thank you."

"No problem."

I go back to the nurse's station. I call Carmel and tell her that I'll pick her up tomorrow morning around ten. We'll have breakfast, then drive down to Jericho. I'll make reservations.

I hang up and open *Robinson Crusoe*, but I can't concentrate. I put the book down and reach for the newspaper and read the article about the Copts, who believe that Christ has only one nature, partly divine and partly human, as opposed to other Christians, who believe that Christ has two natures: one divine, the other human.

Supper is served: alphabet soup, boiled beef cubes, undercooked boiled potatoes, avocado salad, and nondairy chocolate pudding. Hadassah Benedict, for some reason, doesn't eat her Alephs.

"Why aren't you eating your Alephs?"

"I'm shrinking."

"I thought you were dying."

"That's why I'm shrinking."

"I guess you'll just have to be a little patient."

"What do you mean?"

"Nothing. Why aren't you eating your Alephs?"

"They taste funny."

"Don't be silly. All the letters taste the same."

"Not the Alephs."

"Do whatever you want."

I walk back to the nurse's station. Immanuel Sebastian and Ibrahim Ibrahim are today's patients-on-duty. They're washing the dishes, but I'm not in the mood to check on them. I can hear them talking in the kitchen, and I can hear the water running in the sink, so I guess they're doing their job. "They wanted to make an example out of me," I hear Ibrahim Ibrahim's voice. "A token of our thirst for blood. That's why they shot me in the leg."

"Come on," says Immanuel Sebastian.

"I'm serious. They didn't shoot to kill."

"Don't be so paranoid," says Immanuel Sebastian. "You're not the only one who killed someone. I killed someone too—

but you don't see me walking around bragging about it, do you?"

"Who did you kill?"

"Who? Is that what they taught you over there?"

"Whom did you kill?"

"My mother."

"You didn't."

"I swear to God."

"You killed your own mother?"

"With a toaster," says Immanuel Sebastian. "You see, I used to be an alcoholic, but then I switched to psychedelic drugs, and I was having these flashbacks to blackouts. Didn't know what I was doing. And one day, I can't even remember why, I just threw the toaster at her while she was taking a bath."

"And she got electrocuted."

"Of course not. It wasn't even plugged in. It just hit her on the head. Killed her instantly. One of those old, heavy toasters."

"That's horrible."

"It wasn't that bad. The real problem was trying to get rid of the body."

"What did you do?"

"I got rid of it by not getting rid of it."

"I'm sorry?"

"I just left the corpse in her apartment, kept it refrigerated—so that the neighbors wouldn't smell anything. I kept paying the rent, left some automatic lights on, came for occasional pretend visits, regularly sent her some fake mail, regularly came to pick up the fake mail—it all went so smoothly, I thought I could keep doing it forever. But one day—it was one of those really hot summer days—I loaded her into my car, trying to take her to the beach, just to make it even more convincing—and I got pulled over by the police."

* * *

My parents got divorced a few years ago. My mother remarried an Iraqi Jew who has multiple myeloma and a Ph.D. in Arabic poetry, and my father a Polish-American non-Jewish woman he had met on one of his business trips to Boston. My mother and the Iraqi are still married, but things didn't work for my dad and the Pole. He brought her to Israel, and they were actually living together for a while, but they didn't get along, and after a few months she went back to Boston and my dad had the open-heart surgery. That's the valve replacement I told you about. They let him choose between a mechanical valve and a pig's valve. He chose the pig and got his marriage annulled, but his mother—my grandmother— had already sat the seven days of mourning as if he were dead. According to Jewish law, if you marry a Gentile, you're as good as dead. So my grandmother, who in her old age became a born-again Jew, had to publicly mourn the so-called death of my father for a whole week, and from then on she acted as if he didn't exist anymore. I wanted to talk to her, ask her if she was really serious about it, tell her that the marriage was officially over, ask her if a metaphorical bereavement can be revoked—but she wouldn't talk to me either. I went over to her house a couple of times, but she wouldn't open the door. Maybe she thought my father was with me and that we were trying to trick her into seeing him. Maybe the son of a Jew who marries a Gentile is also considered dead. Or maybe it had something to do with the valve. I don't know. In any case, I never saw her again. And neither did my father.

And when she died, we sat for an hour. But not out of revenge. We just didn't know she'd died. Walking up King

George Street in downtown Jerusalem on his way to the bank, my father ran into a friend of his mother's, a very old woman with dim blue eyes and a number on her forearm, who apologized for not calling him earlier, when it all happened.

"What happened?" asked my dad.

"Your mother," said the woman.

"I had no idea," said my dad, and they both started crying in the middle of King George Street, right in front of the bank. Then he pulled himself together, said goodbye to the woman with the number, went home, and called Benny Miller. Benny Miller worked with my dad for a few years, until he also became a born-again Jew, quit his job at my dad's office, and went to work for the Jerusalem Kaddisha Company, the General Orthodox Mortuary.

"I need some information about my mother," my dad said to him.

"Sure," Benny Miller said.

So my father gives him my grandmother's name, and Benny Miller goes on the computer and gets all the information for him right away: date of death, place of burial, section, plot.

My father thanked him, hung up, and called me at *The Capital.*

"Grandma died," he said.

"When?" I asked.

"Six months ago."

"So what do we do?"

"We sit for an hour."

Apparently, the Jewish law concerning death and mourning has considered such a case. If a person dies, and the relatives don't hear about it until considerably later, they should sit and lament for only an hour—instead of seven days.

And that's what we did. I was working on a review of the new Monster Magnet album when my dad called. I told the editor-in-chief I had to take a short break. It took me twenty minutes to get home, so we only had to sit for forty minutes. We sat in the kitchen, and my father told me about how my grandmother had escaped from Europe in the nick of time. Or as we say in Hebrew, using soccer terminology, in the ninetieth minute.

It was the summer of 1939, and my grandmother was a student in Prague. The Germans had already invaded Czechoslovakia, and when she found out she was wanted by the Gestapo, she sought the help of her professors, who decided to diagnose her as seriously ill and commit her to the university hospital. When the officers came to the hospital to arrest her, the doctors told them that her illness was not only so serious that she couldn't be moved, but also so contagious that it was best not to get near her. They left empty-handed, but it was clear that she couldn't be passed off as a dying patient for the next six years. So her teachers arranged for her to go and do a semester abroad, at the Hebrew University of Jerusalem.

But first she had to get the approval of the British, who were not too keen on letting Jews into Palestine. The State of Israel did not exist yet, and the land, which had been a Turkish territory until World War I, was now under the British mandate. The British agreed to issue my grandmother a student visa on condition that she returned to her home country as soon as her semester at the Hebrew University was over. They demanded that a distinguished and reliable member of the Jewish community in Jerusalem sign a promissory letter, vouching for her return to Europe.

Through a network of connections and references, she got a Mr. Shmuel Yosef Agnon to sign the letter. He knew—and maybe even the British themselves knew—that it was a complete lie: *I, future Nobel Prize winner, hereby testify that the holder of this letter promises to happily return to the gas chambers as soon as she's done being a diligent exchange student.*

But before she could take the boat to Palestine, she had to get permission from the Germans to leave Europe. Adolf Eichmann was the German officer who signed her passport. She had to go through six or seven officers before she was allowed to enter his office and receive the final stamp on her visa out of Prague. The six or seven officers sat behind a long desk, each in charge of verifying a different aspect concerning the applicant's eligibility to leave Europe: one made sure that my grandmother didn't have a pending income tax debt, one made sure that she didn't have a pending social security debt, one made sure that she had no criminal record, and so on, each imprinting a separate stamp in her passport. Finally, when all the authorizations had been stamped, she was allowed to see the boss, Eichmann himself, head of the Central Office for Jewish Emigration, who signed her passport without even looking at her and sent her away. The German policy back then, before the Final Solution, was to get rid of the Jews in any way possible, including just letting them go.

So my grandmother went to the Hebrew University, and Eichmann got promoted. At the height of his career he was in charge of inspecting death camps and other concentration facilities, making sure that they operated smoothly and efficiently. In 1945, when the war was over, he managed to escape to Argentina, where he lived for fifteen years before he was abducted by Israeli agents from his home in Buenos Aires, brought to trial in Jerusalem, sentenced to death, and executed.

By the time my dad got to Eichmann hanging from the gibbet, our forty minutes were over, and I got up and drove back to *The Capital* and finished my review of Monster Magnet. It would have been more appropriate, of course, if I'd happened to be working on a review of an album by Entombed or Grave Digger or Death Angel—but no, I was writing about the new Monster Magnet album, and that's a fact I can't change.

* * *

They've all taken their medicines and gone to bed now, so I'm going over the newspaper again, trying to read a long piece about the casino, which I hope will take me to the end of this shift. Ever since the casino opened a few years ago, there's something about it in the newspapers almost every day. Gambling is illegal in Israel, but now that Jericho is under Palestinian self-rule, it's okay for Israelis to go there. According to the newspaper, it's actually more of a loophole: officially, as far as Israel is concerned, the Palestinian Territories are still an Israeli military zone, which means that technically, Israelis who gamble in Jericho are breaking the law. Which is why last week, a member of the Knesset, the Israeli parliament, proposed that Israelis should be banned from the casino. The proposition was immediately dismissed, because even though the casino was built by an Austrian company, it's basically an Israeli-Palestinian coproduction put together by businessmen, lawyers, politicians and security agents from both sides. That member of parliament castigated "the abnormality of retired Palestinian terrorists protecting Israeli compulsive gamblers from Muslim zealots." But apparently the proposal was also rejected because 95 percent of the gamblers in Jericho are Israelis, which means that if Jews were banned from the casino, there would be no casino.

Meanwhile, the only people banned from the casino are the Palestinians themselves. Gambling is against Islamic law, and the Palestinian Authority, which collects 50 percent of the revenues, decided that it would be best if Palestinians stayed away from the casino. Other reasons why the Palestinian Authority doesn't want Palestinians in the casino is because lots of Israeli girls go there every night, and it might not be a good idea for practicing Muslims to be around Jewish sluts. However, Israeli Arabs, even though they're Muslims, are allowed in the casino, whereas Christian Palestinians, even though they're Christians, still can't go there.

But it's getting too confusing for me, so I get up and wander around the unit, looking for something to eat. There's nothing in the staff kitchen. Some leftovers from supper on an orange plastic plate in the patients' kitchen, but it doesn't look too good: cold, shriveled beef cubes and a semicrusty pile of avocado salad gone black, scavenged by an industrious assembly of little black ants. I dump it all in the garbage and throw the plate in the sink. This is what they do when they're too lazy to wash the dishes—which is practically every time you don't watch them. They save some inedible portion of food in the kitchen, pretending that someone might want to eat it later, just so they can wash one less plate. But what's really disgusting about it is that if I don't throw it away, someone will actually eat it. They get up in the middle of the night, and I guess they're hungry—or, more likely, they *think* they're hungry—and they eat the stuff. And if they get up in the middle of the night and the food is gone, they greet me in the morning with extended vituperative homilies, saying that I'm a vile tyrant and that I have no right to throw their food away and that I'm worse than the Nazis. But Dr. Himmelblau tells me to tell them that when they have a place of their own, they can eat whatever they want, whenever they want—but as long as they're in the hospital, they have to abide by the rules of the unit.

I make myself a cup of tea, go back to the nurse's station, and try to read the rest of the article about the casino. Last week the ancient Jewish synagogue in Jericho was desecrated by local Arabs, an act that led another member of parliament to propose that the army demolish the casino in retaliation. The article also supplies a list of all the Palestinian security organizations, most members of which, according to the newspaper, are "graduates of Israeli prisons." There are eighteen official Palestinian security organizations: National Security, Preventive Security, Special Security, District Security, Presidential Security, Public Security, General Intelligence, Military Intelligence, Military Police, Civil Police, Air Police, Border Police, Civil Defense, Coast Guard, Chairman's Guard, Special Airborne Force, General Security Administration, and the Joint Security Committee. Each of the above organizations has two separate branches: a Gaza Strip branch and a West Bank branch. In addition, there are several semiofficial security apparatuses operating in the Palestinian Territories: the Civil Militia of the Palestinian Liberation Organization, the Military Wing of the Islamic Resistance Movement, the Islamic Jihad, the Martyrs Brigades, and the Marxist-oriented Popular Front for the Liberation of Palestine.

There are some strange noises in the unit. Like a mumbling and a dragging of furniture. Is the TV still on? I put the newspaper aside and get up, but the TV is off, and everybody seems to be asleep. And now it sounds like somebody's tapping on a metal object. And a faint slapping sound. I pace around the unit, passing by the patients' rooms, but the noise has stopped. I stand outside Hadassah Benedict's door for a few minutes, but I can't hear anything. A jackal is howling in the wadi outside, joined by another one, and another one, but then they stop, and the only thing I can hear is the ticking of the big clock in the dining room. Maybe just some cockroaches in the kitchen.

I fold the newspaper and put it away. I shouldn't be wasting my time reading the newspaper every day. I should focus on writing. I should come up with some good quotes to put on the first page of my book. Poignant epigraphs to hook those literary agents right from the start. Something from Baudelaire, for example:

> *Life is a hospital where every patient is obsessed by the desire of changing beds. One would like to suffer opposite the stove, another is sure he would get well beside the window. It always seems to me that I should be happy anywhere but where I am, and this question of moving is one that I am eternally discussing with my soul.*

Or maybe something more contemporary, something by Gilbert Sorrentino:

> *The idea of a novel about a writer writing a novel is truly old hat. Nothing further can be done with the genre, a genre that was exhausted at its moment of conception. Nobody cares about that "idea" any more, and Dermot knew it. To rescue his shambles of a book he added scenes of gratuitous sexuality, so crassly done as to cause all but the most debased reader to throw the book down in dismay and disgust.*

Or maybe a shorter quote. People don't like long texts. In this fast-and-furious, pedal-to-the-metal, six-lane highway we call life, who can afford to read lengthy, time-consuming books with too many pseudo-reflective asides, self-referential ruminations, and amateur linguistic interludes? Here's something short and neat by Eleanor McNees:

> *Words are like elements that, if properly acted on, will grant grace and communion with God.*

But Eleanor McNees is an academic. She doesn't really know what she's talking about. Ensconced in her ivory tower, she's disconnected from real life, from the people, from the literary needs of those who feel and yearn and fight and cry and live and die. So maybe a quote from a more down-to-earth bunch of people would be more appropriate:

Time melts away in this living inferno,
Trapped by a cause that I once understood.

Slayer. My favorite band. Or maybe something from Thomas Szasz, my favorite psychiatrist:

For millennia, people accepted theological tyranny because the priest promised them protection from the unceasing terrors of an eternal life in the hereafter. Today, people accept therapeutic tyranny because the doctor promises them protection from the unimaginable terrors of an increasingly long life here on earth.

Or something by an Irishman. Flann O'Brien, for instance:

A satisfactory novel should be a self-evident sham to which the reader could regulate at will the degree of his credulity.

Or a famous linguist. Hermann Paul:

The element most sharply distinguished from the rest is, in the first place, the psychological predicate, as being the most important of all, containing as it does that which it is the final aim of the sentence to communicate, and on which therefore the strongest emphasis is laid.

SCREAM QUEENS OF THE DEAD SEA

Or something by Flannery O'Connor:

I once received a letter from an old lady in California who informed me that when the tired reader comes home at night, he wishes to read something that will lift up his heart. And it seems her heart had not been lifted up by anything of mine she had read. You may say that the serious writer doesn't have to bother about the tired reader, but he does, because they are all tired. One old lady who wants her heart lifted up wouldn't be so bad, but you multiply her two hundred and fifty thousand times and what you get is a book club.

I look at my watch. It's already a few minutes past ten. I go to the staff kitchen, wash my empty teacup, wipe my hands on the paper towel for a little longer than necessary, standing there for a minute or two, waiting to hear the cockroaches in the kitchen again. I'm concentrating hard, but I still can't hear anything. Which is a little disappointing. For a moment it felt as if I were on the verge of enhancing my sensory perception, acquiring the ability to detect noises heard in heaven and on earth, maybe reach some understanding that has so far eluded me. But I guess I'm just tired.

I grab my backpack from the nurse's station, swipe out, and lock the door behind me. The night is cold, and my ears are freezing as I walk to the Justy, but I'm happy thinking about not having to be here tomorrow. We'll go to Jericho. We'll have fun, away from the unit, away from the suffocating tentacles of Jerusalem, away from all these human cockroaches.

CHAPTER 9

It's always hot in Jericho. And even though it's only thirty minutes away from Jerusalem, we decide to spend the night, pretend like we're actually going away on a big trip. We have some clothes and our toothbrushes and the little tube of lubricant that Carmel keeps in her heart-shaped makeup box, and we're on the Jericho Highway, windows rolled down, hot wind playing with Carmel's hair. She takes off her coat and jacket, remaining in a blue Harley Davidson baby doll T-shirt. I put my right hand on her left thigh. The Justy rolls down the empty road.

Jericho, along with Gaza, was one of the first two cities we handed back to the Palestinians a few years ago, and the first thing the Palestinian Authority did was build this huge casino in the middle of the desert. We're ten minutes away from it now, but I need to get some gas, so we pull into a gas station near a settlement called Genesis Land, where they sometimes stage reenactments of famous Biblical stories about Abraham and Isaac and Jacob. While I'm pumping gas, a teenage boy in sandals, a small prayer shawl under a white button-down shirt, and a white-and-blue skullcap comes up to me, handing me a yellow flyer with bold black print in Hebrew and English:

> *While it is understood that Austrians and others would have no moral problem trying to make bucks off of Jews surrendering G-d given Jewish land to Arabs, Jews who are willing to sell their eternal birthright for a bowl of lentils is a sad commentary.*

We pull out of the gas station and hit the road again. We slice through the Judean Desert, driving past Palestinian villages that look like Roman ruins, Jewish settlements that look like upscale American suburbs, local Arab nomads— the Bedouins—with their little convoys of camels and donkeys, and soldiers patrolling along the road. Jericho, which lies next to the Dead Sea, is the lowest point on earth, and along the road there are signs that tell you that now you're 200 meters below sea level, now you're 300 meters below sea level, and now you're in Jericho, which is 400 meters below, which is about 1,300 feet.

We go through the army checkpoint and enter the Palestinian Territories. The road is narrow and in need of maintenance. When we pull over to get some orange juice at a roadside stand, a tall, skinny guy comes up to us. He looks about my age, maybe a little younger, and he's wearing a white turban, a thick black beard, and a washed-out red T-shirt with a green iron-on that reads: *Islamic Resistance Movement.* He hands us another bilingual flyer, this time in English and Arabic:

> *It is lamentable that the Palestinian Authority believes that the liberation of Jerusalem from the Zionists could proceed from the*

den of iniquity in Jericho. With the money invested in and collected from the Casino of Satan, the Palestinian Authority could have built 150 factories instead, creating jobs and enabling our impoverished workers to end their dependence on the Israeli labor market.

The funny thing about Arabic is that they have no present tense. As a matter of fact, there's no present tense in Hebrew, either. Instead, we use the participle, which is a grammatical form somewhere between a verb and a noun. But the Arabs don't even have that. I mean, they do have the participle, but they never use it as a substitute for the present tense. They just use the future tense: the same form of the verb signifies both the future and the present—which can sometimes be confusing. But I guess it does make some sense, because why would you need the present in a place that relies on the past and looks forward to the future? We have a history and we have an afterlife. The present doesn't matter.

Arabic is also more economical. What takes English seven or eight words to say—*The Reviver of the Female Infants Buried Alive*, for example—is condensed in Arabic into just two words, pithy and precise.

"You guys going to the casino?" the bearded guy asks me.

"Yes."

"Why?"

"We've never been there."

"I live across the street from the casino," he says.

"In Jericho?"

"In Aqbat Jaber."

"What's that?"

"A refugee camp. Have you ever been there?"

"No, not really."

"Do you want to see my motorcycles?"

"Thanks, but we're on our way to the casino."

"I'll make you the best tea you've ever had. Then you can go to the casino."

"Aren't you supposed to be handing out these pamphlets here?"

"What's the point? People don't read them. They just go to the casino like robots."

"But *you* can't go there," Carmel says to him, "right?"

"No, only you can."

"If you could go, would you?"

"It's against Islam, but I would."

"You would?"

"Yes, but just out of curiosity. I've never been there."

"Neither have we."

"So go there later."

"You don't really have motorcycles, do you?"

"I collect motorcycles. And I have a friend—he also collects motorcycles."

"What kind of motorcycles?"

"Classic motorcycles."

I look at Carmel. Motorcycles and tea. Sounds suspicious. I don't think we should trust him.

"Why not," Carmel shrugs.

Stupid girl. Why not? He's a Hamasnik, that's why. He's a natural born suicide bomber. He's been waiting his whole life for this perfect chance to kill himself along with two evil Jews. He joined the Islamic Resistance Movement so he could blow himself up while serving you tea, then go straight to heaven to collect his seventy-two virgins. Stupid, irresponsible girl. Can't you control your reckless sense of adventure for once? We could have made it to the casino and back alive, but no, you had to volunteer to be slaughtered by this bloodthirsty fundamentalist. And there's no turning back now, because the last thing I want him to think is that we're afraid of him.

"Why not," I say. "Let's go."

Hamasnik is an interesting morphological creation: the Arabic acronym for the religious alternative to the PLO, followed by a Russian suffix indicating profession, occupation, place of habitation, or, in this case, organizational affiliation. In the army I had a desk job, which made me a *jobnik*. Which, of course, is a derogatory term used to distinguish soldiers like me from real soldiers, combat soldiers.

"Follow me," says the Hamasnik. His turban is not exactly white. And it's not exactly a turban. It's a green-and-white kaffiyeh, a turban-like headdress that probably signifies his devotion to Islam or something. I just hope it's not a bad sign. He marches into a little papaya grove at the side of the road and pulls out a gigantic BSA from behind the trees, black and heavy, a little rusty here and there, a Harley Davidson sticker on one side of the gas tank, a hand-painted Palestinian flag on the other. Angrily, repeatedly, he jumps on the kick-start pedal, and when the bike is finally up and running, he mounts it ceremoniously and maneuvers it slowly to where Carmel and I stand. He brings it to a shaky halt next to the Justy and revs up the engine with two or three sharp twists of the accelerator.

"Nineteen forty-two," he shouts, beaming. "My name is Ramzy."

"Gilad," I shout.

"Carmel," Carmel shouts.

"Ready?" He revs up the motor again.

"Wait a minute," I say. "It's not dangerous for us to go to the camp, is it?"

"Not if you're with me," he smiles.

We get in the car and follow Ramzy, watching him riding at a slow, steady pace ahead of us, turning back his head every minute or so to make sure we're still behind him. He gets off the main road and onto a dusty dirt road that takes us through a thick citrus orchard. The sharp smell of oranges and lemons fills the car, and Carmel stretches in her seat, arching her back, putting her hands on the back of her neck. She closes her eyes and breathes through her nose. The sun is on her face, her skin looks fresh and radiant. She's smiling at me, and I'm thinking about her little straight teeth and her small nipples, and about the funny way she was looking at Ramzy when he invited us to join him for tea, and about shoving my cock into her comic-book mouth, and about all those bumps and dips and rocks on the road, and how bad they must be for the Justy.

And all of a sudden we find ourselves in the camp, surrounded by hundreds of low, squalid hovels. The whole place smells. We follow Ramzy to his house, driving very slowly through the unpaved alleys. His house, which seems to be right in the middle of the camp, is just a tiny shack that looks as if it's about to tumble down any moment. He tells us to park our car right where we are, in the middle of the street, and orders one of the little kids playing in the alley to stay and watch it, make sure nobody touches it. He parks his bike in the backyard, which is just a narrow gap between his house and the next-door shack, and takes us in.

The inside of his house looks surprisingly pleasant: a two-bedroom apartment, clean and tidy, carpets on the floor and on the walls, and little light-blue china ornaments with verses from the Koran on bookcases made of cane. The front door is painted aqua-blue, against the evil eye.

"Do you live by yourself?" Carmel asks.

"I live with my family: my mother and my brothers and sisters."

"How many brothers and sisters do you have?"

"Eight."

"Including you?"

"Including me—nine."

"Where are they?"

"At school."

"And where do you keep your motorcycles?"

"We have a small garage here in the camp, me and my friend. Close to the mountains."

"Why were you hiding your bike behind the trees when we first saw you?"

"It's against the law to ride a motorcycle here."

"Against the law of Islam?"

"Against the law of Palestine."

"Why?"

"Security."

"The army won't let you ride your bike?"

"Not the army. The Palestinian police."

"Your own police?"

"Exactly."

"Why?"

"I don't know. I used to ride my motorcycles every day before the Israelis withdrew, but when the Palestinian Authority took over, they decided that only police and security could ride motorcycles."

"So what do you do?"

"We pay the policemen a shekel or two, and they let us do whatever we want. But it's better if they don't see our bikes. Let me make you some tea."

He asks for our permission to leave the room, and when we nod our blessing, he disappears into the kitchen. Carmel and I remain in our seats in the living room. I look at her, but she doesn't say anything. She smiles. I don't smile. I guess I'm a little tense. I wouldn't say scared. Maybe a little nervous, but not scared. I bet he has lots of knives in the kitchen.

Ramzy returns with a silver tray loaded with three cups of tea and a bowl of carobs. The tea is extra-sweet and extra-strong, with a hint of cardamom, and the three of us sip it slowly, Ramzy holding the bottom of the glass with four fingers, laying his thumb across the rim. He speaks almost perfect Hebrew, but I think he knows I know Arabic. He probably knows I was in the army, but if he doesn't mention it, I'm not going to, either.

"Where's your father?" Carmel asks.

"In prison."

"What did he do?"

"Nothing. He's just a member of Hamas. Islamic Resistance Movement."

"How long has he been in prison?"

"Eleven years. The Israeli army had put him in prison in the first place, but when the Palestinian Authority took over, instead of releasing him, they didn't release him."

"Why?"

"Because they don't believe in Allah. They claim to be Muslims, but they act like the worst infidels. You want to see my motorcycles?"

"Sure."

We get up and go out, Carmel and I putting our sunglasses on, Ramzy fixing his kaffiyeh on his head. He spits a couple of words in Arabic to the kid-turned-sentinel, reiterating the strict order to keep watching my car, then leads us through the dirty alleys toward the outskirts of the camp, where the shacks are a little less crowded, the stench of sweat and human waste a little less pungent. He takes us to a place that looks like a deserted stable, where in one of the wooden sheds his motorcycles are stored, and in another—his friend's.

"Who's that friend of yours?" Carmel asks.

"Just a friend."

"Does he live in the camp?"

"Not exactly."

"Is he some sort of silent partner?"

"I guess you could say that," Ramzy smiles.

"Sounds mysterious," Carmel says.

"It's not. It's just safer that way."

"Okay," Carmel smiles back. "So what exactly is this place?"

"It used to be a horse ranch, but they shut it down."

"The army?"

"The owners."

"Who were the owners?"

"Just some guys from the camp who wanted to open a horse ranch. They had horseback riding summer camps for Jewish and Palestinian kids. Believed in peace. They had a horse named Typhoon, the most beautiful horse you've ever seen. Almost as beautiful as Al-Buraq, the prophet's horse."

"What happened to it?"

"It took the prophet to heaven and back. You can see its hoofprint on a sacred rock in Jerusalem, near the Wailing Wall."

"No, what happened to Typhoon?"

"Oh. It died. All the horses got sick and died."

"Didn't the owners take them to the vet?"

"We had a vet who used to come down here from Jerusalem every week, but last year, when the army put Jericho under curfew and blocked all the roads, the vet just couldn't come."

"Don't you have a local vet here?"

"He's afraid of horses."

When I was little, my father used to tell me the same bedtime story every night. There once was a king who received a very special gift from a strange knight: a mirror in which you could see openly who was your friend and who was your foe. I think I need one of those mirrors now. The strange knight had other supernatural gifts for the king: a flying horse, a sword that could cut through mail, and a ring that would make you understand the language of the animals. My father said that the flying horse was an aircraft, the sword was an armor-piercing projectile, and the ring—military intelligence.

"But that'll never happen to my motorcycles," says Ramzy. "I don't rely on any outside mechanics."

"You fix them yourself?"

"Who else would fix them for me?"

"Are they all in running condition?"

"The BSA—yes. The Triumph, the Matchless, and the Norton—not yet. But they will be."

"When did you start collecting them?"

"We used to collect classic cars, my friend and I, but the desert destroyed them."

"Wait a minute," says Carmel. "The desert is dry—isn't that supposed to be good for antique cars?"

"Yes, dry is good. But it's too hot. The sun just killed my cars."

"How hot does it get here?"

"In the summer? Around forty-five, maybe forty-six degrees. Sometimes even forty-seven."

"That's hot."

Ramzy strokes his beard. I look at the mountains surrounding the camp. They took us on a field trip to one of the
settlements in this area when I was in the army. We listened
to a talk given by a self-proclaimed biblical analyst, who
showed us that if you read the Pentateuch skipping fifty-
something characters at a time, it would still make sense. But
I'll tell you all about it later, because right now Ramzy is lecturing us about the desert and the heat. Forty-seven degrees
Celsius is almost 120 degrees Fahrenheit.

"And there's also sandstorms," says Ramzy. "And sudden
floods. And camels."

"Camels?"

"Oh, yes. Camels can be a real nuisance here. My friend
had a 1974 Corvette—bright yellow, beautiful, almost mint
condition. The camels ate it."

"They hate it?"

"Ate it. They just love fiberglass. He parked it right next to
my house when he was visiting me one day, and when it was
time for him to leave, we found two camels chewing on it."

"So that's why you told that boy to keep an eye on my
car."

"No, that was because you have an Israeli license plate."

"Which means?"

"Which means that if it's unattended—that is, if there's
nobody there to tell the people that you're my guests—
they'll either steal it or burn it. Now let's go up."

"Up?"

"To Mount Temptation."

"Temptation?"

"One of the temptations of Christ. He climbed up there
when he went away for his forty days of solitude."

"Listen, we're actually on our way to the casino."

"I'll show you the casino. You can see it very clearly from the top of Mount Temptation."

"We were thinking of seeing it from the inside."

"It'll only take a minute. We have a cable car."

"A cable car?"

"Yes. It takes you from downtown, where the traffic light is, straight to the top of Mount Temptation."

"What do you say?" I turn to Carmel.

And please, Carmel, please don't say "why not." Be sensible. I'm counting on you, Carmel. Make some excuse, say that we really have to go, say that someone's waiting for us at the casino. Can't you see what he's trying to do? Couldn't slaughter us in the camp, so now he wants to be our special tour guide, lead us to his secret abattoir on top of this god-forsaken mountain, slit our throats while chanting verses from the Koran. In the name of God, the Compassionate, the Merciful, I hereby spill the blood of this ex-soldier and his sexy girlfriend, and may the King of the Day of Judgment provide me with the seventy-two young girls that I now right-fully deserve, Arab or Jewish, I don't care, as long as their hymens are intact.

"Why not," Carmel says.

Ramzy looks at me.

"Why not," I shrug.

"Good," he smiles. "Let's go."

We walk back to the camp, where Ramzy suggests, for safety reasons, that we leave his motorcycle parked in the backyard, take my car, and drive downtown together, all three of us. We get in the car and take another narrow dirt road, which, after about ten minutes, turns into Main Street. I just hope he doesn't touch my steering wheel.

"Here comes the traffic light," he says.

It's a traffic light all right, but there aren't many cars around. Most of the people ride bicycles: old, squeaky little bicycles, with the seat and handlebar pulled all the way up. We pass by a big mural showing a palm tree and a mosque, with a metal crescent on top of a minaret. A man with a mustache and a unibrow is praying on his hands and knees while a barefoot woman in a red dress is flying in the air. Ramzy suggests that we stop for lunch. There's a great hummus place here, Abu Nawaf, that we just can't afford to miss.

We park on the street, and as soon as we walk into the restaurant and sit down, before we even get a chance to order, Abu Nawaf himself, a fat man of about forty, cross-eyed and sweaty, comes out of the kitchen with three bowls of hummus with fava beans on top, and a few small plates of side dishes, naming each of them as he puts it all down on our table: pita, falafel, goat cheese in olive oil and parsley, roasted eggplant in garlic and lemon, stuffed grape leaves, pickled beets, Syrian olives, Arab salad.

"What's an Arab salad?" Carmel asks.

"An Arab cuts it," says Abu Nawaf.

"They're from Jerusalem," says Ramzy.

"Welcome," says Abu Nawaf. "Eat, please. This is everything I have. No menu."

We eat in silence, and I must admit, the food is good. The best hummus I've had in a very long time. But I'm a little nervous. Abu Nawaf is huge—looks like the local Polyphemos—and I wouldn't be surprised if he decided to have a Hebrew male nurse and a female university student for lunch today.

We finish eating, Carmel scooping up the last bites of her hummus with some pita bread, me picking up the last olive off the plate. We're watching Abu Nawaf clear the table, disappear into the kitchen, then come right back with four cups of thick, bittersweet coffee and an apricot-flavored water pipe. He sits down and passes the pipe around, and Carmel and I take a few puffs each, even though we don't normally smoke.

"So," says Abu Nawaf, spouting two long jets of smoke out of his nostrils, "have you two seen Ramzy's motorcycles yet?"

"Oh, yes," says Carmel. "I love motorcycles."

"And have you met his Jewish friend?"

"What Jewish friend?"

"You didn't tell them?"

"Of course I told them," says Ramzy.

"Your secret friend is Jewish?" asks Carmel.

"He's a Samaritan," says Ramzy.

"An American?"

"A Samaritan. A Palestinian Samaritan. From Nablus."

"So what is he," I ask, "a Palestinian or a Jew?"

"He's a Palestinian Jew," says Ramzy.

"And he doesn't even speak Hebrew," says Abu Nawaf.

"What does he speak?"

"Arabic, of course," says Ramzy. "And Samaritan."

"He only prays in Hebrew," says Abu Nawaf.

"That's right," says Ramzy. "The Samaritans practice a very ancient form of Judaism. Which is why most of the orthodox Jews in Israel don't recognize them as Jews."

"So is he Jewish or not?" I ask.

"Oh, he's Jewish," says Ramzy. "They have their own Pentateuch, and slightly different dates for the Jewish holidays, but basically, it's the same religion as yours."

"And you accept them as Palestinians?"

"Oh, yes. They've been here for ages."

"But they're Jews."

"So what? There are Muslim Palestinians, there are Christian Palestinians, and there are Jewish Palestinians."

"But you said that the Christians and the Jews were infidels."

"They are," says Ramzy. "But they're Palestinian infidels."

We pay Abu Nawaf and ask for his permission to leave. He nods and shakes our hands. Ramzy says we can leave the car parked in front of the restaurant—Abu Nawaf will keep an eye on it—and walk to the cable car station, which is just a few blocks away. He takes off his green-and-white kaffiyeh and tells me to throw it across the dashboard—just to be on the safe side. I do as he says, and we cross the street and walk through a big outdoor market where at most of the stands they sell only oranges and grapefruit. When Ramzy stops to buy a pack of cigarettes, I signal for Carmel to come closer.

"Do you think they really have a cable car?"

"I don't know. Do you think they really have a Samaritan friend?"

"Of course not. They must have had something in that hookah."

Ramzy comes back with a pack of *Farid* cigarettes, and we both smile at him.

"We're almost there," he says.

I look at Carmel. She looks at me. Is it finally dawning on her that we're walking into a trap? Should I put a stop to this ridiculous game and tell Ramzy that we're going back to the car? It doesn't look like Carmel is going to do anything about it. She doesn't even look concerned. Maybe it's my duty to protect her. If we get there and they don't have a cable car, I'm calling the whole thing off. A cable car! Does he really think we're that stupid? A cable car in Jericho, where they have no sidewalks, no sewage system, one traffic light, nothing to eat besides hummus and oranges, and ten times more bicycles than cars.

"There it is," says Ramzy.

"What?"

"The cable car."

I look at it, then at Carmel, then back at the thing. It's a cable car. Three red cars. Bright red. Going up the mountain. On a cable.

"Haven't you ever ridden in a cable car?"

"Me? Of course I have. I'm just a little surprised, that's all."

Ramzy buys the tickets, and when the three red cars come down, we board the middle one and sit by the big window. Ramzy lights a cigarette, even though there's no smoking in the cable car, and we start moving up, slowly. I look at the city growing smaller down below, trying to see if I can spot my car, make sure it's okay. Of course, pretty soon we won't need the car anymore, since Ramzy is going to butcher us on top of this stupid mountain.

But when we actually get to the top, the place is crawling with tourists, most of them Christian pilgrims, I assume, speaking in English and Spanish and German, and I even hear some Hebrew here and there, and a monk in a brown wool robe greets us with a smile, and some more tourists.

"From here," says Ramzy, spreading his arms in the air, "you can see everything. Right there, on the other side of the Dead Sea, is Jordan. When Palestine was under Jordanian rule, King Hussein used to come to Jericho every winter with his Princeton Tigers cheerleader wife, Queen Noor."

Carmel and I exchange glances again, but Ramzy doesn't seem to notice.

"And down there—see all those arches and columns?— that's Hisham Palace."

"Where's the casino?" I ask.

"Wait," says Ramzy. "We'll get to the casino."

"When was the palace built?" asks Carmel.

"In the seventh century, in the early days of Islam, when the Muslim empire stretched from Arabia to Spain."

"And who was Hisham?"

"The emperor. This was his winter palace."

"Where was his summer palace?" I ask.

"In Damascus."

"Can you see Damascus from here?"

"No, Damascus is far away. But you can see the synagogue."

"What synagogue?"

"The old synagogue of Jericho. Right there. Among those who helped build Hisham Palace were Jews, and when the palace was completed, Hisham rewarded them by giving them permission to build a synagogue."

Oh, so now he's playing the all-knowing scholar. Is he going to educate us before he slays us? What's he trying to prove? And why does Carmel pretend like she's interested? Why does she keep asking him all these questions? Don't encourage him, you idiot.

"And what's that?" she asks.

"That hill, down there? That's Tel Sultan."

"What is it?"

"Some kind of ancient settlement, ten thousand years old. Discovered and excavated only fifty years ago."

"Did you say ten thousand years old?"

"That's what archaeologists believe."

"Who lived there?"

"Who knows. Some guys from the Neolithic period."

"And where exactly did they find the Dead Sea Scrolls?"

Is she serious? Does she really care? Maybe she's just testing his knowledge. Maybe she wants to see if he's really as smart as he thinks he is. I just hope she doesn't start lecturing to him about Robinson Crusoe or dead astronauts.

"Oh, that's over there," Ramzy points out to the desert, "in Qumran."

"And what's that over here? Are those caves?"

"Those are the caves where the monks used to go for forty days of solitude, imitating Jesus Christ in his original cave."

"And where's the original cave?"

"Up here, in the monastery. Let's go see it."

"Wait," I say. "Where's the casino?"

"I almost forgot. Sorry. There it is, down there. It's called Oasis."

Ramzy is pointing at a white marble building, not very elegant, rather bulky, with mirrored walls, beige glass windows, and a big sign on top that probably says *Oasis*, but I can't really tell from up here.

"It's referred to in public as a hotel," says Ramzy, "even though everybody knows it's a gambling house. It's actually built on land that belongs to the Islamic endowment, so you can imagine how uncomfortable it must be for the Palestinian Authority to mention the word *casino* when they try to justify it to real Muslims."

"And what's that building next to it?"

"That's the real hotel: the Jericho Resort Village. But I guess you'll have plenty of time to spend down there. Let's go up to the monastery."

Ramzy points at some rock steps, steep and narrow, carved into the side of the mountain.

"This will take us all the way up there," he says, smiling.

Why is he smiling? And why is he being so nice? He's not supposed to be nice. And he's not supposed to know so much. Christians, Muslims, Palestinians, Neanderthals. What does he want from us?

"It's called Karantal," he says.

Carmel nods.

I don't get it. Why is she being so attentive? Is she genuinely curious? Are they having a private dialogue now? Can he tell that I couldn't care less about imaginary Samaritans or American college girls turned Arab queens? Now I bet he'll explain to her why the stupid monastery is called *Karantal.*

"*Cuarenta* means *forty*," he says. "Hence the name: *Karantal.*"

Carmel smiles at him again. I'm tired. I want to get out of here. I want to tell this Arab buffoon that his time is up, thank you very much. We're leaving.

We enter the monastery, and Ramzy speaks to one of the monks in a strange dialect that I don't understand. Sounds like a mixture of Arabic and Greek, but maybe it's just my imagination. He guides us through dark corridors and a series of high-ceiling halls, and I force myself to pretend as if I'm admiring the frescoes and the stained glass windows, as if I'm having fun, as if I really want to be here.

And all of a sudden—I think Ramzy can sense my unease now—the tour is over, and we're gliding down the mountain in this silly red capsule again—Ramzy is smoking again—into a city that seems to be closing down. It's getting dark, and just like in Jerusalem, everybody seems to be hurrying home. We walk back to the car, a little faster than before, me still nervous, Carmel looking excited, Ramzy humming some Arab tune that I think I've heard somewhere before. Abu Nawaf is closed now, but the Justy is still here, right where we left it, in front of the restaurant.

"It's been a pleasure," says Ramzy. "Thank you for being my guests."

"Thank you for being our guide," says Carmel.

"Wait," I say. "We're taking you back home, right?"

"I can walk to the camp from here."

"Are you sure?"

"Absolutely. I have to stop by the mosque. You two drive to the casino, before it gets dark."

I open the car and give him back his green-and-white kaffiyeh. Carmel gives him a short tight hug, even though she must know that it's probably not the smartest thing to do in Jericho, in the middle of the street. When I extend my arm for a handshake, Ramzy puts both his hands on mine and shakes it for a long time, as if to suggest that we've formed some kind of special bond.

"Drop by any time," he says. "You know where to find me."

"We will," I say.

We get in the car, and I'm not waiting for the engine to warm up, I just pull the choke all the way up and drive.

"Thank God it's over."

But Carmel closes her eyes and leans back in her seat, not saying anything, pretending as if she's tired, or as if she didn't hear me. So I keep my hands on the wheel— in a few minutes we'll be at the casino—and I'm thinking about the phrase *green-and-white*: is it the same as *white-and-green*? Not necessarily. You always beat somebody black-and-blue, never blue-and-black, even though both phrases signify the same colors. And if you're watching an old movie, it's always in black-and-white, never white-and-black. And if you're in England, you always eat fish-and-chips, never chips-and-fish. The objects the words refer to are the same, but semantically, the phrases are not identical.

But I guess I'll have to postpone further repudiation of referential theories of meaning, because right now we're pulling into the casino complex and checking into the hotel, and Carmel wants to stop at the gift shop to get some moisturizer before we go up to our room.

"Let's put our stuff upstairs first."

"I need moisturizer. It's dry as a bone here."

I follow her into the gift shop, but once we're inside, she starts looking around, wasting time, checking out all kinds of stupid souvenirs: pebble necklaces, wooden flutes, wicker doormats, blue glass statuettes, white gypsum garden gnomes.

"The cosmetics section is over here."

"I'll be there in a minute," she says.

So I'm standing here in front of a myriad of cosmetic products, trying hard not to be impatient. They have tons of lotions and soaps and shampoos here, all containing special minerals from the Dead Sea, but the interesting thing is that they have everything twice: from *Ahava*, an Israeli cosmetics company, and from *Zara*, a Jordanian manufacturer from the other side of the border. Both are intended mainly for tourists. The *Zara* package has the same text in Arabic and English. The *Ahava* one has the same product description in thirteen languages: Hebrew, English, French, German, Spanish, Italian, Swedish, Finnish, Russian, Czech, Norwegian, Portuguese, and Dutch. I'm looking at an Advanced Mud Masque:

Found in its natural form on the banks of the Dead Sea, our special natural mud, which contains an extremely high concentration of minerals essential for healthy skin, is comprised of layers of sedimentary clay formed over thousands of years.

I wonder how they say *Dead Sea* in all those languages. Should be easy: *Mer Morte, Mar Morto, Mar Muerto, Toten Meeres, Dode Zee, Döda Havets, Dødehavets.* The only texts I can't decipher are the Russian, because I can't read Cyrillic characters, and the Finnish, because it's not an Indo-

European language. *Mutanaamio.* No, that must be *mud mask.* Maybe *Huuhdstä.* I don't know.

"Ready?" Carmel says.

"What?"

"What are you doing?"

"Reading."

"The package? Don't tell me you're translating again."

"I wasn't translating. I was looking for a moisturizer for you."

"I got my moisturizer. Let's go."

"Why are you getting the *Zara* moisturizer?"

"What's wrong with it?"

"Get this," I point at the *Ahava* box.

"That's a mud mask. I need a moisturizer."

"So get an *Ahava* moisturizer."

"You get an *Ahava* moisturizer. I'm getting this one. Are you coming?"

The cashier rings us up, and I'm standing here, lethargic and useless, our suitcases in my hands, waiting for Carmel to collect her change. We climb to our room on the third floor—the elevator is out of order—and somehow I just know it'll be crummy: lumpy bed, leaky toilet, dusty curtains, no view. Jerusalem is only thirty minutes away. We can just grab our stuff and drive back home.

But when we walk into the room, it looks okay—more than okay, actually—and I'm a little disappointed. Everything's clean and tidy, the bathroom is spotless, the whole damn place is immaculate—I forgot it was built just a few months ago—and we even have a view, a perfect view—too perfect, almost unreal—of the Dead Sea and the mountains behind it and the clear sky with all the planets and constellations, including the three stars that make Orion's sword, which, unlike the much brighter sash, are always hard to see in the city.

"So," I sigh, throwing Carmel's suitcase on the bed. "What do you want to do now?"

"Have sex?"

"Is your husband still alive?"

"Why do you ask?"

"You haven't mentioned him in a long time."

"And you think that now is a good time to do it?"

"Have sex?"

"No, mention him."

"Your husband?"

"Yes."

"What's happening with him?"

"Nothing. Nothing you don't already know. Yes, he's dying. No, he's not dead yet. Need more information?"

"I just thought I'd ask."

"Why? Do you want him to be dead already, so you wouldn't feel guilty anymore? Or would you rather have him kept alive, so you could still feel some excitement?"

"You know what? We don't have to do it."

"Have sex? It was your idea."

"My idea? You suggested it."

"And if I hadn't, you probably never would've thought of it yourself."

"What exactly do you want, Carmel? What did you bring me all the way to Jericho for? To have a fight?"

"You seem to be enjoying it. I get the feeling that you'd rather fight with me than fuck me."

"That's ridiculous. Why do you have to say that?"

"Why do you have to mention my husband?"

"Me? You're the one who keeps telling me about him,

updating me on his condition: the doctors said this, the doctors said that. Stop bringing him up, and I won't ask you about him."

"Stop being so obsessed with him. You knew I was married when we first got together, didn't you?"

"Yes, but you said he was dying."

"He is."

"Then how come he's still alive?"

"How come you care all of a sudden?"

"Is he going to die or not?"

"Are you going to fuck me or not?"

"How do you want me to fuck you?"

"Whichever way you want."

I slap Carmel across the face and tell her to take her clothes off. She removes her Harley Davidson T-shirt and her bra, then her shoes and jeans and socks and panties, dropping it all on the carpeted floor. She stands naked in front of me, not saying a word. She brushes her hair backward with her fingers. She looks smaller in the nude.

I tell her to turn around and get down on her hands and knees. I take out the little tube of lubricant from her makeup box, squeeze a few drops into the palm of my hand, and insert my middle finger in her ass. She groans. I rotate my finger inside her, pushing it in and pulling it out, in and out, in and out. She rests her shoulders and her right cheek on the beige carpet and reaches back with her hands to grab her own buttocks, stretching her asshole open, pink and tight.

I keep pushing my finger in and out. She closes her eyes and presses the right side of her face deeper into the carpet. I reach for the remote. *The News in Hebrew* is on the Jordanian channel. The newscaster, an old Arab with gray hair and a black mustache, says that the Israeli army has made another incursion into the Palestinian Territories today, demolishing fifty-eight houses, leaving more than four hundred people homeless. I spank Carmel and push my finger deeper into her ass. She tries to squirm away, but I wrap my arm around her waist and spank her again. I change to the Israeli channel. The anchorwoman, a thirty-something brunette with straight hair and a cute smile, speaks beautiful, fluent Arabic. She's sticking her tongue between her teeth, overpronouncing all those sexy interdental fricatives that we don't have in Hebrew. She says that only thirty-four houses were knocked down, houses from which terrorists were throwing stones at our tanks. I spank Carmel again, this time a little harder. And again, harder still. I click to the hotel's movie channel, where they're showing *Star Wars*. Obi-Wan is trying to talk Luke into leaving his home planet to join the rebels. Luke says no. Doesn't want to be a hero. I take my clothes off.

Carmel props her elbows on the floor, her face still buried in the carpet, her ass sticking in the air. I squeeze some lube onto my penis and stroke it. Empire troopers attack Luke's farm, destroying his cabin, killing his aunt and uncle. I push the tip of my cock into Carmel's ass. She squeals. I push it further in. Luke decides that he wants to be a Jedi Knight after all. Carmel clenches her little fists. I tighten my grip on her pelvic bones, pinning her ass to my dick. She presses her toes hard against the carpet. I stare at her asshole stretching around my dick, swallowing it in, ejecting it slowly, then taking it in again. She's mumbling something into the carpet. I'm sweating. If she had big breasts, they would pendulum above the carpet. The princess is trapped on the Death Star. Darth Vader is blowing up her planet.

I remember when *Star Wars* first came out. I was so impressed by it, I went to see it four times. The plot seemed so complex. I used to sit by myself in the movie theater, trying to figure out who was fighting against whom. My mother was angry when she found out I was wasting my pocket money on the same movie over and over again. And a science fiction movie, with no real human beings—just robots and astronauts and spaceships and laser beams. She said I should read a book instead. And not a Stanislaw Lem book. A real book, with people and emotions.

I'm standing on the tip of my toes now, knees bent, descending on Carmel from above. I'm squeezing her ass cheeks, kneading my fingers into her clammy flesh as I keep sticking my dick into her. Now they're in the garbage masher. A drop of sweat is rolling down my forehead, hanging at the tip of my nose for a second or two, then splashes onto Carmel's back. I watch it glisten on her spine. I pull out of her, squeeze out a few more drops of lube, and stick my cock in her butt again.

She's screaming that it hurts now. I apply more lube. The rebel pilots are trying to find the Death Star's weak spot. When I was in the army, one of the classes I took at the Intelligence Academy was called Military Doctrine. The lecturer was a fat lieutenant colonel with a soft voice and two fingers missing. The first day, before we even knew his name, he marched in slowly, examined our faces for about thirty seconds, then threw out a question: "What do we need an army for?"

"To protect the country from clear and present danger," we said. "To safeguard the sovereignty of the state. To defend our borders, our citizens, our national interests." He listened, nodding now and then, then said: "Bullshit. The army's purpose is to kill as many people as possible in as little time as possible, spending as little money as possible."

Carmel's asshole doesn't feel so smooth anymore. I pull out and reach for the lube again, but when I squeeze a few more drops onto my cock, I realize that it's not a greasing problem: I'm getting soft. I try to stick it back in anyway, but it doesn't work. I stroke it with my left hand, pulling at Carmel's hair with my right, twisting her neck, hoping that the pained expression on her face will make me hard again. She's biting her lower lip. Sharp lines are etched around the outer corners of her eyes. But I'm still going soft.

I reach for the clicker. Maybe they have a porn channel here. I keep my finger pressed on the button, going quickly over everything they have—but nothing seems to suit my needs. The movie is over, and so is the news, and now there's a man trying to pack fresh eggs on a moving assembly line into cartons of twelve. The eggs are moving too fast. He can only get two or three into each carton, and most of the eggs get to the end of the line unpacked and fall to the floor. Everything's a mess. The man yells for his supervisor to come and rescue him, but the supervisor is hiding in the back room, laughing. The man is helpless. He's desperately trying to save the eggs. They keep breaking. There's a red switch that's supposed to stop the machine. He flicks it off. The eggs keep moving. He flicks it off again. The eggs keep moving. The switch is fake. The camera is behind the mirror. The supervisor is laughing.

I flip Carmel over, lay her on her back. She closes her eyes. I grab her ankles and lift her legs in the air, pinning her knees to her breasts. I try to stick my dick in her ass again, but it's not working.

I give up. I get up, wipe my brow with the back of my hand, and walk to the bathroom. My dick is sticky. I smell of sweat. I just want to pack my stuff and go now. If she wants to stay, fine. She can stay. I'm leaving. I lock the door behind

me and get in the shower. The pressure is good and soothing, but I'm hungry, and I feel the blood pounding in my
temples. I close my eyes and try to clear my mind, letting the
water hit my face for a long time.

A few minutes go by, and I think I feel a little better. I
shampoo my hair twice, soap up and rinse down twice, then
spend a few more minutes just standing under the running
water, trying to see if I can remember some of the lyrics from
the new Cradle of Filth album. "Pulled from the tomb, her
spirit freed, a tourniquet of topaz glistened at her throat."
"Cruelty Brought Thee Orchids." Which, of course, is a simple transformation of the deep structure of a noun phrase, a
verb phrase, a noun phrase, and a prepositional phrase: *Cruelty Brought Orchids to Thee.*

And here's a simple declarative about Ibrahim Ibrahim
with three pairs of identical words occurring in the same sentence: *Ibrahim Ibrahim had had a hell of a time in hell.*

I step out of the bathtub and stand in front of the mirror.
I dry off and shave real slow, enjoying the good mirror they
have here, which is shiny and new and clean and sort of
makes everything a little bigger. I know that prescriptive
grammarians, high-school teachers, and other language
purists would probably say that you can't say *I shave real slow,*
and that the correct form is *I shave really slowly*—but I don't
care. If adjectives can function as adverbs, let them.

When I'm done shaving, I wash my face in the sink, put
on some of Carmel's new moisturizer, wrap the towel around
my waist, open the door, letting a short gust of colder air col-
lide with the dense steam in the bathroom, and walk into the
room.

"It's not bad, this Arab lotion of yours."

My clothes are still scattered on the floor, just the way I
left them.

"Carmel?"

Her clothes are gone.

"Carmel?"

I look out the window. The Justy is in the parking lot. Where is she? She must have gone down to the lobby. Probably needed to go to the bathroom. She'll be back in a minute.

I get dressed, put my shoes on, lie on the bed. The TV is off. Did I turn it off? It's eight-thirty. She'll be here any minute. Probably went downstairs to get a bottle of mineral water. I get up and walk to the kitchenette. I walk back. I look out the window again. I touch the TV, the nightstand, looking for clues, signs, a note, evidence of struggle, drops of blood. Nothing. I slump back on the bed. Maybe she went to the casino. Got tired of waiting for me to come out of the bathroom and went to the casino by herself. I'll give her another ten, maybe fifteen minutes. If she's not back by then, I'll go look for her.

I close my eyes. My head hurts. Maybe I'll just take a quick nap. Fifteen minutes, no more. I'll try to have good dreams, wake up feeling better. I'll dream about records. I'll go to a record store that specializes in heavy metal. There they are, all those rare records that I've been desperately looking for. A special edition of Venom's first album, *Welcome to Hell*, with previously unreleased bonus tracks and demo versions. An early Arch Enemy bootleg, with live tracks and cover versions of Priest and Maiden. And picture discs of Cannibal Corpse's *Butchered at Birth* and *Eaten Back to Life*, which I've never seen before. And they're cheap. I expected them to cost a fortune, but I can actually afford them. I grab them all and walk to the register. The cashier is a cute gothic chick, with glossy black hair, white skin, a pierced eyebrow, and lots of rings on her fingers. I hand her the records, smiling, letting her know that I like the way she looks.

"I'm sorry," she says. "You can't have these."

"Why not?"

"I'm afraid I must ask you to leave."

"What do you mean? I've been looking for these records for years."

"Do you know these bands?"

"Are you kidding? I listen to them every day."

"Do you know the lyrics?"

"Of course I know the lyrics. You want me to recite them for you?"

"This is a very extreme form of music."

"I grew up on this music! I've been listening to it all my life!"

"Are you familiar with heavy metal terminology?"

"Of course I am! Power metal, thrash metal, doom metal, black metal, grindcore, speedcore, necrobuzz, technodeath. Need I go on?"

"We drink human blood here."

She's smiling, and I notice that her teeth are all red, and I realize that she's Elizabeth Bathory, but I don't say anything. I just pull out a two-hundred-shekel bill, hoping that the sight of cash will make her change her mind.

"Your money's no good here. But you can have these for free if you join us. We need young recruits in Human Resources to serve in our FFS."

"FFS?"

"Fresh Flesh Stockpile. With a good chance for promotion."

Two guys dressed in black come out from behind the counter, and I know it's time for me to do something, but before I get a chance to start running, I wake up.

I check my watch. Ten-thirty. Can't be. I check my watch again. Ten-thirty. I look at the clock radio on the nightstand: 10:28. I get up, wash my face, make sure the keycard is in my pocket, and walk out of the room.

CHAPTER 10

The casino is hot and noisy, packed with overdressed, sweaty people, and I'm having a hard time figuring out where the tables are and where the slot machines are, where the bar is and where the food is, who's an employee and who's a guest, who's a croupier and who's a gambler, who's an Arab and who's not. The walls are coated with the reflections of women holding drinks in their hands, most of them leaning on the arms of fat men. They're all looking at me, and I'm beginning to feel a little out of place.

I buy myself a martini and start looking for Carmel. Too many faces. "That ugly model from Germany—she was supposed to come here for the grand opening," says a girl with small ears and too much makeup to a man shorter than her, "but she canceled." "Fuck her," says the short man. The girl kisses him. He laughs, putting his arm around her neck in a half nelson. Actually, he didn't say "fuck her." He said "let her go to Azazel"—which roughly means "she can go to hell" or "to hell with her"—but since there's no Azazel outside of Israel, "fuck her" seems to be the closest translation.

I don't really like martinis. "Fourteen days of reserve duty," says a man with gold-rimmed glasses and thick sideburns to his blackjack partner, "starting tomorrow. So I thought I'd go throw them some change before I kick their asses." I like the olive at the bottom, though.

A tall woman is leaning against the bar, smoking. Long hair, long legs, miniskirt, minipurse. I take a sip of my martini, and I reach with my finger to the bottom of the glass, trying to fish out the olive, but there is no olive at the bottom. Big breasts, a blue-and-white pin on her minipurse, left over from the last election: *A Strong Leader for a Strong Nation*. I smile at her. She blows smoke out of her nostrils. Smiles back. This is the old slogan. It's a good slogan, his public relations advisors told him, but it might be interpreted as having megalomaniacal, maybe even fascist, undertones. He took their advice and changed it to *A Strong Leader for the Future of the Nation*. The woman touches her neck, running her fingers across her collarbone, adjusting the black minipurse strap on her bare shoulder. I move away. I need to find Carmel.

How come there's no olive in my martini? Maybe someone stole it, fished it out of my glass while I was busy ogling the Strong Leader woman. I need to find Carmel. Find Carmel, then kill grandma in her sleep—without waking grandpa in his grave. Too many mirrors. Why do they have to put mirrors on the walls? Why would you want to look at yourself? I wonder what Dr. Himmelblau would say if she saw me here. What would my parents say? I didn't kill grandma. Neither did Eichmann.

A German Jew by the name of Adolf Goldberg came to Israel after the war. His friends told him he might want to think about changing his name, get rid of unpleasant connotations. He took their advice and changed it to Adolf Silverberg.

I need to find Carmel. Maybe she's hiding. Maybe she's wearing a mask. A mud masque. Maybe I could smuggle some mud from the Dead Sea back home. Hide it in one of her bodily orifices. I remember the time I caught her in bed, naked, all by herself, playing with a false idol. She sat on it and said she was having her period.

Too many people. With such self-pronounced prestige and sophistication, you'd expect the floor to be a little less sticky. You'd expect the followers of the prophet to be a little more compassionate, a little more merciful. Maybe I should ask about her. I'm looking for my girlfriend. Brown hair, nice tits, sore ass. Either lost or kidnapped. Maybe I should call the police. But then I would have to decide which police to call. The Palestinian police? Should I talk to them in Arabic? Maybe I should call the army. Did she go with Ramzy? Did she get tired of me? I bet she's on the back of one of his motorcycles right now, zooming through dark orchards and lush vineyards, her arms around his waist, holding him tight. Maybe I could get the army to demolish his house.

The fool. Doesn't realize she's using him for her own self-righteous recklessness. He's smart, but probably overwhelmed. Infatuated with some passing Hebrew pussy. He's giving her an oral dissertation on Samaritans and Nortons, she's asking him questions about monks and pistons. They make love in a little clay cabin in the camp, praying to the prophet in a mud mosque downtown.

Poor Ramzy. What have I got against him? He's not my enemy. Polite, knowledgeable, hospitable. Showed us around, took good care of us, offered us his friendship. So how come I hate him? How come I picture him in the hospital?

Immanuel Sebastian would probably eat him alive. Play with his mind, ridicule his faith in Allah, harass him with his usual nonsense about not believing in anything.

Abe Goldmil would try to make him see the light. He'd make him memorize his sonnets, then recite them all at a special initiation ritual in which Ramzy would denounce Islam and convert into a disciple of Julie Strain.

And next month, when it's time for us to go out again, I'd take him downtown with the rest of the patients. He'd be stopped and searched, like every Arab that goes to downtown Jerusalem, but I'd tell the soldiers that Ramzy is not a regular Arab. I'd tell them he's okay, he's with me. We'd go to Shalom Snack, where they have good sandwiches and lots of mirrors on the walls, and watch ourselves watching Maccabi on TV. And if we have time, while we're in the neighborhood, I'd take him to get a haircut. Have you ever been to a barking barber?

Then we'd take the bus back to the hospital, where Amos Ashkenazi would most likely try to do something annoying, like flaunt his vocabulary, or change the channel, or pick his nose—but I'd just tell him to put on his purple pajamas and go to bed, otherwise I'd call Dr. Himmelblau. We'd pass by the kibbutz on our way to the Haven, and I'd tell Ramzy all about my stupid reporter. Beaten by a baboon. Spineless coward. So what if some ape has a better command of English than you? You're a writer. You can't worry about what your mother might think.

Ibrahim Ibrahim would try to bug Ramzy with his chronicle of the snake and the soldiers.

Desta Ezra would look at him with her big, accusing eyes. Uriah Einhorn would tell him his tedious life story. Every day.

At least Hadassah Benedict wouldn't bother him. She's dead.

According to Dr. Himmelblau, this is where Ibrahim Ibrahim killed the little female soldier. Somewhere in the Jericho area, right by the Dead Sea. This is where he stabbed her to death and was shot in the leg. I wonder if I could find the exact spot. Should have asked Ramzy to show us the murder scene from Mount Temptation. Ibrahim Ibrahim. Stones in his kidneys and a snake on his chest. They took the stones out, but they couldn't get the snake to go away. Children of the stones. Cast them every day at the soldiers. Cast no shadow, sneak up in the dark, grab and stab, pray and slay. Sent to the other side of the Jordan River. Snake a stubborn soul. From Jordan to Moscow. To Russia with a snake on his shoulders, funded by the Authority, paid for by the president himself, the man with no land, the old commander who was kind enough to furnish him with a letter saying that Ibrahim Ibrahim was one of the fearless children of the stones, a little warrior bravely wounded in the uprising against the enemy, so please treat him right, and the Authority hereby promises to pay all expenses.

Ramzy was right. People just go through the motions like robots. Is that a tautology? Is *A Corpse Without Soul* a tautology?

I wouldn't want them to drive him crazy. I'd have to get him out of the hospital. Escape, but not to sickness. We'd go someplace where we could talk about history and archaeology and books and bikes and Arabic word formation. He'd throw stones at the soldiers and run away. Run as fast as you can. Run for your life. Kill and be killed. Dump her body in the Dead Sea.

Jaguar, from England, had a song called "Run for Your Life." Riot, from Canada, also had a song called "Run for Your Life." And Hellion, of course. I liked Hellion. The singer called herself Ann Boleyn, and there were rumors about her putting a curse on members of Hellion who had left the band. She had long black hair, black fingernails, black toenails. I remember a picture of her dressed like a schoolgirl—white blouse, plaid skirt, white sneakers, white socks—nailed to a wooden cross, blood dripping from the corner of her mouth.

Silly me. Nothing sinks in the Dead Sea. Everything floats. Flotsam and jetsam. Dump a body, and it's bound to rise right up. Back from the dead, rise from the grave. Sick of life. Sick of it all. Seek and destroy. Destroy her so that he would be destroyed. A corpse without soul. A soldier girl. A woman in uniform. A little fighting girl in khaki. Let the blood run red. Let the girl be dead. A little enemy soldier girl. Kill her and be killed. Sick and destroy. Slay the snake that's on his chest.

He stabbed her twice. She was waiting for the bus. Standing at the bus stop, waiting to die. That's the spot. That's the stop. Stop and stare. Hot wind in her hair. Ripped her pretty stomach inside out. A woman in uniform. A little fighting girl with khaki eyes and khaki hair. Cold sweat trickling down his neck. Warm blood seeping from her chest.

The soldiers saw it. Waiting for the bus on the other side of the road. They crossed the street and shot him. He thought he was as good as dead. He thought they'd never let him live another day. Kill the snake that's on his chest, destroy the serpent in his heart, slay the demon in his soul.

But when they shoot, they don't shoot straight. He feels their fingers on his skin. They pull his shirt, twist his arms.

They drop him to the ground, they kick him in the head. But never shoot him dead.

I need to find Carmel. Where is she? Got tired of attempting to tempt me to torture her. She's far away now, gone to Jordan to see the queen, gone to Norway to eat the whales, gone to Wales to study Welsh.

I should go to Wales, like my mother tells me. I'm a good boy, can't escape it. Stranger in a nonstrange land. Married girlfriend, dead-end job, hog-hearted father, renal-catastrophe mother. What's keeping me here? Or maybe to England, to study English. In the middle of nowhere. Middle English. I'd rent a nice place somewhere in the country, read, write, wake up late every morning, lie in bed all day, wait for the beautiful wife of the landlord to seduce me while her husband is out in the woods hunting boars. Or maybe not. No more perfidious affairs. No more fighting for my king. No more Star of Solomon on my person. No more traveling across the country to kill a scary green goliath who really wants to be my friend.

I take another sip. I need to cross to the other side of the gambling hall. Too many people are kibitzing around the tables, blocking my way. I stand on the tip of my toes, craning my neck, scanning the hall. Can't see her. I take a few steps forward, trying to elbow my way between two girls in snakeskin blazers and push-up bras, make it through to the other side. One of them is skinny, the other one a little chubby. "Excuse me," I mumble, trying to squeeze between them—but they push closer. "The monkey in the eyes of its mother—a gazelle," says the chubby one. The skinny one laughs. She touches the chubby one's forearm.

Why would I want to live in English? Hebrew is such a beautiful language. So elegant, so natural. So what if we have no present tense? It's better when you only have two tenses: past and future, good and bad, us and them. Too many tenses—too much tension. And no copular verbs. Who said nouns had to be connected? Keep them separated: sky and earth, sea and land, day and night, man and beast. That's the way it's meant to be.

No olive in my martini. I must find her. I know where she is. She's with Ramzy. It's late at night, and hordes of Israelis are storming the casino. He must be at the gas station, handing out those pamphlets. She must be with him. I saw the look in her eyes. I saw the fire in his pupils. I know where to find them.

I put my empty glass on the bar and squeeze among the gamblers, pushing forward, pressing on, kicking ankles, stepping on toes, clutching at shoulders, rubbing against cleavages, making my way out, slowly, slowly.

The air outside is good. It's cooled off a little. I take a few deep breaths and walk to the hotel—but she's not in the room. Of course not. She's with Ramzy. I wash my face, go downstairs to the parking lot, get in the Justy, and drive to the gas station.

Everything is dusty and dark. No lights, no traffic, just the desert. I'm rolling down the road, windows rolled down, soft breeze blowing in my face. I look at my watch. Almost four in the morning. The palm trees bend slightly in the wind. The Dead Sea is black. The air smells of sulfur. The pale neon sign of the gas station flickers in the distance. Extraterrestrials?

When I was little, maybe six or seven, I used to hide under the table when my parents fought. I couldn't understand why they had to have these doomsday fights every weekend, why they couldn't just get dressed and go to a movie, or cook a big dinner and sit down and eat, or shake hands and say goodbye. Later, when I was a teenager, I would lock myself in my room and chain-play heavy metal records with the earphones on, catching their screaming and crying only when I turned sides. But when I was six or seven, all I could do was hide under the table, hoping they didn't break too many dishes, didn't smash the TV, didn't stab each other. I used to wish for a flying saucer to come and land in front of our house, something big and extraordinary that would make them stop and stare in amazement as I was taken to outer space. But aliens don't land in residential neighborhoods. They usually land in places like this, in the middle of the desert, late at night, by eerie salt lakes, on empty roads, with only a fugitive girlfriend and an antigambling activist to witness the visitation, and maybe an incompetent assistant nurse.

I turn on the radio, but all the stations are playing melancholic music again. On Army Radio One, an old man with a shaky voice is talking about the origins of the swastika. Holocaust Day is coming up, and everybody's getting ready, invoking mandatory memories, engaging in national debates, sinking into unifying sadness, preparing for the annual culmination of it all, at ten o'clock in the morning on Holocaust Day, when we have the traditional two-minute siren, during which all the people of Israel, all over the country, all at once, stop and freeze and stand in silence and count very quickly from one to six million and think about the victims with agony and vengeance. And the weird thing is that every year you're startled by the siren as if you're hearing it for the first time. You know it's going to go off—you've heard it a million times before—but for some reason, it always takes you by surprise. I usually hide somewhere in advance, normally in the bathroom. Or if I'm home alone, I just don't get up. But I guess I'll have to stand in silence with everybody else this year. Set an example for the patients.

Last year we were all watching TV in the game room, and when the siren went off, Uriah Einhorn freaked out and started screaming and running for cover, and Hadassah Benedict laughed at him, and Amos Ashkenazi started scolding her for profaning the memory of the dead, and Immanuel Sebastian told him to shut up, you can't talk during the siren, and Desta Ezra started crying, and Abe Goldmil said that since his grandfather died in Dachau, he's exempt from standing with everybody, and Dr. Himmelblau said that if I can't perform a simple task, like getting them to stand still for two minutes, how can I expect them—or her— to respect me?

Two years ago, when I was still attending the Hebrew University, I excused myself from my early morning class a couple of minutes before ten o'clock—I think it was Advanced Topics in Phonology—and went to the Humanities restrooms. There were big posters all over the campus inviting students to a panel discussion facilitated by the Department of Jewish Philosophy: *Where was God during the Holocaust?* On one of the posters, on the notice board next to the restrooms, someone had hand-written with a black marker:

a) In Berlin.
b) In Beverly Hills.
c) On vacation.
d) In the imagination of the believers.

I pull into the gas station. It's closed. I park next to the closest pump, diagonally, and look around. No one's here, just crickets chirping, and the wind rustling on the warm asphalt, and the big sign shining in colorless neon, and Ramzy standing by the air pump, a stack of undistributed pamphlets in his hand, looking tired. I turn off the engine and step out of the car.

"Is she here?"

"You lost her?"

"She's not here, is she?"

"Last time I saw her was yesterday afternoon, with you, when we said goodbye."

"She's gone."

"She'll be back."

"I need her."

"Right now?"

"Right now."

"What for?"

"I need to ask her some questions."

"What kind of questions?"

"I don't know. Just questions."

"What about?"

"I have a paper to write."

"For school?"

"Yes."

"What about?"

"What do you care?"

"I'm just curious."

"Epic Narratives."

"Epic Narratives?"

"The great masterpieces of world literature."

"Homer?"

"For example."

"Was Homer a woman?"

"I don't know. We didn't talk about it in class."

"What did you talk about?"

"The *Odyssey*."

"I don't like Odysseus."

"Why?"

"Why is it okay for him to have sex with that little nymph on the island for seven years while his wife must wait for him at home, passive and loyal and chaste?"

"Ramzy, I'm looking for Carmel."

"What do you need Carmel for? I know all about the Epic Narratives."

"You don't know anything about Epic Narratives."

"Try me."

"Have you taken anything other than Suicide Bombing for Beginners? Have you read anything other than *The Terrorist's Guide to Successful Slaughter*? Have you read *The Epic of Gilgamesh*? *Beowulf*? *Sir Gawain and the Green Knight*?"

"Same thing. In *Gilgamesh*, goddesses, prostitutes, and other magical female creatures suggest that women are simply nonhumans. Meanwhile, the brave king, capable of sustaining a seven-day erection, fights for his right to sexually own every virgin in the land."

"Ramzy."

"In *Beowulf*, bloodthirsty warriors who call themselves true believers must vanquish those who don't subscribe to their faith, butchering both the monstrous pariah and his mother."

"Ramzy!"

"And in *Sir Gawain*, the female is either an ugly old sorceress who tricks the hero into betraying his host—or a two-timing temptress that he must resist if he wants to keep his dominance intact."

"Stop it! Enough! My class is not about Epic Narratives!"

"Then what's it about?"

"It's about Robinson Crusoe!"

"Oh. I haven't read *Robinson Crusoe*."

"You haven't?"

"Sorry."

"Then you can't help me with my paper."

"What's so important about your paper?"

"It needs to be done. I have to finish it."

"Why?"

"So I can move on."

"Where to?"

"I don't know. Just move on. Advance."

"You don't want to advance."

"What do you mean?"

"If you really wanted to advance, you would have finished the paper a long time ago."

"I'll finish it."

"When?"

"Soon. And then I'll go. You'll see."

"Go where?"

"Somewhere. Anywhere. Wales, Finland, Hollywood. It doesn't matter."

"You don't need a paper to go to Hollywood."

"If I don't write this paper, I'll have to stay."

"Then stay."

"Why should I stay?"

"It's your homeland."

"I thought you believed this was *your* homeland."

"It's my homeland, too."

"Then we're neighbors."

"Yes."

"And friends."

"No."

"Why not?"

"You can't be my friend."

"Why not?"

"I'm an Arab."

"I'm not afraid of Arabs."

"You're not afraid of lunatics, either—but you can't be their friend."

"Why not?"

"Because they're not you. They're lunatics."

"They're people."

"They're abnormal people. They're outcasts, runaways, apostates. You have nothing to do with them. You belong to the people who belong."

"But I write."

"So?"

"In English."

"So you're a traitor—but you still belong."

"I don't go to the army anymore."

"Aren't you on reserve?"

"I was discharged."

"How come?"

"I pretended I was crazy."

"After being a soldier for four years."

"But I had an office job. I never fired laser-guided missiles at famished kids with stones and slingshots. I worked with dictionaries and lexicons."

"And you still do. Here, in the State of Israel. Where you belong. Where you have a duty."

"What's my duty?"

"To crush your enemy. To be cruel to your neighbor. To get rid of the pernicious burden in the heart of your beautiful country. Does it really make a difference whether you perform or shirk this duty?"

"Of course it does. I made a conscious decision. I got out. I'm in control of my own life now. I escaped from the army to be the master of my fate."

"By faking an illness you don't gain control. You simply become the pretend master of an imaginary symptom. You're putting on an act. It's not rebellion, it's a show. You're not an escapee. You're an escape artist."

The neon light breaks on Ramzy's face in a strange way, and I notice that his eyes look purple. Or maybe I'm just tired. I look down at my shoes, then at the pumps, the palm trees, the scratch on the Justy, then into Ramzy's eyes again— but they're still purple.

"No wonder we hate you so much." My voice is shaking. "What makes you think you're the all-knowing voice of con- science? You disgust me, you smug, pretentious Arab. You're worse than my girlfriend."

I put my hands in my pockets and close my left fist on the car keys. Ramzy's beard points forward in a glossy shade of black, his eyebrows stretch thick and long under his stupid turban. I feel like saying something nasty, something really nasty—like "go to hell" or "you son of sixty thousand whores" or "should have learned how to operate those smart missiles instead of wasting my time studying your stinking language"—but I don't. I just turn around, get in the car, slam the door, open and slam it again because the safety belt got stuck in it, and drive away.

It's about five-thirty when I get back to the hotel. People are beginning to leave now, coming out of the casino, their eyes all puffy and red, packing themselves back into their cars, climbing up to Israel. Dawn by the Dead Sea is beauti- ful. No fish, no fowl, no waves, no life—but somehow it's the only place that makes some sense, the only place where you are neither here nor there, the only place where you can speak the language of the living dead. I can smell the fresh salt and the cleanliness of the desert morning even inside the hotel, as I climb the stairs and walk along the hall and slide the keycard in and walk into the room. The sun hasn't come up yet, but its rosy fingers, as they say in the book that Ramzy doesn't like, are on the window curtains and in the kitchenette and on the bed, where Carmel is lying.

I close the door behind me. She sits up Indian-style and puts the blanket over her shoulders. She smiles. I don't.

"I've been looking all over for you."

"I went down to the casino."

"I didn't see you there. I drove all the way to the gas station."

"I was right here."

"Where?"

"In the casino."

"Why didn't you tell me?"

"You were in the shower."

"You can't just disappear like that."

"I didn't disappear. I just went out for a little while."

"Without saying anything?"

"I needed some air."

"Couldn't you just wait for me?"

"The room got too small."

"Did I hurt you?"

"Don't be silly."

"Are you sure?"

"My knees hurt," she smiles again, "but other than that I'm as good as new."

"Your knees?"

"You gave me rug burns," she laughs. She gets up from the bed and hugs me and kisses me, but I don't kiss her back.

"What's wrong?"

"You disappeared," I say.

"But I'm back."

"You just got up and left."

"So?"

"You didn't say anything. You just left."

"So?"

"No apologies, no explanations."

"Are you angry because I didn't return the favor? We could go buy a little strap-on thing when we get back to Jerusalem."

"I don't think so."

"A *big* strap-on thing?"

"I don't think so."

CHAPTER 11

I'm sitting at a coffee shop in Amsterdam, and King Diamond comes up to me, asks me if I'm ready to order. He has his usual corpse-paint on his face—white all over, black around the eyes and mouth, an upside-down cross on his forehead—and he says that if I'm here to see the show, the show is canceled. I ask him why, and he says: "Problems with our lyrics. The committee thinks the language is inappropriate." I tell him that I came here all the way from Jerusalem, so what am I supposed to do now? He says that Amsterdam is a nice city and that I might want to visit Anne Frank's house. I tell him that I'm not in the mood, and I try to get up, but I'm glued to my chair. He says he's been working at this coffee shop for almost thirty years now, and it's company policy: you can't leave before you order. So I order a cup of coffee, but he says he's sorry, they're out of coffee. So I order some cheesecake, but he says that they just served the last slice. I ask for a soup and sandwich, but he says that the kitchen is closed. So I ask for a glass of water, but he says that due to the recent drought, there's a shortage of water in Holland. I tell him that I'm very thirsty, but he says there's nothing he can do about it. I want to scream at him but my mouth is dry and I can't swallow and he just laughs and walks away and I try to get up again but I'm still glued to my chair and I wake up.

It's two in the afternoon. We packed our stuff this morning and sped away from the casino, back to Jerusalem, ascending to the city in uncomfortable silence. I dropped Carmel off at her house and drove home. It was raining. I took a shower and listened to Mercyful Fate's *Don't Break the Oath*. Made myself a cup of tea, played air guitar to "Come to the Sabbath," drank my tea, felt a little better, set the alarm for two o'clock, and took a nap. Mercyful, not Merciful.

I drink a glass of water and get dressed. No time to eat. No time for uninvited visitors. If there's a slow tractor ahead of me today, Odelia will give me that nasty look again, and the patients will suspect that I'm just as irresponsible as they are.

I put my coat on, lock the door, get in the car, start driving to the hospital. And sure enough, here's the yellow tractor, fat and slow, slouching toward the kibbutz, and I'm stuck again. I slow down and try to find something good on the radio, but all the stations are still playing sad music, and for some reason, I don't feel like listening to Nokturnal Mortum or Diabolical Masquerade today, so I just turn off the radio and look up at the sky, where two falcons are circling, quite low. It's still cold, but the sky is clear now, and a soft sun is shining on the road, bringing out the yellow in the tractor. It looks old, spitting black smoke, panting its way up the mountain, dirty and rusty—like the scratch on my door. But

I'm not angry anymore, even if she did it. I don't mind. At first I though it would heal, just like human tissue. I know it's stupid: damaged cars don't just fix themselves. But for some reason, that's what I thought might happen if I just waited long enough. So I waited, patiently, but it only got bigger, longer, wider, deeper. Maybe she stretches it with a screwdriver while I'm sleeping. For all I know, she might be driving to my neighborhood every night to sabotage my little Justy. But even if she does, I don't care.

I look up at the sky again: the falcons are still patrolling overhead—and there's also a rainbow up there, a real one, big and bright. Last year, when I was driving with Carmel on Burma Road, the secret historic route that connected the besieged Jerusalem with the rest of the country during our 1948 War of Independence, we saw an amazing rainbow, bigger than this one, and Carmel said we should stop and make love in the woods, among the trees, which we did. It's an unpaved road that circumvents the highway, cutting through thickets and fields, and it felt good to park the car in the middle of nowhere and do it on the soggy ground, then stand up naked under the rainbow and peel off the pine needles that had stuck to our bodies. But then, when it was over, we got into this stupid fight, I can't even remember what about, and we got home and couldn't stop arguing, and I got angry and smashed my own copy of Agent Steel's *Mad Locust Rising* and had to buy it again later.

Something strange is happening with the falcons. They're flying too close to each other, almost bumping into each other, and all of a sudden one of them is pouncing at the other, midair, chasing it away, and I'm not sure if it's a game or a fight. The tractor slows down, enveloped in its own smoke, preparing to make a right turn into the kibbutz. It's blocking my view. I have to slow down now, watch its brake lights. It's making a wide turn, and when it's gone, I try to locate the falcons in the sky again, but I can't see them. I scan the horizon, stretch my neck in all directions, but they're not out there anymore. Stupid birds. No wonder they're an endangered species.

The guard opens the gate. I wave at him, but he doesn't wave back. I park in front of the unit. Five minutes early, in spite of everything. Good. I walk in. Odelia is on the phone, probably with her husband or one of her kids. She hangs up, stands up, and, while putting on her coat, gives me the usual update:

Immanuel Sebastian: ate, took his medicines, watched TV, quiet.

Abe Goldmil: ate, took his medicines, wrote in the kitchen, quiet.

Uriah Einhorn: ate, took his medicines, sleeps most of the time.

Amos Ashkenazi: ate, took his medicines, mumbles to himself, quiet.

Hadassah Benedict: ate, took her medicines, says she's dead, other than that quiet.

Desta Ezra: quiet.

"See you tomorrow," she says.

"Wait," I say. "What about Ibrahim Ibrahim?"

"He's gone."

"Gone? Where did he go?"

"I don't know."

"When did that happen?"

"Yesterday. They took him away."

"Who?"

"I don't know. Dr. Himmelblau was with them."

"With whom?"

"I don't know. People."

"And they just took him away?"

"Yes."

"Where?"

"I don't know. What are you asking me all these questions for?"

"Are they bringing him back?"

"What do I look like, the boss? Ask Dr. Himmelblau. I'll see you tomorrow."

I sit down. Hadassah Benedict peeks into the nurse's station, looks at me for a second, then withdraws back to the game room. I dial Dr. Himmelblau's number.

"Yes?"

"Where's Ibrahim Ibrahim?"

"Who?"

"The Arab."

"Oh. He completed his observation period."

"And?"

"And that's it. He's no longer with us."

"Where is he?"

"Back where he came from."

"The refugee camp?"

"The military facility."

"Did you ever get his file?"

"Of course."

"Where is it?"

"We didn't pass it along."

"What do you mean?"

"We considered it on a need-to-know basis."

"Didn't you want me to translate it?"

"There was no need for that."

"How come?"

"We had all the information we needed to make a decision."

"And what was the decision?"

"I just told you: to terminate his observation period."

"And do what with him?"

"Release him to the army."

"But that means that he's going back to jail."

"Where he belongs."

I hang up. Should I call Carmel? No, she'll probably call in a minute or two. I walk to the dining hall. Immanuel Sebastian and Abe Goldmil are sitting at the table, looking at Abe Goldmil's notebook. I stand there for a few seconds, but Abe Goldmil doesn't request my permission to read me a new sonnet, so I walk across the hall and into the kitchen, where Uriah Einhorn is standing, holding a blue plastic cup half full of tap water.

"What are you doing?"

"Could you maybe give me a sleeping pill?"

"Where's Ibrahim Ibrahim?"

"Am I the keeper of my sibling?"

I give him what I hope he realizes is a reproachful look. He shrugs. I walk away, back to the game room, where Amos Ashkenazi and Hadassah Benedict are playing Monopoly.

"Where's Desta Ezra?"

"She's taking a shower," says Hadassah Benedict.

I walk back to the nurse's station. I sit down, waiting for Carmel to call. The newspaper's on the shelf, but I don't feel like reading it. I tap out Iron Maiden's "Where Eagles Dare" on the Formica desk. She still doesn't call. I open the newspaper. Having claimed for many years that information regarding nationality definitions for identification registration was confidential, the Freedom of Information Commissioner at the Ministry of Interior Affairs agreed yesterday to publicize the official list of national identity options. Specifying 132 nationality definitions recognized by the Population Administration, including over a hundred countries and states, as well as different religions and ethnicities, the list, however, allows neither an Israeli citizen nor a permanent resident to register as *Israeli*. Among the recognized definitions are *Abyssinian, American, Arab, Basque, Bolivian, Canadian, Druze, Irish, Italian, Jewish, Libyan, Maltese, Maronite, Micronesian, Taiwanese, Under Inspection, Undetermined, Unknown, Unregistered*, and *Unspecified*.

I call Carmel.

"Hello?"

"Ibrahim Ibrahim is gone."

"Who?"

"The Arab."

"The one who killed the girl?"

"The one who killed the girl."

"Where is he?"

"Back in jail."

"Does Dr. Gimmelfarb know about this?"

"Himmelblau."

"Whatever."

"Of course she knows about it. She's the one who sent him back there."

"So?"

"It makes no sense. I go to Jericho for one day, and when I come back—he's gone."

"Don't you think she knows what she's doing?"

"But he's crazy."

"But she's the doctor."

"That's exactly what I don't get. Any idiot could see that he was completely off his rocker."

"That doesn't sound like a very professional diagnosis."

"He's insane. He thinks a snake is choking him. How could you kick such a nutcase out of a mental hospital?"

"She's a psychiatrist. She must have years of experience when it comes to telling the difference between a real lunatic and a guy who's just trying to get away with murder."

"He thinks that Robinson Crusoe is a Jew. He's out of his mind."

"He killed a girl."

"He killed because he was psychotic."

"He's still a killer."

"An *insane* killer."

"What's the difference?"

"The law says that there *is* a difference."

"Forget the law," Carmel says. "Let me give you some examples. When the Nazis killed the Jews because of a false belief in the supremacy of the Aryan race—that was murder, right?"

"Right."

"And if a man kills his wife because he falsely—or rightly—believes that she's having an affair with someone else—that's murder, right?"

"Right."

"And if the prime minister is assassinated because the killer honestly believes that he's doing the country a great service—it's still murder, right?"

"What's your point, Carmel?"

"My point is that killing is a crime, no matter what the motive is. Crimes do not cease to be criminal because they have a racial motive, a romantic motive, or a political motive."

"So?"

"By the same token, crimes do not cease to be criminal because they have a psychotic motive."

"So who decides who goes to jail and who gets to stay in a mental institution?"

"Dr. Götterdämmerung."

"Himmelblau."

"Whatever. The point is: you have no choice but to trust an experienced professional to provide an accurate diagnosis."

"But if people should be judged by their actions, and if everybody is responsible for their own behavior, then there's no scientific basis for any psychiatric diagnosis."

"Still, someone has to decide."

"So why Dr. Himmelblau?"

"Why not?"

"Why not me?"

"She's a doctor."

"But she's not making an objective, unbiased decision."

"But she's the doctor. It's *her* decision."

"Which means that it's not a *scientific* decision. If a human being has to decide, it's never going to be a purely medical decision, free from moral judgment."

"What's wrong with her decision?"

"It makes no sense."

"Even if it makes no sense—it's reality."

"Says who?"

"The DSM."

"The DSM is just a book."

"A book that lists psychiatric conditions and criteria for diagnosis."

"A book that was written by people. People with subjective opinions. People with social and political views."

"People who played the game, Gilad. People who completed their academic education and became doctors. You can't even finish your *Robinson Crusoe* paper."

"But if she's sending a guy to military prison, she's diagnosing him politically, not medically."

"So write your stupid paper already, finish your degree, go to graduate school, get your Ph.D., become a doctor or a lawyer or something—and then maybe you could keep your killer friend in the nuthouse."

I look out the window. It's cloudy again. And cold. I don't like this kind of weather. I think I like it hot. Like in Tel Aviv. I lived in Tel Aviv for a year, the last year of my military service. They'd moved me back to the Military Intelligence Academy to teach Arabic to new recruits. I rented a tiny studio apartment in Tel Aviv and started enjoying the city. Sure, it's hot as hell in the summer, but you can always go to the beach. And you'll never freeze to death in the winter, like in Jerusalem. Of course, when I say "freeze to death" it's purely hyperbolic. I guess that Canadians or Russians would laugh at me for thinking that a couple of degrees below freezing is very cold. But I don't care. Let them laugh. I'd like to see them survive a summer in Tel Aviv.

In Tel Aviv I discovered Daniel Almog, my favorite Hebrew poet. I'd known about him—I think I'd even read some of his poems—but it wasn't until I moved to Tel Aviv that I began to appreciate his poetry. There was something about the city that inspired me to start collecting his books, reading them over and over again, memorizing his poems:

by cracks through which notes are inserted
to communicate with short-tempered idols
inflicting unconditional pleasure on subjects
held captive on familiar grounds working
on far-reaching tunnels fortified passports
soap guns wax wings old files nails sharpened
to utilitarian perfection homemade trumpets

to blow down bricks punch a hole in the
wailing of olive bodies not getting the hell
out to quote old Dave rhyme neither white
nor burning time neither right nor running out

One day—a typical Friday afternoon in Tel Aviv: hot, sticky, mellow—I was flicking through the weekend newspaper in my apartment when I spotted a small ad in the classifieds: *Poet Daniel Almog Seeks Translation Assistant.* Like I told you, Hebrew is a language that distinguishes between male nouns and female nouns. The *assistant* in the ad was female, so I called my co-instructor—the second lieutenant I was teaching Arabic with—and invited her over for coffee. We talked for a while, mostly about different ways to construct the passive, then I asked her to call him.

He wasn't home. I told her to leave a message. He called back an hour later. I picked up the phone. I'd be lying if I said I wasn't excited. Daniel Almog was calling my house. And I talked to him. He asked if he could speak with Shira, and I said "sure" and handed her the phone. I know it doesn't sound like much, but some communication did transpire between us, even if it was brief and practical.

"Do you know French?" he asked her.

"No."

"German?"

"No."

"Russian?"

"I'm sorry."

"English?"

"Yes."

"Is it your mother tongue?"

"No."

"Can you type?"

"I'm afraid not."

"Never mind," he said. "Come over."

She hung up. "Old lecher," she said.

"He's a great poet," I said.

A few months later, when he died, all the newspapers wrote that he was a hopeless womanizer.

Shira called me: "You see?"

"He was just lonely," I said.

"Just write your paper," Carmel says, "instead of wasting your time on this stupid book."

"I thought you liked my book."

"Well, I don't."

"Why not?"

"To be honest with you, I think that times like these call for a more serious and responsible approach to literature, an approach that, in the face of the atrocities perpetrated by our enemies, emphasizes our collective faith in unity and humanity."

"So you don't like it, huh?"

"I don't want to discourage you from your project, of course, but I feel that playful metafiction and self-referential prose are contraptions that belong to happier days, days that will surely come in the future. Right now, however, when our troops risk their lives every day to protect your very ability to write literature, you should definitely tone down your sarcastic and critical voice, keeping venomous irony and thankless parody to a minimum."

"But you liked the sex scenes, didn't you?"

"As a matter of fact, I wasn't too keen on your pitiful attempts at writing erotic scenes, most of which I found highly offensive. Quite frankly, it's not sexy. It's repulsive."

"It serves a purpose."

"Well, I understand that you're using sex and violence as a rhetorical device that may or may not reflect common codes of behavior, both personal and political—but do you really have to sodomize your girlfriend to prove a point? I must admit that I was quite shocked at such a distasteful display of literary lewdness, and I'm afraid that you risk alienating many of your potential readers."

"Who cares about the readers?"

"Not to mention all those misleading inconsistencies and inaccuracies."

"Like what?"

"Like certain characters who, if I understand correctly, are supposed to represent the so-called chameleon-like nature of the moral minority. You have to understand that the shift to hawkish positions is perfectly understandable during wartime."

"Is it?"

"Of course it is. It's an act of faith. It's what saves us."

"Then I guess I'm not saved."

"I guess you're not."

"I'll talk to you later."

I hang up. I get up, pace up and down the station for a while, then stop and stare at the desk. I pick up the newspaper and drop it to the floor. I pick it up and put it on the chair. I stand on the chair. I don't know why. I'm just standing on the chair. I look around. Everything looks smaller. I keep climbing. I put my right foot on the desk, testing its willingness to hold my weight. Then the other foot. I'm standing on the desk. I could reach the ceiling if I wanted to, but I keep my hands close to my body. The Formica complains.

"You can't build a house if you don't own all the streets in the city," I hear Hadassah Benedict say.

"What about a hotel?"

"Let alone a hotel."

Uriah Einhorn appears at the door. He's holding an orange cup, extending it in my direction, but when he sees me on top of the desk, he freezes. I look at him, but I don't say anything. He looks up at me, but he's not saying anything either. Immanuel Sebastian and Abe Goldmil approach the nurse's station. Abe Goldmil has his brown notebook in his hand. They stop at the door, on both sides of Uriah Einhorn.

"What's going on?" says Immanuel Sebastian.

"I don't know," says Uriah Einhorn. "Is this a part of his job?"

"I don't think so," says Immanuel Sebastian. "Unless they changed the code."

"What's happening?" I hear Hadassah Benedict say.

"Come here," says Immanuel Sebastian.

Hadassah Benedict joins them, followed by Amos Ashkenazi.

"He's standing on the desk," says Immanuel Sebastian. "They'll kick him out of the hospital."

"Finally," says Hadassah Benedict.

"He'll have to find another hiding place," says Amos Ashkenazi.

"Where do you think he could go?" says Abe Goldmil.

"He'd have nowhere to go to."

"Nonsense. He can go anywhere he wants."

I look at them from above, examining their faces. They look tired. Do I see Desta Ezra at the back, standing on her toes? Maybe I should go to Africa. Not a great heavy metal scene, but the weather is probably warmer than Finland.

The closest I've ever been to Africa was when I went to Sinai. I'd never been there when it belonged to us. The only time I went there was after we gave it back to the Egyptians.

I drove my Justy to the border, parked it near the fence, crossed the checkpoint to the other side, and took an old Peugeot taxi to a little village on the Red Sea called Devil's Head. After a few days of perfect rest—swimming in the sea in the morning, talking to the Bedouins over hot tea in the afternoon, and at night, on the beach, listening to traveling musicians from Sudan play instruments I'd never seen or heard before—I took another Peugeot taxi down to Dahab to snorkel in the Blue Hole. Then I climbed Mount Sinai, where I met a Catholic girl from Argentina who was literally following the footsteps of the pope. He'd been there a few weeks before—a historic visit to all the holy places in the Middle East—and Delfina, tall and full of energy, with green eyes and good English, was doing a private reenactment of the recent papal tour. We climbed all night to watch the sunrise from the summit, and I remember thinking hard of something to say, something profound and insightful, something that would capture the majestic intensity of the moment, something that would sum up the essence of being in the presence of Moses and the pope, something that would impress the Argentinean.

"You know," I said, "when you think about it, sunrises don't really exist. The sun doesn't move, so naturally, it can't rise. Or set. It's just more convenient for us to organize the world in terms of the illusionary movement of the sun. And if you think about it, words don't exist either. It's just more convenient for us to organize language in terms of sentences and words, which, in reality, are merely agglutinations of clauses and phonemes."

"You should go away," says Hadassah Benedict.

"Why?" I ask.

"Because you can," says Abe Goldmil.

"Where would I go?"

"You like heavy metal, right? Go to the Midlands, the birthplace of heavy metal."

"Or London," says Hadassah Benedict.

"Or Detroit," says Immanuel Sebastian.

"Or Los Angeles."

"I don't want to go to Los Angeles!" I shout.

"Why not?" says Abe Goldmil.

"It's a stupid place!"

"It's good enough for Julie Strain."

"I'm not a Julie Strain fan!"

"Then go to Wales," says Amos Ashkenazi. "Bug the Welsh with lectures about Welsh."

"Wales would be too cold for him," says Uriah Einhorn.

"Then just go away," says Amos Ashkenazi.

"Why don't *you* go away?" I say to them.

"Where can we go?"

"Out. Don't you want out? I'll open the door and let you all out. Just escape. I don't care anymore."

"We don't want to escape."

"Of course you don't!" I shout at them. "Because you're crazy!"

"No," says Abe Goldmil. "Because we've already escaped."

"And now it's your turn," says Hadassah Benedict.

"But I *am* escaping!"

"Where are you escaping to?"

"Here!"

"You're on your way *out* of here."

"Says who?"

"She'll fire you," says Uriah Einhorn. "You're standing on the desk."

"She'll never know," I say.

"We'll tell her."

"She won't believe you."

"She'll fire you anyway," says Immanuel Sebastian. "You're out of here."

"The book is not over yet," I warn them.

"The book is no escape," says Abe Goldmil.

"It's in English!" I shout.

"It's fiction," says Abe Goldmil. "It's a *production* of an escape."

"It's a show," says Hadassah Benedict.

"Get out! All of you! Get out of my station!"

But they all just stand there, staring at me, as if they've never seen someone standing on a desk before. So I stare back at them, looking at the way their little heads glow in the fluorescent light, catching the first warm rays, blazing like the lower peaks surrounding Mount Sinai. And I'm standing there for a long time, and it's getting hot, and all of a sudden I realize that I'm alone. Delfina had left the moment I finished delivering my profound linguistic observation, looking at me with the kind of pity and disgust usually reserved for really bad cases of leprosy. She must be climbing down now with the rest of the pilgrims and tourists, her long legs carefully on the rocks, making her way back to earth. And I'm standing here all by myself, waiting for something to happen, for thunder or lightning to strike some knowledge into my heart, for the hand of God to come out and give me a sign, a hint, the revised ten commandments, directions to Hollywood.

But nothing happens. It's just hot, hot and purposeless, so I look at the sky, and I'm thinking about my father, and how sometimes the human brain must take control over a pump that used to belong to a pig, because the stupid swine-spigot wouldn't do anything on its own. And I'm thinking about my mother, and how sometimes you just have to plug yourself into a strange machine that wakes you up at night, just to kick-start your own stuck strainer, get your liquids moving. Because if you don't, nothing will happen.

And I'm still standing here, on top of the mountain, waiting.

Uriah Einhorn walks out of the station, holding his empty plastic cup with both hands, and Desta Ezra steps forward and looks at me for a few seconds, then walks away, shaking her head, and Immanuel Sebastian says to Abe Goldmil that the new one still needs work, especially the line where you compare her to a sunflower, and they turn around and leave, and Amos Ashkenazi says to Hadassah Benedict that he wants to buy Ben-Yehuda Street, but Hadassah Benedict says that Ben-Yehuda is expensive, do you have money, and Amos Ashkenazi says that he just passed *Go*, and they both step back into the game room.